ANGEL TEARS

D.G. RADFORD

Copyright © 2022 by David G. Radford

All rights reserved.

No part of this book may be reproduced in any form or by any electronic or mechanical means, including information storage and retrieval systems, without written permission from the author, except for the use of brief quotations in a book review.

ISBN: 9798359814089

PRINTED IN THE USA

I dedicate this work to anyone I have had as a student, to my own teachers, to Carol and to all the colleagues I have had the grace to work along side. I also dedicate this novel to the characters found within. They have a literary life to live and I learned so very much while recording some of it.

CONTENTS

1.	The Stranger	1
2.	The Future is in Color	12
3.	Some Other People to Keep Afloat	18
4.	Corn	25
5.	Two-Timer	39
6.	Buckland's Bad Day	66
7.	Chance Encounters	75
8.	Larky the Dog	99
9.	The Party	109
10.	The Back Nine	168
11.	The Brown Palace	201
12.	The Princess	244
13.	A Space at The Table	270
	Acknowledgments	285
	About the Author	287

1

THE STRANGER

Not more than three miles from his condo, a man sat on the sand staring at the horizon line where the ocean met the sky. Four years ago he had gotten a divorce. He continued to be stunned by it. To him, it felt as if he had ridden a rocket through the ozone without a windshield. It was only recently his feet could touch the ground, and by now he knew his insides had changed. He was far less of what he once was and more of a stranger. More a stranger to his kids, more a stranger to his ex, more a stranger even to himself. Over the last four years, enough time came and went for him to have caught up to himself. He hadn't. Things were different now.

He knew things he didn't know before. For one, he knew the world could end. His world, anybody's world, could fall apart in two splits of a second. That quick, it could all be over. He knew that for sure. Deep down everybody knows they walk on thin ice. But his days had made him painfully aware that not everybody had gone ahead and fallen in.

He also knew there was a great spirit that really existed, and he could get help if he would only ask or, as often as not, beg. It was a spirit that would help out, but he had to carry the heavy load. The spirit could buy him some time, and it had these last four years, so no doubt he had healed up a bit. No doubt.

Healed a little, but that feeling of being lost? He's had an impossible time shaking that. He got lost at the moment of separation from her. When he had to live for months away from the family in the first of several apartments. When the judge rapped the gavel and the divorce was finalized. When he had to leave the kids at her door after a weekend visit. He just couldn't hold on to himself and he got lost. Simple as that. The torque and acceleration and stardust had worn him away. So, he came down to the same town but to a different place than he had ever been. He sat on the sand. He kept his eyes fixed to the horizon. It was a beginning.

There were some parts he liked about this stranger he was getting to know. This guy went to the beaches more. All over, from Watch Hill, East Beach, Horse Neck, Falmouth Heights. Any beach was a good beach. He visited with them like steadfast friends. When the weather broke, the early spring winds off the sea blew away the ghosts he picked up each winter. Each year he was at the ocean later into the fall and earlier in the spring. He went when his two sons were with him and he went when they weren't. On the weekends when his boys were with him they were likely to walk the beach, throw the Frisbee or a baseball, or build complex sand cities, their skin darkening as the sands warmed.

Half the time, though, he was alone, and the day would come each year when he would cut through the water up to his waist, knife into the Atlantic and feel that blue chill race down his spine. With that level of commitment he would stay in a while, until the ocean seemed almost warm to his body. Then he sat on the sand, his large red towel wrapped around him while the sun dried him and bleached his brain. The crisp air was dense from being piled up by the light breeze coming in off the sound. This was a sky with low clouds running just above the horizon line. The sun seemed no bigger than a brass button. It had most of the sky to itself, but seeing it was early spring, the lingering winter chill took most of its heat. In a week or so the water would be right for the boys, he thought. And little Russell would complain that he didn't have any real chance and Dad wasn't supposed to be the first one in again this year.

Russell was his little soldier. The rain ran heavy on the day he was born. Connie's water broke two months early. She looked up from her oatmeal wide eyed as she stood up. Her denim dress was wet at the waist, her voice full of fear and amazement she breathed, "Daniel, call Doctor Slater while I get the suitcase packed."

She continued issuing orders. "No, no. Taylor, you get the yellow blanket from the closet in your room and spread it out on the couch for mommy."

" Connie, you stand right there. Don't move," he said, trying to take command of the situation.

Young Taylor spread the yellow blanket on the couch for his mother as instructed. "

"All right, all right, we're fine. Now, just sit on the couch, okay? I'll get the suitcase packed and call Doctor Slater. This is unbelievably early huh?"

By the time he contacted Doctor Slater and set up the suitcase, Connie had assigned Taylor to get her coat. "Is everything in the suitcase?" she asked.

"Don't worry it's all here. If there's anything else we need, we're only ten minutes from the hospital. Taylor, grab your jacket."

The three of them went out into the splattering rain and were soaked through before they could get into the car. Two-and-a-half-pound Russell Bainbridge joined them on this earth before their clothes could dry. Russell spent months in the hospital, placed in a small transparent plastic tent. When he would stop breathing an alarm rang and someone would pat him on the bum and he would start breathing again. His little arms shook and his little hands clenched into tiny fists. Connie stayed beside his incubator most days. Most nights, too. She would cradle their little boy and lean him towards the plate glass window. There was a stocking cap on Russell's head no bigger than a thimble, Connie's soft cooing noises filling his ears, her comforting mothering smile beckoning close to his new eyes.

On one of these visits, with Russell as usual behind the plate glass window, her head rose from Russell in the incubator. She looked through the glass and stared directly into Bainbridge's eyes, fixing her stare. The longer she looked the more it felt as if she was accusing him. He had somehow failed as a father. Without words she was pouring out that this was his fault. Russell came too early because there was something lacking in his dad. Something Connie was seeing now for the first time. This was on him. Something in the Bainbridge blood. Certainly nothing like this had ever happened before on her side of the family. This is your son, your fault, your blood. Her eyebrows knitted. She blinked several times all the while holding her stare. Abruptly, what could, under normal conditions, be construed as a thin smile, took hold and she returned to her Russell. They never actually talked about the incident. He figured, probably wrongly, that if what he had been thinking was true, he'd hear about it again.

He and Taylor stood on the other side of that glass window many times. He would tell young Taylor that once his brother got going he would be just like everyone else. Taylor believed him because his dad had said it and because Taylor believed it his dad did too. Now little Russell was, in fact, just like everyone else. He played soccer and baseball. He beat on his older brother incessantly and could spit from between his teeth. This year Russell learned to whistle.

Thoughts like these caused the worms to wake up in his stomach. But this stranger he had become knew it was time to pack it up and keep moving. Once the worms came out the only thing to do was to keep moving. He worked his arms through his heavy sweater, rolled up his towel, tossed his last two cinnamon rice cakes at a bossy seagull two feet from him and walked the beach, his eyes hidden behind dark sunglasses.

He reached Putter's Sea Grill, got to the long dark oak bar, and went to the corner near a wide window, which gave a view of the ocean and a large trawler in the distance working its way through silver water. A pack of Marlboros rested against the cash register. He leaned across and took a cigarette and was fishing out a pack of matches from a small cup when he heard, "So I see you've still managed to quit smoking, Daniel."

"Francis," he said, "I'm doing this for you. It is one less you'll have today. You will be thanking me for this when you're seventy."

"Bainbridge, bartenders don't live to seventy."

"Why is that?"

"They get to know too much."

He pulled on the cigarette and blew the smoke between his lips in a long sigh.

"Well, believe me Francis, mistakes are made. You might just slip past the bastards. Listen, do me a kindness and switch the music to a country station will you? And bring me a big cold draft. Please. While you're over there."

"Seeing as you look so pitiful I'll put it on while you're here. "But you know, the season's beginning. This soft folksy stuff is the atmosphere in here for the next four or five months. You've got to remember lad, that's a New England seacoast you're looking at out that window. I don't serve a lot of people from

Texas, including you. That's what it has come down to for you, has it? Beer and songs about trucks and dogs that run away, that's what makes you happy? And by the way, lad, you can't goddamn smoke in here."

"Whoever came into a bar to be happy, Frank?"

"Oh god, drink this and shut up. The winter is over. That counts for something, don't it? And put that cigarette out or go outside."

There was a woman eating at a wooden table near a small window. Her bronze hair was pulled back by a white bow and hung below her shoulders. She wore a white t-shirt and brushed green vest and there were thin gold rings on each of her fingers, though none of them a wedding ring. Maybe. She was pretty and about his age. Francis had just tuned in the country station when she looked up from her dish of scallops, melted cheese and green peppers.

"Francis, could you turn that up just a smidge more, hon?" She added, "That exact song right there has been my favorite song for months."

With the cold beer in his fist, he went and sat in a chair beside her, leaving the cigarette smoldering in a little white dish near the pack of Marlboros. "Now tell me, doesn't that boy sound like Elvis."

She didn't seem uncomfortable when he sat near her. She smiled, actually, then slanted her blue eyes in a playful way and said, "I'm so glad someone kept that voice alive. It had to be a country boy, of course. Francis must like you. He hasn't had that station on for two weeks or so. He swears the sun is here and the tourists are coming. Are you a tourist?"

"Pretty much. In a lot of ways you are right about that. Lately I can't find the bathroom without a map. Actually, Francis and I go back a few years. It seems I'm in here more and more each year. I sold him a house just four blocks from here and was here pretty regularly then. I was his real estate agent. We got to know each other a lot better at that point. I did go to high school with him though. Not that knowing him has been a major plus. You haven't wrecked that place yet have you Francis?"

Francis was directly opposite them wiping his bar with a damp rag and watching these two birds get to know each other.

"I think it is a wonderful house Dan. Why don't you come by and give me an appraisal?"

"Francis," she said with false indignation. "You're not going to sell that house. You just finished sanding all the floors and getting that kitchen straight."

"No, no," Daniel said. "Francis has me evaluate his house every year. Come to think on it, I'm starting to suspect he didn't believe me when I told him he was getting a good deal on that place. What does it take for you to trust somebody, Francis?"

"A driver's license and second form of ID."

"Oh, come on now, Francis," the woman jested in mock disbelief. "Long legs and a tank top would do it and you know it."

"Aubrey, behave. Be sweet. You are sitting near a friend of mine. Daniel Bainbridge, since I noticed you've been too awkward to introduce yourself I'll bail your butt out again. This sweet thang beside you is Aubrey O'Donnell. A northern redneck such as yourself."

He jumped in before Francis owned this conversation, managing to steady her eyes on his as he said, "Well now, in spite of his forceful introduction it is a pleasure to meet you, Aubrey O'Donnell."

They both pulled away from the look. A black duck pounding his wings two feet above the waves shot into the water and disappeared. She looked back to see if he had seen what she had seen.

"It won't come up for a long time you know. It drops from the air and swims under water longer than I could ever imagine," she said. The black duck's head broke the surface about 200 yards from where it had disappeared.

"Over there," he pointed in a short half stroke of his hand and arm. "I wonder where they lay their eggs. For that matter I've never seen a small one or a baby sea gull either. Both birds seem to show up in the sky fully grown."

"Well it has been my observation everything starts out small and gets bigger." She held back a grin and pulled her eyebrows up. "In any case I'll have to look closer this spring for the little ones."

She took money from her purse and left it beside her plate.

Bainbridge offered, "Can I buy you a dessert? Or some tea or something."

"No, but that is so nice of you. Perhaps another time." She slid out from her table and stood beside him for a moment. He smelled lime and spice from her clothing as she stood there. "It was nice talking with you." Her blue eyes took him in. He could tell she liked what she was looking at. "And Francis, tell Patty the food was great. Her bread is especially good tonight. Have a nice afternoon fellas."

"Bye Aubrey, "said Francis.

When she was gone the place went empty. There was country music playing and a big window and the ocean working against the beach. There was Francis slicing oranges into wedges at the bar, but the place felt empty. He'd stood when she had been talking to Francis. Now, he crossed to the bar, took one of the orange slices, and bit into the meat of it. Francis studied him with a silent smile. He began slicing another whole orange into eight precise wedges in about as many seconds. Still with that grin, he broke the quiet with, "Ah, aren't all women beautiful Bainbridge?"

"Strange you should ask me that question. I'm not sure I've

got this woman thing down just yet. Every daddy's little girl is a beauty. I know that much. It's just when she grows up and eventually moves in with another guy, now that's when it can get ugly. At least sometimes anyway. Women. What do I know. I do believe a woman can be the most beautiful creature on this earth. And I need to meet one as soon as I can, Francis. But god, they can leave a real mark."

"You just did meet one you bean head. And you let her just go out that door without getting a single piece of information about her. What's it been, three, four years since your divorce went through. You've got to start showing up when the game is being played lad."

"I've got her name don't I? Aubrey O'Connell."

"O'Donnell. And I gave you that. She was Roullard there for a while but took her last name back. Danny me boy you've got to be more thorough. There are plenty of shiny pebbles at the bottom of the brook, but you must search them out a bit. Try to get their phone number or where they work or something. Don't you remember any of this?"

The wolf inside him remembered all of this. The wolf in him was relearning how to range this land. Learning to lope along at a steady, unremitting pace. And yes, the unremitting was the harder part. Added to that was finding out exactly when and where to break through the parts of him that were locked down. His loneliness had become thick like a mist, a loneliness that clawed out pieces of him until his insides were left with worms and emptiness and more worms. His wolf blended into all of this to the point of being invisible.

His business, made up of clients, an office, a tech guy/office manager, and a team of two or three agents, would seem to be a type of connection and you wouldn't be wrong to think so. But this became automatic, a veneer of personality. Business can be a predictable pattern of exchanges. During the first year of his divorce he relied completely on the momentum of his business to run on its own. He found himself with a second nature: one which completely disassociated business from all the other aspects of his life. Russell and Taylor were with him fully. When he was with them, he had people. But it was clear to him even with his best efforts, space between them was widening. Four years made him see the unavoidable fact that their lives were mostly spent in a world apart from him. He admitted that it broke him every time he saw it happening. He could feel the weight of loneliness. It pressed down fast and heavy, breaking bones in his spirit. There were nights now where he woke to a loud cracking noise. He could never be sure if it was real since there was no one else there to hear it.

This animal, this wolf inside him picked up vibrations. Sensed all manner of signs no words could express. Because of it he knew he was getting close, closer. He could feel her heat. She was near. With Aubrey he could smell lime and spice, and the tangy smell of scallops carried on her breath, and in it all, the subtle differences between desire and fear. The hunt had to lead somewhere. She's close.

"You know," he said to Francis, "when I was shot out of the cannon and into the ozone, I got a good look at the earth. Not too many people know this Francis, but the earth isn't round really, not a perfect circle. It's pushed in from the top and the bottom a bit."

"What the hell are you talking about?"

"There were a few times, not too far back, when I seemed to be floating way out in space by means of a thin silver cord. And I mean way out. During one of those launches, I saw the earth as plain as I'm seeing you, Francis. More like a heartbeat than a circle."

"I don't want to know that. Nobody wants to know that.

You've got to bring your reality quotient up a few notches. Lad, I'll tell you what you should want to know about."

"Really, what would that be?"

"Aubrey's address and phone number. How could you let that moment go by and get so little out of it?"

"I got the feeling she likes me."

"And?"

"Hey, enough. Give me what you've got and I'll act on it right now."

"Right now?"

"Yep, right now."

"Well, I don't know her phone number or home address but I do know she owns the candle shop or stone store or the gift thing or the whatever in the center of town."

"Great, that's terrific. I mean all I have to do is pop into every gift shop in town until…"

"Bainbridge, stop your whining, just do what you said you would do and get out of here. I'm sick of the country music and I'm changing it anyway."

As he was leaving Bainbridge asked, "What is it about country music that bothers you so much?"

"My main reason is all the men are singing through their noses and it all sounds like its coming out of the same nose. There's more, but don't get me started," he said, then added "Git" in an exaggerated two syllable southern accent.

2

THE FUTURE IS IN COLOR

There were two rows of small clear jars. Each contained an oil of a different color - A red, a blue, a light blue, a yellow. Some had two colors in one bottle, like mauve and green, or pink in one half and red on the bottom. She told him the colors remained separated unless the bottle was violently shaken. Once the bottle was still again, tiny balls of the two colors could be seen returning to their original level.

She smiled and almost whispered, "Now just choose three colors or combinations of color from each row. Be relaxed and select the ones your eyes are drawn to. Avoid as much thought as possible."

"Only six? You have about twenty jars in both rows."

"Yes, there are a lot to choose from, but find three from each shelf. Now be a big boy and follow the rules."

"There are so many colors and little bottles. I can't even make a decision on whether the socks I put on were deep brown or dark blue. I'm sorry. This might not work for me."

"Try to use your eyes to feel something rather than to just see it. Let the colors tell you which ones to pick. Calm yourself and listen and look. Feel the colors. You'll do just fine, relax, there are no wrong answers. Take the time you need."

He tried to follow her, but she didn't really understand. She was pretty and he hadn't been with pretty since landing back here on earth. The smell of the bayberry and cinnamon candles she sold in her shop was pulling his mind to other little shops in other seacoast villages he had spent time in during his life as someone else.

He wanted to be friends with her already, not meeting just now and having to learn about each other. He wanted her to have known him for a long time and in this afternoon, finally, they were going to admit that they liked each other. Liked each other a lot, actually. Instead she was someone he had been with for no more than an hour. He was just becoming familiar with the way her face cut through space and the wetness in her voice. He knew she was strong enough to talk truthfully to someone she'd just met. More importantly, she could talk truthfully to someone she had known since time began. He was working hard to figure out exactly how he had come to this conclusion when she said as encouragement, "See, when you give yourself a moment you can find some peace and think about it, can't you?"

"Alright then, in the back row I like that one and that one and that light blue one next to it is trying to tell me something."

"Good. Very good," she offered as she took each one he selected and placed it almost reverently in front of him on the high counter which separated her and the bottles from him.

"I've always loved green. Put it beside the light blue one there, if you please. And the two-toned one and the scarlet red one on the end."

"Are you sure these are the ones you like the most?"

"Oh yes," he said.

"It would be all right to change any one of them or all of them if you wish."

"No, no. What we have before us are the colors that represent the inner me for today. I swear. So what do you think of me now?"

She came around the counter to tell him what the little bottles and their colored oils had to say about him. She stood shoulder to shoulder beside him. A long moment suspended itself as they adjusted to the warmth the two of them experienced. Beside him she stared in deep reflection at the bottles lined up on the counter. She then turned to face him as if to finally tell him what his arrangement of colors revealed. He shifted to the side to face her and noticed the luminescent quality to her blue eyes. She drew in on herself in an effort to find a stranger's truths inside her. Then he felt the palm of her right hand come lightly against his solar plexus. A sauna-like warmth radiated from her hand almost instantly relaxing his chest. He became aroused and grew large in spite of himself. Then her delicate touch was gone. He leaned closer to her and said, "Why did you do that?"

"I could tell you would let me. I suppose I needed to touch the person who is in front of me because, you see, there are at least two of you. The colors you've chosen talk about two different people. There is no continuity between what you pulled from row one and row two. I can sequence the personalities you own but you just came into my boutique. It is important to know which one of you is here, and a touch can convey so much so quickly, don't you think?"

"Well which one is me here?" He asked.

"The one that is alive," she said.

"Well, I don't know what you're talking about really but I suppose being the live one is a relief to both of us. Yes, I am the kind of guy who likes walks on the beach, theater, sunsets, candlelight, and everything from classical to country music." He saw she was amused and continued. "And a woman's hands inside my blue jeans as I read the Sunday brunch section on my phone. Did I mention rainy afternoons?"

"Oh, you sound so familiar."

"Well, I should by now seeing what has been going on at this counter so far."

"Aha," she laughed. "Alrighty then, let's just see if the colors can tell us a tad more about you than you would find by reading your own ad in the personals."

An Asian couple and their boy came into the shop and walked past them. They began a slow inspection of the books, cards, tie-dyed shirts and small statues of angels. He looked out the glass door that closed as the customers came in and saw a large mutt at the end of a leash trot by on the sidewalk across the street. The leash pulled a guy in black spandex and roller blades. His crash helmet looked like a blue plastic tear drop which tapered at the back of his neck. He felt a huge space open up beside him and he turned his head to see Aubrey moving back around the counter to face him.

"Now," she began in a wonderfully low voice, "the totality of these selected colors speak to a person divided, scattered. Your spectrum wildly shifts, as if a rainbow had touched the earth and created an earthquake. Whatever issues you are into, they will not end. You will merely grow bigger than they are. Or not. There are many sunset colors here. It is the time of day you are at your best. What thoughts or feelings come to you then are your truest guides for the day."

He became aware that the Asian family had stopped browsing and were collectively intent upon Aubrey's narrative. The woman was nodding in mute agreement while her husband's round face rose above Aubrey's display of angel statuary. Bainbridge held a practiced smile and a look of inquiry on his face. For an instant the boy caught his eye. The young one rolled his eyes upward in exasperated pity and then the boy went into the boutique's second room. Bainbridge's body began to separate from him. What was he doing here. Who were these people and why was it that at that moment he was listening to this woman telling him things about himself? He could hear the click of a switch in the back of his mind and actually hear inside his skin the sound of a furnace start up at the base of his spine. His tongue dried up as heat began to fill up his gut. He heard the Asian woman say, "She is very good Timmy. I would like her to do me next." With effort he ignored these people and tried to hold himself in by anchoring his eyes on Aubrey.

"You know, free yourself of regrets and look to the future," she told him. She scanned him trying to find out if he was following her. "The future hasn't happened yet so there can be no regrets. Your last two colors meeting in this little bottle are separate from each other as you can see but in a very real way they are together here in this glass. Do you understand what I'm saying? No? Well then, it is like this. They are not green and blue. They are saying see us as one. You can. It is possible. That is why you selected them."

"I've lost you. It is not your fault. I've got a very short attention span these days. I've eaten hamburgers with more intelligence than I have lately."

"That's alright. It's okay. Relax. Don't worry."

The woman had come up beside him and pushed a hundred dollar bill across the counter saying, "Excuse me, when you are finished with this man I would love for you to read the bottles for me please." Bainbridge looked down at the sheen of her silken black hair. A bright ring of light on the crown of her head from the recessed light above seemed like a halo to him.

Aubrey's door rattled open. "Keep the dog outside," Aubrey commanded as the man with rollerblades coasted up to the counter. He seemed to tower over them all. His wraparound sunglasses and teardrop helmet, his blue nylon jump suit, the black knee pads, wrist guards, and elbow pads made him appear like a kid's life sized transformer hero. Everyone at the counter twisted their heads upward to witness this presence roll toward them.

"Hey Aubrey. Don't you worry. Earl is outside. I'm just wondering if you're going to be hungry later. I can bring you some take out on my way back through town."

"That's nice of you Paul but a friend and I are going out when I close up. Or maybe it's the next night. I'm not sure, but no, no food thanks," she told him. "Paul this is Daniel and the lady beside him is Holly. Folks this is Paul Roullard. Among other notables is he is a wonderful plumber and my ex-husband, and apparently working for Meals on Wheels today."

The woman beside Bainbridge seemed disturbed. "How did you know my name? I've never met you before."

"Yes. Well those things just happen."

The woman looked back at her husband saying, "She is *very* good."

3

SOME OTHER PEOPLE TO KEEP AFLOAT

It will be more than once we get into who is the main character in a story like this. You, after all, are in the story now. What you bring to the story makes you a contender for main character I'd say. All I'm saying is how you take things may not be how I take things. If I have to say it out loud, then I'm a main character as far as I'm concerned. True as it may be, let me throw Bucky and a seagull into the mix.

I made Bucky a project of mine ever since I went to work at the plant. He's only a little older than I am so there is that. He's lean and cute with brown eyes that hop around like two sparrows. His diet is horrible though. Truth be told his lunch usually consists of iced tea and a large order of fries. So eventually I told him, "Bucky, you're packing your face full of oil and salt. Monday through Friday it's the same thing. It adds up, every working week of your life you eat the same thing. You're a walkin' dead man," I told him. "You are lean, sure, but this can't be all you are eating in a day is it?"

He told me, "My mom makes a huge meal almost every night

– can you believe it?" He does have a silly ass endearing smile, *but my god*, I said to myself, *the man still lives at home.*

A couple of months into working there, I'd seen Bucky a few times, especially in the cafeteria. If I was there, he'd come over. Usually we'd talk about somebody we knew at work, but I was also beginning to see that he was one of those "save the planet" guys. When he would start in on it I really didn't give him much time back then. I was too busy learning my job and trying to fit in to be taking on any big causes. He had gone off on the relative rate an Iceberg takes to melt out in the ocean and the variables that would go into that equation when I said to him, "Wait, wait. Look around you Bucky, is there anyone in this place, including me, that is thinking or wants to think about a melting iceberg right now? Just look around and tell me."

He did look around. He sat there and started his head bobbing from one end of the entire f-ing cafeteria to the other. At the time he wore his hair in a man bun. It looked ridiculous. He's an engineer. He is the plant's facilities manager if truth be told but you'd never know it from looking at him.

This is where we work. We all try to play the adult game here. Most of the time we win that game, but not always. I'm 25 and I know he's a few years older. We get paid to be here. This is not a Formica table in a high school somewhere. This is a Formica table we eat our lunch at and then go back and do some pretty complicated work.

At the beginning I had mixed feelings about him. I wanted him to notice the salad I'm munching on or the fish tacos or whatever. And I also felt he should be talking about me more, but no. Something always seems to come with him. Like the time he spotted that seagull. That's right, a seagull outside on that ledge. Right there at that window. A big old bird gawking in on all of us eating lunch. Swear to God.

Bucky said, "Look, it's a gull."

And I said, "You're right it is a gull. What do you think of this sweater, is it the right color on me?"

Then he said, "There's something strange about that gull."

"We are no more than two miles from the ocean, Bucky, a few sea gulls in the parking lot is a fairly common sight."

"That's true," he said. "But this one is standing at that window looking at a cafeteria full of people eating. What can he be thinking? Cheryl, Cheryl! No, no, look," Bucky says. "There's something wrapped around his head or something."

We both got up from the table and walked towards the window. That bird just stayed there. Right there staring at us. A fierce eye. A wide snowy white chest and slate grey folded wings. Then I see what Bucky had already noticed. One of those six ring plastic beer holders was wrapped around his head and beak. The plastic ring was that milky transparent stuff. You couldn't notice it wrapped around his white head right off. But that is what it was alright. The rings worked to net his head and tied his beak almost shut.

"He looks weak and angry," Bucky said. And I agreed with him.

People at other tables were beginning to notice him since we moved toward the window. About forty people eventually started gawking back at the bird standing outside on the windowsill. When it seemed like he had the entire room's attention the bird started marching back and forth along the sill. It was like he was on patrol.

"Oh Jeez," said Bucky. "We've got to do something. I've got to do something. Somebody's got to do something."

He walked out the exit door to the back where the bird was. Once outside Bucky walked really slow toward the sill, his arms outstretched. It looked like some sort of silent horror movie. The gull wasn't moving now. It was staring at this fool creeping up on him. Bucky got about a foot away and the gull jumped off the sill, ran along the lawn, flapped his wings to get over the three foot shrub line and it didn't make it. The poor thing got tangled up instead. Then it kinda flopped over the other side and began strutting around the parking lot.

A bunch of us had joined Bucky out there trying to casually catch the bird while it managed to strut along, keeping its dignity while we're lurking around pretending there's nothing we like better in the world than standing in the parking lot, and if we just happen to catch the bird fine but that wasn't the least bit our intention.

Finally the bird had enough of the running around the parking lot game. It got a good start and flapped his weary wings. He was getting going and he got about four feet off the ground when it hit the grill of a huge blue garbage truck that was barreling into the parking lot towards the trash bins at a billion miles a second. Like a bug on a windshield the bird was spread out and suspended on the grill for an instant that seemed to last forever. Then it dropped down below the bumper and fell under the center of the truck. As the truck whizzed on down to the other end of the lot, the bird's body was rolling to a stop on the pavement.

Bucky reached it first, yelling, "Damn it! God damn it!" I guess everyone figured that was that because they all went back to finish their lunches. I can still remember even Ann from Human Resources looking at me with eyes full of pity. She shrugged her shoulders turned and went back in with all the rest of them. That left me standing beside Bucky as he knelt and cradled the dead sea gull in his hands. We looked at it in a silence that went long enough for me to feel uncomfortable. The bird didn't look too bad except that it was dead, of course. Half the top beak was broken clear off and the plastic rings were still tight around his head.

"Damn it. Too bad. Damn it," said Bucky as he began to

unknot the plastic from up and under and around the gull's head. It was gross. When the bird's head was free of the plastic holder, Bucky handed it up to me without even looking or saying please. Nothing. So I was standing there holding this disgusting plastic wrap and I'm whining, "Oh, come on, Bucky. What am I going to do with this?"

But Bucky wouldn't talk now that I was stuck with this miserable plastic thing. He got up, still cradling the dead bird, and started walking small circles around the area where the bird got hit. I said to him, "Bucky, what the Christ are you doing?"

And he said, "Looking for the other part of the beak. What do you think I'm doing?"

"Oh come on, get a grip," I said. "I'm going in."

And I did, heading to the trash can near the condiment table to get that gross plastic thing off my hands as soon as I was in the door. People were milling inside the doorway, wanting to see the plastic and gape at it or whatever. But I told 'em, "You are all a bunch of sick people." And I got rid of it.

Jesus, Mary, and Joseph, the whole pack of them were insisting I show it around. But no. I threw it in the trash anyway. I noticed once it hit the trash no one bothered to go over and fish it out either.

I went back over to the window to see what Bucky was doing and he wasn't out there. Finally, I spotted him coming out of the maintenance department with a shovel in one hand and the bird in the other. He came over to the grassy area that ran from the parking lot to the cafeteria, went to that border of three foot shrubs over there, put the bird down and started digging a hole. It was a sick man I was looking at.

Mr. La Montaine showed up outside. He is the regional manager of the entire plant. The man liked to wear three piece suits and he did look good in them. He was always in a world class hurry, that one, you can tell. And so the whole place is in a hurry. Seemed like we struggle to make the product as good as possible, which meant in about half a year we were learning a new way to make the same damn thing. I'll admit, most of the time it was for the better. La Montaine is the guy who tries to explain it all to us. He's the guy that decided whether we kept doing what we were doing or were going to change it up or add another product line or whatever.

He was outside. I couldn't hear what he was saying but I could see La Montaine lean in to inspect the bird. Then it was pretty clear he wanted Bucky to toss the body into the trash bin down the way because La Montaine raised his arm and pointed directly at it.

I could see he was starting in on Bucky for digging up the factory's lawn. You could see La Montaine's arms flapping and every so often he pointed a finger at Bucky or the bird. All Bucky was doing was sometimes nodding his head yes, sometimes wagging his head no. All the while, Bucky kept digging.

Eventually La Montaine raised his arms to the clouds and stormed off, shaking his own head in disgust. There would be a price to pay for that, I'm sure. La Montaine made a lot of things more difficult than they had to be. You know what Three Piece did yesterday? It was all over the plant today. He's got a two car garage, you know. Oh yeah, big house, two car garage, the whole enchilada. Alice is his secretary and she has her morning coffee with me. She knows everything first and then spreads it around to the rest of us.

He was in his usual rush. He popped into his car, grabbed his controller, pushed the button to open his garage door and backed out. Right through his garage door. He came to a smashed up stop in his driveway, looked out his windshield and saw the garage door on the other side is wide open. He'd pressed the wrong button. So, he came in late and driving his wife's car, and Alice had to carry him through an entire day again. The man's doing the best he can, I suppose. And this place is humming.

That's the way it went. Basically. I didn't see Bucky the rest of the day. At the end of the shift I went down to the cafeteria and I saw the little round brown patch on the lawn through the big window. I went soft or whatever cause I went over to where I threw the plastic ring holder in the trash. It was right there. Yes, so I took it. Tonight I cut one of the rings out of it and I made a bracelet. But I don't think I can wear it for more than a day really.

This plastic bracelet is a reminder, my little moment to remember, after all is said and done, Bucky is a good soul. It just shows up on him. I do I see the effort he makes to do a right thing.

You are here now; you might as well see it through. If you want to know the town then you've got to know something about the people in it. They are complicated and Bucky is no exception believe me.

4

CORN

You may know my first wife, Aubrey Roullard. She was Aubrey Roullard because she was married to me, Paul Roullard. Now, of course, she's back to Aubrey O'Donnell.

You could say it was a poke in the eye – divorce. Actually it was best for both of us and we knew it. Hey, we're both proud we gave it a try. We stay friends though. Or I think we do. No reason to blame anybody. We just didn't fit. I don't have to think about it much if I'm busy. It is a plus. I could work day and night, night and day. Day, day, night, night. It's not that I want to, but I could. When times are good, I'm working. Even when things are down I find the work around town. You know, at this decently early stage in my life I've got more money than I know what to do with. I never thought I would say that. Even after our divorce I had the three apartment buildings within four blocks of each other. Think about it. I own them. This isn't bragging. Sometimes I'm amazed at it myself. Lots of people have more, and plenty of people don't have anything.

I'm 38 and a few nights back right here I'd say, in some delusional sense, I almost met my second wife at this very same place. And that would be about a week ago. If I really had married that girl I met that night I'm pretty sure it would have worked out. That's probably the delusional part. Funny how that goes. I only talked to her for a few minutes but I'll be carrying her around for a lifetime - again probably. I certainly carry my ex-wife around in my head, and if there is room for her there is room for anybody.

That's why I don't give myself a lot of time to think. I try not to overthink things but in trying to not over think things I'm still thinking. So, I'm a damn closed loop. As an example I tell you I can go round and round about Gerard dying on me. About a week ago she got added to my circuitry. But if I were to think about it, mind you, well, marrying her could have been the best thing that ever happened to me and it could have happened as far as I was concerned. If it had gone just a little bit, a smidge, differently. If that idiot hadn't showed up, who knows?

I should have just watched her. I could've had my beers and shoved off, gone my way, tucked it in for the night. I went to Putter's Pub for no good reason. I'm working all day and it's next to impossible for me to just go home and zone out. I can't just kick up my heels. That's my problem right there. Seventy miles an hour down to zero. It's tough. I'm not one of those guys who wants to go home eat his spaghetti, walk the dog, watch the tube and shuffle off to bed. I need to blow some steam. Not every night, but I'm alive. On occasion I like to go stupid like every other guy. He who lives to work is going to burn out fast. You know that. I know that. I do what I can to minimize the damage.

It was videoke night down here. Putters is where I met Cheryl. Her face absolutely filled the 65-inch screen. Her face reminded me of what I had been looking for since my brother died. An easy smile. Cheryl's eyes never once looked directly at the camera. They dodged from side to side. Two eyes that were guilty of petty theft. She had a smile you want to see happen as much as possible. She hid something behind that smile you could tell. Something funny, probably.

The emcee asked routine questions, keeping the video interview with her going. He was good. He'd get people to say some of the damndest stuff. He starts with something like, "If you were a movie star today, who would it be?" And pretty soon you're telling him how many times you've had sex this week or why your boss doesn't deserve the job. While you're talking, your face is up on 65-inch screens all around Putters and you are the star.

She was saying how cruddy she was feeling. "Yeah, my friend, Bucky, was to meet me here but the little stallion isn't here now, is he? I hate that you know."

"So what do you suppose happened to Bucky?" asks the emcee.

"Who cares," she says, "I'm sick of men saying they are going to do something and they don't do it. They're losers, complete losers."

"Well we're all glad you made the Putters Pub visit aren't we gang?" And all those bothering to watch her on screen and follow the emcee shout out a ragged collection of oh yeahs and whistles and clapping. "So you basically hate men is that it?"

"No, no, no. I basically hate one man tonight. He's really missing out you know." And again, whistles, snorts, clapping. The crowd was warming up to her. Her face filled the large screens. A beautiful woman. I was warming up to her. That curly brown hair that fell across one side of her face like wood shavings.

"As you can hear from all this whistling we all want to know exactly what this Bucky fellow is missing out on tonight?"

She slowly stood up and put her hands on her hips and in the poutiest, sultriest voice said, "Well, what do you think he's missing, big boy?" She loved the camera and the camera loved her right back. She was a goddess of videoke. She leaned towards the camera for her snifter and every man saw cleavage lolling into her low cut, powder pink sweater. She remained standing. Swirling her drink against the sides of the glass. A guy in a baseball hat at one of the far tables got to a microphone.

The emcee said, "We got a question from the crowd. Hello, sir. How we doing tonight?"

"Yeah, fine, amazing, yeah, amazing. Listen, my buddies and I want to know if she'd like to join us at our table. Since her friend didn't show up and all."

The camera stayed on her and she was shaking her head long before the guy was finished. "My momma told me about boys like you. Basically I personally never did listen to momma but tonight, you know what, I think I will."

"What's that supposed to mean? I'm a nice guy and I axe you out is all."

"Well, that's your problem right there. You're a *nice* guy. What American gal wants to go out with a nice guy. I mean really. Basically."

The women in the room piped in from every table and corner of the bar. Go girl and laughter and that's right and right on sister right on. "You know, I'll tell you and your friends there a secret. Like, what we want is to be with a baaddd boy. A dangerous man. The only Marine in the place. And a bother to the law doesn't hurt either. Women want to discover the nice guy in there that the world just can't see. You think you're a tough case and we want to be the only one that knows your soft spot. You ought to be taking down notes. Who else would tell you this but me."

"I'm not hearing no," the guy at the mike said while pulling his baseball hat lower, almost to his nose.

"Nah," she said, "It wouldn't work. For one thing you've got to come alone to places like this. You've got to learn when to leave the whole team back at home."

"So I guess we can take it you two aren't happening tonight," said the emcee. "Thanks for being on with us here at Putter's"

The baseball hat standing at the mike pushed in one last time, "Listen, I'd like to buy the lady a drink."

"Sure," she said as she sat down and finished what she had in her snifter. "But that's my point. You're a nice guy."

The emcee moved on and the camera worked through the crowd until I spotted a side shot of my own slope-nosed mug coming into close focus on the big screen. I tried to hide by remaining as still as a beetle. I studied the tiny bubbles in my half raised glass as if I'd lost a contact lens in there. It did no good. It never does at Putters. The camera moves around like a one-eyed beggar. The rat faced camera guy had decided it was my turn. It was going to be my TV moment. I heard some women's voices chirping good natured approval. This and my beer was all I had going for me. The emcee settled beside me like a new family in the old neighborhood.

"How you doing?" He asked.

"Fine."

"Are you a Putter's regular?"

"Nah, well maybe. I don't know exactly. What do you mean by a regular?"

"Ah ha, a born emcee, reversing roles and asking me the questions. Are you married?"

"No, not yet."

"Does that mean you've got someone in mind, someone you're dating or whatever?"

"No, it means nada." The camera shifted to my left hand and my fingers drumming the bar top. My fingers looked huge, like five party wieners doing the wave. "I'm not married and I'm not going out with anyone right now either. Pitiful isn't it?"

"No. Putters is packed with single people tonight. Am I right?" There was some cheering and applause to the emcee's statement. "What's your name?"

"Paul."

"Paul, what's your favorite thing to do – besides coming into Putters?"

"I like spaghetti," I heard myself answer. This seemed to rock the joint. Bursts of laughter were flaming out all over the bar. I realized I hadn't come close to answering this guy's actual question. I wanted my face on that TV to fade to black. I got nervous. Then I went stupid.

"So, you like eating as your favorite thing to do? Is that it?" He was trying to be helpful. I appreciated that.

"I said I like spaghetti. Eating spaghetti hasn't killed me yet."

"Have you had some close calls with other food groups? Are there peas and carrots lurking out there to assassinate you?"

"No, I haven't any close calls. My brother had a close call eight months ago and he's dead now."

"Your brother is dead? My dear god, I'm sorry. Tell us what happened..."

So, I said it into the mic and on to the TV screen and around the half buzzed crowd at Putters. I was tired of keeping it in. Tired in the knees from carrying him inside me. First time you hear this it may come across as a lot to blow out at a bar. But first off, this is Putters and just for a minute I wanted everybody at that bar to carry a piece of the load. I said I was tired, so yes, I let some of it seep to this thin little man wearing a white tuxedo shirt and holding out the microphone like a Geiger counter.

"My brother and me, we meet up and come in here, or used to, a lot you know. We've been hanging in here long before

Putters put in this videoke thing. We had a beer. Maybe three. He came over to my place. We were starving so I offered to cook up some spaghetti but nooo, he spies the makings for tacos in my fridge. The pasta was already in the water on boil. The sauce was heating up. But he wanted Mexican. Gerard always made life difficult. So, I said fine. I didn't argue with him. I said go ahead and cook up whatever you want and I pulled out a new box of Rio Chi Chi taco shells from the cupboard and tossed it to him. I'd say he cooked up about a pound of my hamburger. He chopped up my lettuce, shredded some of my best cheese, packed it all into three or four taco shells, then glommed on salsa, mild salsa.

"I ate the pasta. Not him though. He munched through those tacos, begging me to take a bite. Swearing they were the best he'd ever eaten. 'The Mexicans know what food works with beer,' he said. I stuck with my pasta and he ate tacos. All of them. He made a mess of my counter. Shredded lettuce and bits of hamburger and cheese scraps melted onto the electric coils of the stove, salsa drying on the tablecloth. Gerard cooks and the whole world has to clean up after him."

"I get it. I remember now. I read it a while back," said the emcee. "He was one of those that ate the Rio Chi Chi taco shells."

"Yeh, he's one of those that ate the genetically altered corn Rio Chi Chi put into its shells. It should have been me but it was him. That goddamn corn was supposed to go to cattle. Not my brother. He died that night at his place. He was a human being not an animal. The next night after work I went over to his place. He was on his couch. Dead. His teeth and fingernails were glowing in the dark for Christ's sake."

"Oh, man, that's horrible... Listen folks, we'll take a break right here. We will be back at you and in your face in about 20 minutes. So drink up and stay tuned for more Putters videoke.

You're the star here at Putters. And again, I'm sure I speak for everybody here, sorry about your brother."

My face washed off all the screens and the sets went black. Some Rock-a-Billy music came out of speakers high up on the wall. It was a feeling like when the priest closes that little shutter in confessional. What the hell had I said all that for? I needed beer. And I got it free from the barkeep who nudged the mug along the counter with his fingertips but wouldn't look at me. Nobody would look at me. I thought, sure you'd watch me in close up on the screen but you can't look at me live. Shit. I missed my brother and I couldn't get past the blue hazy light coming off his fingernails, his teeth, his eyes.

There was a presence beside me. It smelled of ivory soap and lemons. She had sandwiched herself between me and the next stool. Her snifter rested next to my beer mug. It was the videoke goddess from before my little star turn.

"Hi, you poor baby, you call me Cheryl. You know you need to get your mind off of that thing with your brother."

"Absolutely."

"So, you want to play pretend for a while?"

"Pretend what?"

"Pretend we are a married couple and we are just out at the bar for the night."

"Absolutely."

"We'll pretend, okay? You're not married already are you?"

"No, not at all. Are you?"

"Would I be asking a man to marry me if I was already married? How dumb is that?"

"So, we're married then."

"Yep. Isn't this fun," she said. "Did your brother really pass on?"

"Yes. Yes, the corporate lawyers will probably argue even that. My mother is suing everybody. Rio Chi Chi, Monsanto

Biotech, the grain elevator, the farm that grew the corn. On and on. I think in a way it keeps her mind off the cold fact that Gerard is dead."

"That is so… unbelievable. What a way to lose your brother." She leaned her chest against my arm. "God you don't know what to eat anymore. For that matter, you don't even know what you're eating when you do eat. Sweet Mary and Joseph. You poor baby. Keep damn science out of my body, that's what I say. Don't you? Hey, let's think about something. Like… where do we want to go on our honeymoon?"

"That sounds great but aren't we pretending to be a married couple out at Putters tonight?"

"Sure, but we go on a honeymoon once a year. So, where are we going this year?"

"We can do better than Putters this year. I've got plenty of dough," I found myself saying, "I'm a plumber you know." And feeling like I had to compensate for that somehow, "What about Athens, or somewhere in Italy. Want to go to Cancun? California wine country?"

"Let's do them all." Her eyes twinkled.

"Yeah, that's an idea. A very good idea. This year let's do a honeymoon that lasts an entire year. We'll just kick back and go to a bunch of great places."

"I bet you look great in a suit."

"Do you always ask strange men to marry you?"

"You're not a strange man. You are a sad one."

"I'm probably both if I had to be honest with you."

"Don't be honest with me. Let's not start that. Men can never be really honest. You guys have that x and y chromosome thing going. The short version of the story is you're always at war with yourself. Can you believe how hard this makes it for a woman? Watching you guys struggle. Certain men have no idea what we women fight through to keep you guys from tearing yourselves apart. And everyone around you for that matter. A certain man should have been here about an hour-and-a-half ago but do you see him around here? Honesty? Men are short on that. No. He said he'd meet me here but he's a lying sack of shit. Oh, god, did I say that?" She took out her lipstick and brushed it along her lips, then pressed her lips together. A quick unconscious act. Her lips were gorgeous and now pink like her sweater. "Be a sweetie and get me another snifter of brandy or whatever."

Something big was standing close behind us. I could feel its heat on the back of my ears. I was trying to get the bartender's attention and saying to her at the same time, "My name is Paul Roullard by the way. I figure if you're my new wife you'd want to know more than the fact I was a plumber." Her eyes opened wide but she was looking past me to what was standing behind us. I don't think she actually ever heard my name.

"Well, look what the cat drug in," she hissed.

I turned to look over my right shoulder and saw a big lanky guy with a sheepish grin shifting his weight from one leg to the other. "Bucky, you left me alone in here all night. No matter what else you say you left me alone in here. You jamoke."

"Cheryl, I've got a good reason. Don't get so miffed." The guy tried to lessen her irritation by putting a paw on the shoulder of her sweater and sort of unconsciously picking off burrs of tiny pink fuzz.

It seemed to calm her down. "What have you got to say for yourself, you mook?" She said in half the anger. He'd moved from being a jamoke to a mook. He seemed to be making progress.

"La Montaine was paying me to haul some trash out of his backyard this after. A smashed up garage door, trim boards and twisted metal runners. Everything was going along right on schedule until I tried to start my truck. The damn alternator died right there. Poof! Nothing. Right there at La Montaine's house. The load was already in the truck and everything. Cheryl, are you getting any of this? Look at me. I had to call Triple A. It took 'em forty minutes to get to me. I had them tow the truck to my mother's house. I borrowed her car to get here. I had to clean up, and voila here I am. You happy to see me or what? I'm late is all."

He looked at me and shrugged as if it was no big deal and since I was a guy I'd agree with him that it was a mountain made out of a molehill. Sensing he was sinking fast, I stayed out of it. It seemed to me the mountain was the dirt from the grave he was digging for himself.

"Let me get this straight. You had a choice tonight between going on a dump run or a date with me." She held out both palms of her hands as if they were scales weighing these options up and down. "Dump run or date with me."

"Whoa. Whoa. Whoa. Monty let me out of the plant an hour early and he was paying me extra out of his pocket. There would have been plenty of time, Cheryl. How was I to know the alternator would blow? I didn't see a problem here when he asked me if I wanted to pick up a couple of bucks. Seemed like a no brainer to me."

She shooed his hand from the back of her sweater. "You can't do two things at once. I know you and let me tell you something, you can barely do one thing at once. You're about two hours late, you moron. That's a problem for me. Certain men don't know what's important in life. I'm important Bucky. Me. Not a few extra bucks from La Montaine. Anyways I'm married now so you can just piddle off and forget it."

"Married," he said, his face aghast. "Married to what?"

"I am married to this gentleman right here. We got married about twenty minutes ago."

"Get out," he blurted and he gave me what I would have considered a good-natured shove but I was turning to face him. I had both feet off the footrest as I began to spin on the stool. With nothing to anchor me, his jab against my shoulder sent me into the guy sitting next to me.

The videoke people were setting up again and that rat faced camera man happened to be scanning the bar crowd just as this jerk pushed against my shoulder. It was up on the screens. No doubt about that. The crowd got to see it in slow motion three times. You see a guy with a man bun pop at my shoulder. You see my legs blow out like I'm riding a wild bull. My body collapses back almost into the lap of the guy in the stool to my left. It looks violent. Not that it was, but the screen made it look like the beginning of a class A bar brawl. The crowd sounded hungry. "Oh yeah. Right on. Fight. Fight. Get him. Get up you bum." That's what you get to see three times. My surprised face staring up from a guy's lap and finally the screen went black.

"What the hell are you doing, Bucky. For Christ's sake Bucky."

"Nothing Cheryl. Nothing. I just gave him a little jab is all. I swear just a jab."

"Jab, my ass buddy. What are you trying to do here?" I thumped with my index finger to his chest.

Cheryl pressed her way between the two of us. "Bucky, what did you come for? Really? Was it to ruin everything? What are you pushing him around for? He just lost his brother, show some respect, you ditz."

"He lost his brother? How? Where?"

"Let's not worry about my brother right now."

"Terrible. That's terrible. Lately you can't go anywhere without meeting somebody who has lost somebody. It's probably why we are all back drinking again. My cousin's neighbor died in his swimming pool and the guy was just one town over. And I got an uncle, remember me telling you Cheryl, he died in that Detroit train explosion a while back. He was dressed in a grey suit and going to work. That's all he was doing, just going to work. And now you. I tell you, life ain't what it used to be."

"Please, Cheryl, that's enough," I said.

"No, no. Certain people have no capacity for sympathy. And this certain person can ruin a perfectly good night just by showing up late and acting like a side of beef."

"Hey, I'm sorry to the both of you. Sorry. Really. I didn't mean anything by it. I'm surprised is all. Surprised. Confused. Confused. Surprised. That's right Cheryl, confused. Are you two married? What are you talking about here?"

"Forget about it. You've embarrassed me to the point I want to melt. Get me out of here. Can you do that Bucky? Put it all together enough to do that will you? It's time to leave this place and go home. Bucky can you make that happen?"

Bucky looked at me to see if I had ideas of a fight over Cheryl or the push I'd caught from him. "Forget about it," I said.

"Yeah, forget about it," he echoed and he brushed his chest and flashed me a quick peace sign.

"Hon," Cheryl said to me, "I can't tell you how sorry I am for everything. You're a good man. I can see that in you. Remember that. We had fun though. Right? No harm done, right? I got your mind off your brother for a while. That's something isn't it? It was fun to pretend. Right?"

"Yeah. Yeah, really. No harm done. You certainly moved my mind from point A to point B."

"Sometimes that's all it takes. Be strong, sweetie. I'll say a prayer for your brother."

"Yeah, he'll need that."

Bucky said, "Ya know, I could use a beer."

"You could use a mud hut by the riverbank that's what you could use. But you're getting neither one tonight. You're taking me home in your mother's car. God, certain men don't know what's what."

They left just as the barkeep slid Cheryl's next snifter of brandy towards me. Out the door went a potential wife. I know you'd say I'm exaggerating. But I'll tell you, after your brother has turned phosphorescent blue and died there's not much in life that is an exaggeration. The people you can get to meet in this town can drive you crazy good.

5

TWO-TIMER

Bainbridge could not be certain, but it was pretty clear by now that certain couples went over to Connie and others stayed in his camp. These were couples he and Connie went to restaurants with, had over for adult dinners and drinks on the deck when the kids were put to bed early. Four years later, out of that bunch now, Bainbridge could count on La Montaine and Francis for sure. Clearly gone are the Braybecks, the Orlandos, the Marstons. And that's okay. To hell with them. Friends. He was down to a few. There was room for more, admittedly. His condo and his phone were too silent for his liking.

He was walking from his car towards the town's soccer field, walking past Tom Orlando and Paula Marston intent on their kids out on the field. Bainbridge headed into the shadows of the refreshment stand. There were ten town league soccer fields spread out before him but he lingered beside one of the picnic tables under the roof of the refreshment stand.

La Montaine. Monty's wife, Evelyn. Their daughter Susan. They were all seated at a table to his right. The eleven-year-old,

Susan, had on her soccer gear and her face was flushed. She was over-heated from a game just finished.

Bainbridge stepped into the sun and green fields when he heard, "Danny, hey!"

Bainbridge turned back to the three La Montaines. The distance is only fifteen feet from where he heard the call. Montaine has this grimace working for a smile and an anemic little wave he barely let live. This he used to finish up his hello.

"Hi," Evelyn said softly. Susan, who is one year older than Taylor, stared down along the straw into her Gatorade. She was breaking off pieces from an oversized chocolate chip cookie.

Making no effort to shorten the distance, Bainbridge asked all of them, "Did you guys win?"

"No, but Susan and the team played great. Conti Construction won though. It's their season I guess."

Bainbridge looked at Evelyn. Evelyn would only give him eye contact for a second. She busied herself picking up a piece from the broken cookie on Susan's plate.

By moving slowly toward the fields, Bainbridge indicated he wasn't going to stop. He knew this was a relief to La Montaine. "Well, Monty, maybe next Saturday it will be your turn for a win. And Susan, it's how you play the game not the win. Right?"

"So true Danny," Monty offered up since Susan was too busy being a soccer princess. "I saw Connie over there Danny. She's got somebody with her, but hey I don't know."

"It's the game not the win, right?" Evelyn said this to Bainbridge while keeping her eyes occupied on the chunk of cookie she lifted from her daughter's dish.

He was into the green and sunny field now. Rushes of yellow shirts with green shorts hovered around a soccer ball. A coach was yelling, "Don't beehive! Spread out, spread out!"

Bainbridge scanned the fields attempting to locate the group of players with the green tops and black shorts of Taylor's team.

The sun warmed him as did the familiarity of the scene before him. It was late April. The light was crystal. This was spring soccer, more a maintenance league to sustain skills learned last fall but maybe forgotten over the winter. The town organized it. The fields were full of teams. Some of them in mid game, others in two lines before the net. A goalie rolling the ball out to a player racing towards it kicking it with the side of the foot. The ball rifled high and wide. Parents and grandparents on lawn chairs or blankets lined all the fields.

Bainbridge enjoyed taking his boys to these games. It used to make him feel wholesome. Colors of yellow, pale blue, pink, purple, lime. These were like banners that waved down and back across the fields. Cheers and applause reported that somewhere an important goal had been scored. He felt a part of it then. Now he didn't feel it so much. It wasn't that he forced himself to go. He wanted to go. His boys were playing. Often, when they were staying over, they would suit up and head out to the fields from his place. It was a work-around for all of them. Connie insisted she got continuing credit making sure there were the shin pads and the clean uniforms and juice boxes. Connie got the boys to the fields on time. Connie, Connie, Connie. He noticed this year when he took the guys to the fields from his place she didn't come to those games.

He stood off from them. Closer to the goal defended by Putters. Russell left Connie's side.

"Hi dad," he said in a small voice that he never used before.

"Russell, how you doing?" He put his hand affectionately down on his son's shoulder. An urge to collapse to his knees and bring Russell to him and sob nearly overwhelmed him. Bainbridge rode above the impulse and in words that seemed hollowed out he managed to say, "What did you have for breakfast today?"

"Mom made scrambled eggs and toast. I think."

"Now, that's terrific. Breakfast is the best meal of the day isn't it? Hey, Bay Bank could give Putters a real problem out there today. Don't you think?"

"You know Dad, Bay Bank has won three games in a row."

"Well, that sounds like an immoveable force. How's your big brother doing? Is he up for this game or what?"

"He and mom were arguing about being late getting ready for the game this morning."

"That's too bad."

"He's always late getting ready. This morning he couldn't find one of his socks. Mom found it in the hamper and said he should have found it. He's got one clean one and one dirty one and he's not happy."

"Well, we all know how he gets Rus. Main thing is to show up and play as best as you can. It's not the clothes. It's the guys in the clothes that counts."

Russell began to rummage in the pocket of his shorts. "Dad, I got something for you." He pulled his hand free of his pocket and opened his little fist. In his palm were several cubes of Bubblicious gum, an empty wrapper, which blew away and onto the field, a few pennies, a dime and something he very carefully took out from the center of his cupped palm. He reached up and gave it to his dad. It was a blue piece of sea glass nearly the size of a penny.

"Blue sea glass, Russell, what a find! Terrific. Absolutely beautiful. And huge. Blue sea glass this size is impossible to find, Rus."

"Wait, Dad, wait and see this one. See dad, there's this tiny one?" Russell placed a tiny droplet of glass into Bainbridge's open palm. The sea had rubbed the glass into the shape of a perfect tear. These are known as angel tears, the rarest of finds on a beach. It rested beside the blue glass until Bainbridge's hand began to quiver and he closed it into a fist. He could barely see Russell. It was as if he were looking at his son through an aquarium. He put on his sunglasses and knelt into a catcher's stance to bring himself down closer to his son's height. A voice cracked loud behind him as he hunkered down.

"Dan, this is, ah, ah, well now, this is funny, I'm actually doing this. I practiced this a couple of times; this is just embarrassing. Sorry, sorry. Let me try this again. Danny, I'd like you to meet Bob. And Bob, this is Danny."

He knew it was Bob. What was she thinking? That people didn't talk in this town? Bob seemed shorter than he did when looking at him from a distance and older, though probably younger than Bainbridge at 37. Following his divorce he discovered everyone on earth is younger than he is.

"Dan. Danny. This is where you stand up and say something."

"Yeah, I suppose it is." While still kneeling with Russell he rubbed the wash of emotion from his eyes. He stood filling his lungs. "So this is Bob."

"Hi Dan, it is nice to finally meet you. You and Connie have some great kids I tell you."

Russell tried to insert a question, "Dad, when can you take us to Race Point or something?"

Bob stood close to Connie, his hands in his jeans and his shoulders frumped over as relaxed as a well-loved teddy bear. "So Bob, everybody in town knows you've sort of moved right into my old house. Hey. I get it, not my house anymore but you've got to admit it's a pretty nice spot don't you think? And tell me something, do my boys call you Bob or Mr. Whatever the hell it is? And what is your last name exactly?"

"Dad, when are we going to Race Point beach?"

"I'm wondering, Bob, when the guys are roughhousing who breaks up the fight. You or Connie."

"That's enough. Let's go. Russell, come on, we're going back down field now." Connie looked at Bainbridge with her eyes shuttered to the width of razors. "You're stupid and you're mean. You're almost yelling. For god's sake get some help."

"Dad. Dad, Dad, when do you want to go to Race Point?"

"No Connie wait. Wait. Bob, do the kids see you shaving in the morning and at breakfast do you talk about business or sports or news? What, what is it you talk to my kids about. Huh? Wait! Wait! Where does everybody sit around the TV Bob?"

They had their backs to him now. Connie was slightly leaning over Russell with her arm across his back and shoulder, ushering him down field and along the sideline like some refugee mother in a damp wind.

"Bob, do you have clothes in my closet now or what? Bob, what are you doing? Talk to me Bob. You haven't said a damn thing. And Rus, Russell, we'll get to Race Point next weekend. When you're with me." Bainbridge barely heard the word Dad from behind. A tug on the back of his shirt turned him around. It was Taylor with the game swirling behind him.

"You ok?"

"Yes, yes son. I am okay."

"What are you yelling about?"

"Nothing, Taylor. That wasn't yelling. It's okay. everything is fine. You're doing great out there. You'd better get back."

Taylor was all dirt smears and sweat. His eyes were clear and they worried over Bainbridge for a long moment.

"It's okay. Really. I was just telling Rus we have to get to Race Point next weekend. When we get together, we'll all go out there for a few hours. Get back on the field will you. Try to win this thing."

"See you soon Dad." And with that Taylor was back on the field and running towards the ball.

Bainbridge had never felt more alone in his already alone life.

He heard a familiar voice at his ear and he turned to see Francis. Francis came to all of Putters' games. Even though he had no kids of his own he sponsored the team and tracked their progress through each season as if he were the owner of a franchise.

"I am reminded of what father Burns told us all this morning at mass," he said. "Naturally, he was talking about Jesus. But I sense it could be about you, Danny boy. If you had been there Danny you'd have sworn the good father was talking directly to you. Let me think. I believe the quote was 'He went amongst his own and his own received him not.'"

"You're not far off the mark Francis. It is times like this I feel further and further away. I'm just thinned out. There is no shape, no substance to me. Have you got a cigarette?"

"No, and you shouldn't be smoking in front of the kids anyway. You used to know that."

"Look at this," said Bainbridge as he opened his palm to show Francis the blue glass. "And look there, an actual angel tear. Russell just gave them to me. You know how hard it is to find blue glass let alone this. That boy can hunt. He just gave them to me. He is a giver that one. This will get me through a week I swear."

"It sure as hell will. Listen, on another matter, Aubrey has been asking about you. What did you do, so you did go down to her boutique? You rascal. You did, didn't you. She's been asking so many questions about you, I finally said I'd try to push you along and set you up with a date with her. She didn't argue the point, if you know what I mean. I think you should give Miss O'Donnell a call and go out. Like adults. What do you think?"

"I think I better think about it."

"I think you'd better stop thinking and pick up your phone. How hard is that for a real estate guy to use the phone?"

~

Days slipped between each other until mid-week. Bainbridge had a condo listing he knew would go fast. It was right on the canal. Beautiful water views. The sailboats and expensive yachts holding tight to their moorings confirmed you were with people who know the good things. The very good things. At $950,000, a lot of people around here would be extremely interested. Prices had reached a point where people with money knew the value in a good deal. He had two clients in mind and would be calling both of them around four today when they were still likely to be at work. They could drive by the property and be impressed. He would follow up that night around eight, after their dinner hour, to set up a showing time.

This morning could not have come fast enough for Bainbridge. He'd rolled around in bed waiting for a sleep that never came. When light showed at his windows, he got out of bed and called the office. Allen, his tech and office manager, told him he had a showing on that exact waterfront condo in an hour. No problem there. All business is good business. The tie went on and the dress slacks and the business shoes.

Three times last night he had picked up the phone to call Aubrey. And then it got too late and it just would have been stupid. This moment was it. It was early, but early is better than late. He punched in Aubrey's numbers and waited. The phone rang four or five times. He was about to just hang up when her voice came on directing him to leave a message. "Yes, yeah, this is Dan, Dan Bainbridge. Aubrey, you know I was wondering if um, well, I was wondering if you'd like to go out to dinner with me tonight. I was thinking around seven or eight or whenever you want. I think guys pick up their dates around seven, don't they? Maybe not. I'll check in with you later today to see if you like the idea. Or some other day may be. Okay then, hope to talk to you later this afternoon, bye." Jesus Christ, that doesn't even sound like me, he thought.

He drove through the part of town that followed the shoreline and pulled into beautiful Waterline Condominiums. Unit 12. A three bedroom, two-and-a-half bath classic, with an executive kitchen and water views to die for from just about every window. He actually said to himself, "This is going to be a good day. I can feel it," as he leaned into his back seat to retrieve his trusty clipboard.

Bainbridge stood outside and shared some quiet time with a violet rhododendron big enough to vote and a man-sized azalea bush that was a shocking white in full bloom. That's when he heard the first sound of it. A growl. The flathead growl of a Harley slowing on the main road and turning into the gateway of the Waterline complex.

Two people and their motorcycle came into view. They took a left in the general direction of Bainbridge. The motorcycle gave a husky purr and worked its way to unit 12. The pair, in black boots, faded blue jeans, black leather vests, t-shirts, and wearing matching black helmets with tinted privacy shields, cruised closer, accompanied by an ever-increasing rumble of noise. For an instant they stopped in precise balance, the silence following the engine shutoff sudden, roughly eight feet from where he stood.

Oh God no, Bainbridge couldn't stop the thought from rioting around in his head. These two won't be able to afford this place. Damn. Allen is going to have to do a better job of screening this stuff. I mean, God, this could bung up my whole morning. Ah, damn, I'll find out what they can afford and sell them something nice. We have some decent inventory. This place here will sell in the next day or two regardless of these characters. After he's talked with these two there will be plenty of day left to call the three other clients of his interested in a place like this.

While Bainbridge was passing through his thoughts, the passenger on the back of the motorcycle dismounted the Harley and took off his helmet. His face was round and unshaven. A scraggly beard hung from his double chin. He had a pudgy, pleasant face that contradicted the muscled bulk of his body. Bainbridge put him at about thirty-five. The man was short but massive like an old growth tree stump. His bulky arms were bare up to the white t shirt. Arms that were covered in tattoos. There were more tattoos on that man's two arms than Bainbridge had seen in his entire life. He cradled the helmet under his left arm and walked towards Bainbridge.

The man extended a hand, which was also tattooed beyond the knuckles. Bainbridge shook it with a firm grasp. A hard squeeze was returned. "Yo, how you doin'?" The man gave a broad, likeable smile which revealed a mouth with at least one tooth missing. Oh, here we go, thought Bainbridge, I'm dealing with a guy with more tattoos than he has teeth. "I'm Nick. You the guy from Bainbridge Realty?"

"Yes sir, I am. It is good of you two to come over and take a look at this place. I'm Dan Bainbridge. Nick, I'm sure you are going to see that this is a very special place. You're going to love it. It's a great buy."

Nick turned his face slightly towards the motorcycle and said, "Hey Kate, this is the place. This is Mr. Brainfudge."

"No, Nick, excuse me but the name is Bainbridge."

"Yah, that's it. Kate this is Brainbridge"

Kate stood straddling the cycle. She caught the kickstand with her boot and pulled the bike backwards onto its stand, then lifted her right leg high over the saddle and stood free of the bike. When she took off her helmet, she revealed shiny black hair, bobbed to her chin. She shook it loose from the compression of the helmet, all the while looking at Bainbridge from under her long eyelashes and holding a steady little smile. It was hard, no, impossible for Bainbridge to think. His stomach tightened. He didn't know where to place his hands or eyes. She rested the helmet on the seat of the bike. "There," she said, "Am I irresistible?"

He heard himself saying, "I have nothing but admiration for the way you take off a helmet. You have no competition. No contest. Your plaque will be hanging in our office by tomorrow. Right in our hallway beside our salesperson of the month, welcome, hi. I'm Dan Bainbridge."

"Only for a month? And who is the salesperson of the month?"

"The way things are going? I suppose this month it will be me."

"Then I am in very good company. Sales figures and beauty, are they ever very far apart? I'm Katherine Tabor. Call me Kate, Mr. Bainbridge, or we will never be friends."

Nick said, "Jesus Christ, that's the way it is with us Italians. You have to be family or friends before we can do any business."

She arrived where Nick stood. "Here are the keys. My whole body is purring. I think it's time I bought one of these bikes for myself."

Nick said to Bainbridge, "You like my tattoos do you?"

"Well, yeah, they look good on you."

"Take a look at this one," Nick turned his back to them and pulled the back of his shirt and leather vest up to his shoulder blades. "Do you see it?"

Among the swamp of tattoos he had on his back Bainbridge saw on the lower left, just above the belt line what he hoped Nick was referring to. It was almost a photographic rendition of the Twin Towers. Smoke billowing out horizontally about three quarters of the way up the tower on the right. "My grandpa was in the collapse of tower one. Nice, huh, about every two years I get it retouched. They all fade from the sun or wear out a little bit. Especially around the elbows and hands. Maintenance is a bitch, my man."

"You know, that is the first one I've ever seen like that."

"All mine are very cool believe me."

"Isn't it painful having all this work done on you?"

"What isn't painful? You tell me."

"Nick, you're grossing me out. I haven't even bought this place yet and you're treating it like it's the front yard or something. You're embarrassing me. Pull your shirt down and behave."

Bainbridge came up with something to shift the conversation away from Nick. "That bike looks like a terrific way to get around town. Especially in weather like this."

"It is. What a major thrill! But I don't own it. It's my cousin Nick's."

"Yah, and every time I take her out on the chopper she says she's going to buy one."

"Nick is so sweet, don't tell him but any time I want to drive a bike I can just give him a call and away we go."

"Hey, I'm right here. I can hear you. I hate when you talk about me as if I'm not there."

"Dan. Don't tell Nick, but he is my absolute best cousin. We have a lot of fun. He's my guardian. He's strong like bull."

"She's really a Cuomo, like me, so what are you gonna do? She wants a ride; I give her a ride. If it makes her happy I'm happy."

A cell phone rang somewhere in Nick's blue jeans. He found it, flipped it to his ear and turned a bit to the side. "Wha? No. Ralphy? Is he hurt? Ah for Christ's sake. How stuck is it? Mother of God. Yeah, I'll be, I'll be there. I don't know. Soon."

Bainbridge had lost the momentum here. Nick shut the

phone and turned to them. He showed a meaty grin, "Kate, we gotta go."

"What do you mean, we have to go. Come on, we just got here and I haven't even seen the place. Mr. Bainbridge has taken time out his day to be here. Please?"

"Well, what can I tell you. Ralphy's got the backhoe stuck in a collapsed septic tank we didn't know was even on the damn property. I've got to get another truck over to the site and pull the backhoe out. It could collapse the edge and roll completely into the thing."

"Oh, Nick, damn. Is Ralphy hurt?"

"The little shit is fine. It's the rig I'm worried about. It is half in and half out of some hole in the ground. Ralphy is a piece of work. That scrawny geek can't go a day without finding some way to screw it up. It's like the only thing he's really good at."

"I doubt this was Ralphy's fault. You should be grateful he isn't hurt."

"Maybe. But if that backhoe is busted up I'm going to choke him 'til he passes out."

"Nick, be nice."

"Nice? It would be nice to hang out here and check this place out, but we can't right now Kate. Sorry. But we've got to get going."

"Of course, we will Nick but I'm still driving until we get to my place. I'll come back in my own car. Mr. Bainbridge can you wait and hour?"

Bainbridge could see an option here. In the time it had taken him to think through how he would use the hour, Kate had noted his hesitation and said, "No, tell you what. Nick you take the motorcycle and go take care of what has to be done. I'm going to stay and check this place out. I'll just call an Uber, that's all, see."

Bainbridge was quick with his reply. "Kate, you don't have to do that. I bet you don't live too far away. I'll show you the property and then drive you back to your place, no problem."

"Well aren't you nice. I do live in town, on Inlet Drive?"

"Sure then. Let's take a tour of the place and then I'll drive you right back home. I know that area very well."

"Kate, gotta go, that works for me if it works for you but I gotta go."

"I'll stay with Mr. Bainbridge then." She stood beside him and wrapped her arm around his as if they were a couple about to stroll down a boulevard.

"You take good care of her Brainfridge. Call me later, Kate, and let me know what you think of the place. It certainly looks fine from the outside." Nick returned his helmet to his head then tied Kate's to a metal loop at the back of his cycle.

"You take care and be safe mister," Kate said. "Make sure Ralphy gets to the emergency room if you think there is the slightest need."

"Ralphy is a grown man and if I get my backhoe out of that hole we got work to do."

"Please, Nick? Please."

"Right, all right. If he is hurt at all I'll get him looked at." He kick started the engine and pulled away. Even then Kate and Bainbridge stood arm in arm. One of them relaxed. The other was still scatty from internal waves of heat and confusion.

"Well Mr. Bainbridge let's see the inside."

He unlatched the lockbox on the door saying, "If I'm calling you Kate then there is no reason not to use Dan. That way it's like we've known each other for a long while."

The door opened into a large foyer with a marble tiled floor, then clicked shut with significance. "Oh this is beautiful and bright," she said. "I've been here before but today the light seems to make everything sparkle. And those flowering bushes coming in? I never really noticed how pretty they were before now either. The white one reminds me I have to get my Capri pants from the cleaners."

"So you've been here before and you know the Thorpes."

"My husband and I do know the Thorpes. Well, really my husband knows them more than I do."

Walking just a step ahead, Bainbridge led her into the large living room. Kate went directly to the couch and sat with one leg tucked in under her. Bainbridge joined her. They were looking at an ornate marble fireplace with an oversized painting resting on its mantel. It was an oil portrait of a man in a blue suit and a woman in a green formal dress. The couple stood close to each other and were looking off into the distance a little to the right of center.

"That helps explain how you knew about this listing before it even got into the advertising cycle."

"I think my husband is representing Bill Thorpe in their divorce. My husband isn't really a divorce lawyer. He is more corporate or whatever, but he and Bill go way back. When I talked to Tom on the phone he said the place was going up for sale. I called Monica to let her know I was very interested. She insisted I call you. She's on Marco Island and sounded so broken and blown out, my heart hurt just talking to her. They look young in that painting, don't they? The way they lean into each other they seem so confident. Now they're a little bit older and it has all come undone. Whatever future they were looking at, I bet they can't see it now. She said she won't trust Bill with anything anymore so they have a listing agent and that's you. She said she works exclusively through you. Monica always liked that word exclusive a little too much for my taste." Kate laughed and brushed Bainbridge's arm with her hand. "I personally think Bill would be better off with strictly a divorce lawyer. But they're golf buddies. I think Tom has someone in his firm working on it, really."

"Divorce is never easy. You'd be surprised how many listings come into the office because of a divorce. It is not the happiest situation, believe me. It is probably one of the worst situations you can find yourself in. But you know Kate, in the overall scheme of things, I figure I'm doing everybody some good by helping out. Real estate can be a complex issue. Assisting people through the process lowers anxiety a degree or two."

"I would think that's true. The idea that another person has been put between the two parties. I suppose to them it was a home, and when you arrive they can begin to deal with it as a house."

"Exactly. Monica and Bill are good people. It's the situation that's bad. Who can count the number of problems people face during divorce? I hate to see this happen, but it is and it does. And on the other side of things, it opens up an absolutely beautiful spot for somebody else to enjoy."

She reached over and rested her hand on his for just a moment and said, "You know Dan, I said almost those very same words to Monica."

"What about the rest of the home? Let me take you on my little tour." He was thinking things were going along pretty, pretty good here. Learning that her husband was the well-known lawyer erased any concerns he held that she couldn't afford the place. She was acting playful, but he could sense there was much more force to her than she wanted to use at this moment.

The kitchen was a display of browns. Brown and black granite counter tops, rich cherrywood cabinets, a six-burner gas range, and two ovens. All appliances were faced with brushed stainless steel or hidden behind cherrywood doors. A cherry harvest table was positioned beside a large window, which offered a stunning view of the harbor and its boats. Even the window above the sink looked out at the harbor. A white marble floor with amber tones running through it extended into a room that had French doors and could be used as a study or a dining room. These opened onto a deck, which also had the harbor as a steady companion. The Thorpe's used this area as their TV room. A large flat-screen monitor sat on the mantle of the second fireplace. Bainbridge and Katherine stood near the kitchen table quietly taking it all in.

"So, what do you think of your new kitchen?"

"The few times Tom and I visited were at night. The actual effect of the harbor through these windows doesn't really do it justice until you see it in daylight."

"Do you think you and Tom can enjoy cooking in this space?"

"I'm not going to be cooking here. My mother is. You didn't know? Of course you didn't know. I'm buying this for her. Well she's buying it really. She'll be paying us back."

"Ah," Bainbridge could not help this utterance from sounding deflated.

"What? It doesn't matter who is buying it, does it?"

"No, certainly not, but wouldn't it be better if we had your mother here to see the place?"

"Not really, no. She knows we'll get her something wonderful. She's too busy as it is. She recently sold the farm in Vermont. Lydia is saying goodbye to all her gal pals up there, selling off the machinery and livestock, packing up all her treasures. The people who bought the farm expect to put an industrial office park on it, you know."

"It feels odd to hear of a farm in Vermont being developed into an office park, for some reason."

"IBM has a major presence up that way. Over the years a lot of small communications and computer firms have been drawn to the area like a magnet. She's had offers on her farm for years. Now that dad has passed on she agrees with all of us that it's time to get closer to at least some of the family. Nick could build her something, but this place is available and it is perfect."

Kate began opening the cabinets while she continued talking. "It's beautiful; the maintenance will be taken care of. She loves the ocean and she's only going to be down the road from me. I wish she had done this when Dad was still alive. And Heather was younger then. If they had been living here all along, we could have spent so much more time together."

She went near the kitchen sink and looked through the window at the boats on the harbor. "Lydia loves children. Really. She ran a daycare on the farm for years, right up until Dad got sick. Those two didn't need the money, but if mom isn't busy there can be trouble. She is the most hyper person I have ever known. I'm her daughter and I like to think of myself as intense. But not really when compared to mom.

"The day care business, I think, fit her image of what a farm should have on it. There should be a lot of kids running underfoot. She had four employees until she closed it down. When Heather was younger it would have been perfect for her to be at mom's day care. Except it's more than two hundred miles from here. Another thing is, I probably would have had a hard time getting Heather away from her each day. It would have turned into a huge competition, there is so much mother in Lydia. I wonder if I would have minded really. Anyway that time is gone now for her and for Heather."

"How old is Heather?"

"Fifteen, twenty-five, six. But fifteen, really. Heather is on her own stage where she knows everything about anything. I wasn't aware there was such genius in our DNA until she hit fourteen. For almost two years she has lost the ability to listen to anything but her iPod. But believe you me, the girl can talk. She's not short on opinions. I went from having a darling daughter, a companion really, to living with a person who has only two goals in life: to establish that I don't know anything and to exercise her right, no, her obligation, to point out that I don't know anything at every opportunity. And even when there isn't an opportunity.

"On a good day I find it amusing actually, but it is a phase I need to see end. I'm feeling lonely. I tell her that she has become so smart so early in her high school years it will be a waste of money to send her to college. Mom's arrival on the scene can help me endure this phase with more - panache."

"My two guys aren't like that yet. It sounds frightening."

"What does?"

"I think it's that word panache."

Kate had been opening the ovens, apparently curious to see how clean they were. She came up close to him where he stood beside the kitchen island. She began to draw hearts on the sheen of the granite with her finger. "Ho, ho, ho, mister. You will see."

He adjusted his weight, making sure their bodies touched. She did not move away. "I suppose I will. Until the divorce, I felt like I was at the center of their world but now I feel like I'm sort of orbiting around their world. Even at that, they are not where Heather is. At least not yet."

"I'm so sorry you're divorced. Oh I don't mean it that way, I mean I'm sorry you had to go through a divorce." She stopped her finger painting and clutched his arm with both hands. "I can't imagine how terrible that must be. I wonder how it starts. I wonder what the first signs of it are and, if you knew the signs, if you spotted them, could you change something and put a stop to it?"

"No, it is like trying to stop a cold front from coming in. And you're assuming both people want it to stop. My ex wanted the breakup. She'll blame it on me but it was her. You get to spot the signs of a divorce because they're right there in front of you. You can't do anything to stop it. That is the hardest part to get your head around. When you are in it you can't see any change that is going to do any good."

"Monica says the same thing about what is going on with her. How old are your boys?"

"Taylor is ten, Russell seven. They live in town. So it's not that bad. I get them over to my place alternate weekends, holidays, a chunk of time in the summer. They're great; we are doing fine with this."

She released his arm and went to the kitchen window to look at the harbor. She said, "Your son's name sounds almost like my last name. I love when things converge like that. The longer you live the more you see that there is no such thing as a coincidence in life."

Bainbridge said, "Let me take you through the rest of the home. I think the next stop should be the upstairs bedrooms."

"That's all right, Dan, I'll buy this place right now. I've seen the place all before and it's lovely. Lydia will think it is perfect."

"Really?"

"Really."

"Well come over here Mrs. Tabor and let's get it all down on paper." He pulled a barstool under him and remained at the island. He slipped forms from his clipboard and with an air of formality placed his pen upon the papers. Kate returned to the island and sat across from him. "At this point we have to determine what sort of offer you expect to make and what conditions you want to place on your offer."

"Kate. Remember you are to call me Kate. That is the first condition. I've already talked to Monica and she said the way things are, they have come down on the price and they want what they are asking. So put down that I will pay the price they are asking."

"Let me explain that this is an offer form. Why don't you fill out this part with your full name, address, and last four digits of your social ." He gave her his pen and pointed to the top of the form. When she was finished he took it and pointed to the contingency section of the form. "Now, I'll put that it is a full price offer. Should I write that it is subject to a conventional fixed rate loan? Also, you're going to put down how much as a deposit? Let me point out I will hold your deposit check until the offer is accepted and then place it in an escrow account."

"What do you mean? I am paying cash for this house. What is twenty per cent of this price?"

Bainbridge used his phone to calculate, "That's 170,000 dollars."

"When you take me home I'll write you a check before you leave."

"Really, you will write out a personal check for $170,000 when I take you home?"

"Funds have been moved around, Dan. We knew we were buying something and we made the plans to move forward. My husband loves to move forward, always forward."

"Perfect. Next on the offer form I'll put in 'subject to a building inspection.'"

"I don't know much about construction but I know a beautifully built structure when I see one."

"I'm sure it is, but this is for your protection. If there were any issues this makes the present owner part of the discussion."

"Well, thank you Dan," and she put her arm across his shoulder in a little side hug. "I suppose Nick will give it a thorough once over anyway."

"And I think we can set the occupancy date for thirty days from now since no one is really living here anymore."

"That will be fine. Whether Mom is ready to actually move in then at least the place will be ours."

As Bainbridge was having her sign and date the document she looked up, "I feel great about this. It is almost like I own the place right now. Could we take a final look at the master bath and bedroom before we leave?"

They stood against the doorjamb looking from the master bath into the spacious bedroom with windows that looked out on the harbor. Kate loved the marble countertops in the bathroom. "Adored" is what she said about the long deep tub with air jets. She had been sitting on the tiled pedestal that boxed in the tub and now walked over and was behind him, quietly taking in the bedroom.

She came on to him. Right there. He knew it, or he decided he knew it. She pressed her right breast on his back below his left shoulder blade. He could touch her left breast with the back of his arm if he moved it even a little. Bainbridge stopped thinking. He moved beyond thinking. He turned towards her and wrapped his left arm around the back of her waist. He pulled her the inch it took to be pressed against each other. He saw in her eyes that it would be alright. He watched her for the slightest sign of don't. He moved to her lips through the warmth and smell of her. Her mouth opened with his. They breathed each other's breath and hung on to this kiss. Their hands slid up and down each other's backs and lingered on the waist and searched the thighs. Bainbridge broke from the kiss. Their eyes locked and they swam in that look.

He lifted her t-shirt and it blocked her face. She raised her arms. It slipped off. He hugged her and released her bra. He leaned back and the bra went from her arms to the floor. She was beautiful. He knelt down in front of her. He unzipped her Capri pants and pulled them and her panties down along her legs. She stepped out of them. He slowly ran his tongue between the folds and delicate hairs of her vagina while his hands cupped her buttocks drawing her closer. He licked where she swelled and tasted her going wet and salty. She began to breathe slow deep breaths and quietly moan with pleasure. Her fingers ran through his hair gently rotating his head from side to side and up and down. This directed his tongue to travel where she wanted. She slowly rocked from side to side pushing herself against his tongue. He tasted her milky flow as she came.

He sat back on the tile floor and looked at her while he untied his shoes, pulled them off, pulled off his tie, unbuttoned his shirt, tossing it all in a heap. He looked up at the first woman he had seen naked since his wife. "Oh god you don't know how beautiful you are," he said.

He unbuckled his belt, loosened his pants, then pushed his pants and underwear to the floor. With her fingers again weaving back into his hair, he was pulled upward. Their naked bodies allowed no space but to rub together until he stood. He drove his tongue into her open mouth. Her own tongue worked under his. The taste of her was in his mouth. It was nectar to both of them.

His hands followed the contour of her back until they fell just below the curve of her ass. He lifted her and carried her to the vanity countertop. Once there he carefully lifted her legs to rest on each of his shoulders. He began kissing her thighs and stroking the long run of her legs. Then her stomach, then her breasts, then her mouth.

They seemed to leap at each other, releasing simultaneous groans. He was in her. She was saying wonderful things he only heard as a blur. He slowly retracted and rode in on her then back, then in, her breasts chugging, her shoulders pressed against the large mirror. Bainbridge spotted himself staring directly back at him from the mirror. In his life he had never seen such a look of absolute need and want on that face in that mirror. A second look of recognition was shared by Bainbridge and the man in the mirror. *You are doing this. It is not in your head.* An unavoidable sense of being out of his body became more and more so with each thrust. Deep in his mind he could hear huge waves of guilt and confusion crashing against the back of his skull.

He ignored the man in the mirror and kept his eyes on the glory of her body, her moves, her flesh. They held on to each thrust until he exploded years and years' worth of loneliness and she six weeks of want. Each of them. At the same time. On that marble counter.

They unfolded from each other, stood and held onto each other. They stood in silence until the tile bathroom and their nakedness made them cold. He took her hand and led them to the master bed. As they slid between the sheet and blanket they rested, facing each other and warming again. She said, "This isn't going to be an affair. I won't allow myself to love you. I think you better know that."

"Ouch, that was quick. Oh, well, yes of course, I know," he said, "Are you starting to feel bad about what we did?"

"No, no, well yes, a little," she whispered. "I've never let myself do this before."

"This was unexpected for both of us, I'm sure. But it was wonderful wasn't it? We gave each other permission, I think, I mean I didn't see this coming but wow, this is powerful stuff."

"Yes, we are very beautiful together. I feel so safe in your arms. I feel like this is too beautiful to be a problem."

"And when I bring you home, I know you'll be Mrs. Tabor again," he said. But she was asleep and did not hear him. He watched her breathing in her shallow breaths until he too was sleeping.

A late afternoon sun made the water and sides of the boats in the harbor shimmer in a golden hue. It was the first thing he saw when he opened his eyes. He rolled to the other side and Kate was there looking at him. "How long have you been awake?"

"Not long."

They hugged each other until they were almost back in the arms of sleep.

"I have to go."

"You do, of course you do, yes."

They appeared naked to each other as they retrieved their clothes. It didn't seem awkward to them. It felt more like a married couple dressing for work. With their clothes back on they looked at each other and shrugged and grinned. They moved out to the kitchen. Kate appeared overly amused as he gathered the documents from the kitchen counter.

"What?" he asked.

"No. It's nothing," she said. "It's a private joke I'm having with myself. I'm thinking, if only Lydia knew the extent I'm going to in order to get her a good deal."

"That is a very funny thought young lady. Must say. But here we are. Tell me are we going forward with this offer to the Thorpes?"

"Dan, Lydia will love this place. Absolutely we are going forward. You will make this happen, won't you?" She said while coming towards him in the kitchen.

"Are you prepared to go over the asking price?"

"Whatever number it takes. I trust you on this."

"Speaking as her agent I see no reason this isn't a done deal."

"Done deal. I like the sound of that."

The ride to Kate's home involved hugging the coastline. The sun was past its yardarm. A thin, two-lane road wove through patches of trees onto sudden wide vistas of the sound. The ferry in mid water. Several sails dashing along in the distance. Back into the trees, and finally, Snug Harbor and Inlet Drive. The night arrived just as they pulled into Kate's entryway.

They hadn't touched or said much. They traveled in quiet, taking in the views of what the ride back looked like. She reached for his hand and held it on the seat below the dashboard. The car rolled to a stop at her front door. She took her hand away, looked at him and said, "We did too much today, but I don't have a single minute's regret. You are wonderful. We were wonderful. But I will be staying close to home with my husband. You know what I'm saying, don't you Dan?"

"Yes, of course it's clear. It is also clear I will never forget this day but I get it, this was a one off, an incredible one off."

"That is one way to put it. Anyway, I think it best you wait out here. I'll go in and write the check and bring it right out. Do you mind?"

"Kate, please that is unnecessary. I can hold onto all of this until tomorrow morning. We can get the check then if you like."

"It's only around seven. With the check you can begin to make things happen tonight can't you?"

"Yes, certainly the Thorpes will be delighted to hear your offer. It is early yet."

"Then wait right here mister. I will be back with a check."

In fact she did not return. He never saw her again that night. He waited, keeping his eyes on little things around the car's interior. The proximity to John Tabor and his domain left his eyes furtive but the rest of him felt as relaxed as he had ever been. He felt stunned and content. A sudden tap at his side window got his attention. A girl in a hoodie stood beside his door. He could only make out a bit of her nose and one eye that caught the light from the front door. He pushed the window down as she said, "Is this what you're waiting for?" She handed the check to him and was gone bounding up the stairs like a deer.

This is nowhere to gather your thoughts, he said to himself. This business just went off the charts tonight. My God. He thought of her in that house. He had no idea what she was doing right now. No idea if her husband was home or even in town. Did she have to talk to him just as she walked in and that is why she sent her daughter out with the check. An impulse to charge in and protect her brought him to his cell phone. "Kate, hello, I wanted to thank you for the check. And just see, I mean ask, if everything is fine."

"Of course, silly, I'm tired but I'm fine."

"It's just that your daughter came out to give me the check and....."

"No, no, no, why, was she rude to you? Hold on."

He could hear her talking to someone.

"Where are you mister? Are you still in my driveway? Heather is getting nervous about 'that man' still parked outside."

"To be honest it appears I haven't moved since you left me. I've just started my car. You can tell her to relax. I'm on my way. Goodnight Kate."

"Call me when you hear anything. This is so exciting."

His car turned onto the street. What did she mean 'exciting?' The lovemaking, the condo for her mother in the works, what, both, neither, just a word, just a word at the end of a sentence.

As he worked his way back, he knew he wasn't the same guy he was this morning. How much of the guy he was and how much is this guy he is now he couldn't tell. He'd have to wait it out. It wasn't much later when he sat at his office desk to call Monica about the offer when a thought broke into his busy, busy mind. He hadn't connected with Aubrey, hadn't called her, hadn't taken her out to dinner. His cell phone held a voice message that had to be her. He didn't listen. He deleted. That quickly he was in that place where you just can't set it straight without lying through your teeth. And it was nearing nine o'clock. There was business to be done and his brain was beginning to dummy up like a sleeve of nickels.

When he called to tell Kate that Monica had accepted her offer she didn't pick up and he told it to her voice mail. Eventually the night left Bainbridge to his sleep as it slipped along and was everyone's night.

6

BUCKLAND'S BAD DAY

Buckland woke abruptly from a pitch, deep sleep with his mother's words ringing in his ears. "Buckland, if you are going to borrow my car then I want it back by three. You can make three o'clock, right?." He was snuggled into the sheets and blanket of his old bed in his old room at his mother's.

"Yes. That's fine mom."

"Just so you know. Adelaide and I are going to meet at the Golden Swan for a late lunch." She sat beside him on the edge of the bed. She rubbed his bald head and said, "I wish you hadn't shaved off your lovely head of hair. You are completely bald now. Just like you were when you were a baby."

"Mom, come on now. This is macho. It is just hair"

"Still, I liked you better with your beautiful hair. You looked very stylish in that man bun. You haven't gone and joined a cult, you're not a Nazi or one of those ones that dances at the airport. You'd tell me if you had, wouldn't you?"

"Ma, no one has danced at an airport in eighty years."

"Well."

"There's plenty of guys with shaved heads. It's cool. I told you

I was going to do this. It's gone now and I like to think I did it for a good cause and not just because I look so damn cool this way."

"Don't swear so much. And it sounds silly coming out of a baby's face."

"I told you I sent my hair to Senator Roberts."

"Buckland, I will never understand this. What are you thinking? Really. You cut your beautiful hair and sent it to a Senator. For what?"

"It was a protest. I'm protesting Ma. I told you. He voted against the clean air act and he wouldn't support the Save the Bay fund. He voted against the Water Standards Act, so that was it. For me anyway. He has done nothing. In fact he works to block any environmental issue he can. I had to do something. You want me to sit around and do nothing? No. Of course you don't. So yeah, I shaved my head and put the hair in an envelope. I'm not the only one you know. There are plenty of others who have done the very same thing. There are a lot of us sick of him. You should be sick of him too. We have finally got some people on the town committee. That's a step."

"You start right now growing it back. If you are going to do this politics thing, then you tell me who ever got elected that was completely bald? What does Cheryl think of this new look?"

"Ma, Cheryl's just a friend."

"I know, but what did she say."

"She liked it. She said I looked like I belonged in the army."

"Still. Are these others you talk about men you work with?"

"No, it's an internet thing. Our town committee is connected to committees up and down the state. We are from all over, lots of Zoom meetings. You've heard me yak it up on Zoom a few times. It looks good though mom, doesn't it?"

"Not really but, amazingly enough, no matter what you do to yourself you are still a handsome young man. And listen big chief environmental, I do need my car back by three. You look like my bald-headed baby. Are you sure you're old enough to drive?"

"Please, very funny, but enough. Three is fine, more than fine. I'm just, I just need your Subaru for about an hour actually. Get down to the Autostore and back. That's it. Get a battery for my truck and then slam it in. The truck will be up and running then, finally, I'm sure."

She patted his knee, stood and said, "You've had more than your share of trouble with that truck lately, haven't you. You poor thing."

"Yes I have."

"Buckland, you've been living here and running that plant since you graduated from college. You must have a pile of money saved by now. Why don't you just go buy yourself a new truck?"

"Well for one thing my mechanic fixed everything. You know that. It ran great the last couple of days and then boom the battery dies. It needed a new battery really. Anyway. Nothing else can be wrong with it. Not a single thing. He tuned it up and put a new alternator in it. He checked the wiring. It was running perfect. You know I'm saving that money. Pretty soon, eventually anyway, I'll be running for office. I'm building a political war chest and it's all because of you mom. You letting me stay here gives me a chance to build up some cash for the road ahead. I'm not going to spend any of it on a new truck if I don't have to."

"I love that you are here. If you feel you have the need to run for something well you just go right ahead and do that. As to the truck, I hope that's it. It seems to be one problem right after another with that thing. All that time and money for a few good days doesn't seem right. They build everything so complicated these days. I hope this does it. If it doesn't I'm afraid you'll have to think about getting something more reliable. Buckland, listen to me, do whatever. Just do it by three."

"You bet. No problem. Three is plenty of time."

He was getting up and dressed when his mother left him. She was in sneakers and a walking suit. She planned to meet her friend, Marcia, for a nice five mile walk around the neighborhood. It was a beautiful day for a walk. He felt good about getting up relatively early and starting his day. He felt he was ahead of the curve on this one.

His mother's dark silver Subaru Outback with chrome trim was only about a month old and a beautiful machine. It had four-wheel traction when you needed it which wasn't much around these parts, but still, there must be hundreds of them around town waiting for that one or two days a year when they could get to the grocery store while the rest of the town was snarled up. It was almost like the state car for the paranoid. And in this town there were plenty of overly cautious elderly farts. They must meet somewhere and share notes on what to get to ward off every fear they could cook up. And this Outback seemed to be the committee pick of the year. Bucky was thinking, in a few years when she goes to trade it in, by God, I'll buy it. It's nice. It's tight and peppy. It puts you lower to the road than the truck, but still this is a comfortable ride. He was pulling into the mall parking lot on the side near the Autostore. There were at least two other Outbacks filling spaces just in this part of the parking grid.

Two oversized doors at Autostore opened. The place smelled like clean plastic and he felt the air conditioner wipe off a few degrees. His battery would be here at the best price. Whatever that is.

"Can I help you?" A fifty-something guy with a white shirt and red Autostore vest seemed to really want to help him.

"Well, that would be great. I am here to get a battery for my truck."

"All right. We have batteries right over here."

He followed. They passed one aisle filled with windshield

wiper blades and floor mats. Then, down a second aisle. At the end of it was a display of batteries from two separate manufacturers and the Autostore brand. There were a lot of batteries here.

"What sort of battery do you need?"

"It's a truck. A Chevy. It was running great but then the battery died. It's been one thing after another, really. I just had work done on it but I didn't replace the battery and I should have." He looked at the displays and clearly the Autostore brand was the cheapest. Autostore offered The Heavy Duty for $84.99, the Everlast at $72.99, and the Guardian at a very doable $59.99. "Which one do you think I should get?"

"It all depends. These are all fine batteries. You know what, since it's a truck I'd either do the Everlast or better yet the Heavy Duty. There's a five-year warranty on all of them so really you can't go wrong."

Bucky usually liked the middle of the road and that meant $72.99. But this Heavy Duty for twelve dollars more would give him the sense he'd done everything he could to get the truck back up and running. "All right, I'll take the Heavy Duty just to make sure nothing else happens."

"Great. While you go out and get your battery I'll take one of these over to the service desk."

"What do you mean?"

"I noticed you didn't bring in your dead battery."

"No I don't have my dead battery with me."

"Son, I can't sell you this or any other car truck or boat battery unless you bring in the old one. It's state law. No one can sell you one. You sure you didn't bring it?"

"Yeah, yeah I'm sure I didn't bring it. But let me pay cash for this one. I'll go put it in the truck and come right back with the dead battery."

"Sorry. I wish I could but I can't. It's a state law"

"Oh, come on. I'll bring it right back."

"Sorry, no."

"Come on. No? Well then what if I bought this one and the one for 52.99 too. Then I just gave you that one as my dead battery and take the Heavy Duty with me."

"That doesn't make any sense."

"No? Maybe you're right. How about this one. I pay for the battery and I leave you two twenty dollar bills to hold for me like a deposit or something. When I come back with the dead battery you give me the forty dollars. We can write it up on a deposit slip or the sales slip."

"Sir, I'd like to but I can't. We're a business. We have to follow laws."

"Fine, ok, fine. If I have to then that's the way it is. I'll be back in about twenty minutes. See you then."

"Great. Super. I'll have the battery at the front desk for you."

"Alright then, see you."

Now the time thing became an issue. He grumbled and hustled out of the store and towards his mother's car. "For Christ's sake. I haven't got time for this." He got to his car, pulled the door open, flew into the driver's seat, slammed the door shut, and jammed the key into the ignition. The problem was the key wouldn't turn, nor would it release and pull back out. "Son of a bitch. This is a new damn car. This kind of shit isn't supposed to happen. Come on." He jiggled the key, trying to twist it left right or out.

It was then that he noticed the old woman on the other side of his car window. She just seemed to appear there. She was remarkably short, bony and old. Her eyes went wide and she began screaming something. She was at the level of hysteria where you couldn't understand what she was saying. Trying to understand what this was all about, he partially opened his door. Her screaming flooded in. She pulled a pistol from a huge red leather handbag and aimed it directly at Bucky's stunned fish face. "Get out of my car. Get out of my car young man, get out now. I have a gun." He slammed the door shut and frantically pushed and twisted his key. "Oh god please get me out of here please." He had a goal and that was to get the god damned car started and race away from this crazy old woman.

She held a pistol at point blank range. She held it straight out away from her in a two handed grip. The flab of her upper arm hung loose and leathery along the bone. She had her legs stationed apart in a formal stance.

The muzzle made small circles three feet from his side window. Though muffled he heard her yelling, "Thief! Thief! I will use this, son, I will I swear I will use this! Get out now! Thief! Thief!" Bucky began to lean as far away from the window as possible. He kept his right foot anchored to the floor near the gas pedal. Twisting the ignition key in sweaty spasms, "All right lady. Everything is fine. It's OK I'll be on my way in a second now. Just stay calm, lady."

She couldn't hear Bucky. Her own voice blocked out any voice that may have come across from inside. In a thin nasal tone she insisted, "Stop! Stop this now! I am going to shoot! I mean it!"

There was so much nervous body heat in the car the windows were beginning to fog up. But the pistol he could still see staring at him. "Lady, please put the gun down." Then the scene began to make even less sense to Bucky. He saw what he thought was a light grey blanket flutter down from the roofline and momentarily settle or drape itself on the gun barrel as if it were a coat hook. As it hung there it looked more like a light grey suit coat than a blanket. Just as his inner eye took this in the pistol discharged, his side window exploded into a spider's web of fuzzy broken glass, he felt something tug or punch him where his neck joined his shoulder. A feeling like someone placed a red hot metal rod against his neck roared up inside him. The suit coat seemed to drip down below the outside door panel and again the boney hands gripping the pistol were revealed. Bucky's mind went black like an unplugged TV screen.

When he did open his eyes again he opened them to a world of hurt. A man's face was leaning into his vision. He had a crew cut, a young long face. Bucky realized he was still in the car sprawled across the two front seats. "You're going to be all right, sir. You are very lucky." Much of the EMT's weight rested on a knee positioned between Bucky's legs and hard up against his balls. Bucky didn't want to say anything. But still. "It looks to be a surface wound. You are going to be alright. In two shakes of a lamb's tail we will get you to the hospital, sir, but first I am wrapping this gauze around the wound. Then we are going to pull you out of the vehicle, get you into the ambulance and right to the hospital. Just be relaxed. How you doing?"

"Have I been hit real bad, Doc?"

"It looks like you're a lucky man. But I'm an EMT. We're going to get you to a doctor in two shakes." Bucky hung on to that sincere look in the man's eyes. The right side of Bucky's neck and shoulder burned hot and felt ripped apart. In panic Bucky croaked, "The old woman with the gun."

"The police have her under control. Everything is fine. Here we go."

The passenger door opened and a second EMT hovered just above his eyebrows. She explained she would be sliding her arms under his armpits. She wrapped his chest in her arms. "Try to relax your entire body," she said, "but don't move your head. That's great. You're being so good. Here we go." She began to pull him out of the car. The first EMT got out and came around. As Bucky's legs were about to be clear of the passenger seat the EMT grabbed them and Bucky was hoisted on to a tall ambulance bed. The back of his head, neck and shoulders rested against the woman's breasts until he was released to the stretcher. His head had to fall a few inches to the small pillow. A fury of pain exploded in Bucky's brain. He screamed a long stretched out, "Fuck!"

It was such a pain he'd have liked to die. He blinked away a wash of tears. He grabbed the sides of the stretcher until his knuckles were numb. He saw two policemen. They were on either side of that woman. They both held her by the upper arm and again at the wrists so that her arms were slightly extended from her body. She looked like a turkey buzzard. She was being directed to the back seat of a cruiser. She took small unsure steps like someone barefoot walking into a stony brook. His involuntary scream had forced her to look in his direction. Their eyes met. She looked curious and ultimately confused.

7

CHANCE ENCOUNTERS

Whether we want to admit it or not, when misery is afoot, more than one person in a town is likely to hear its bootheels. Suddenly Kate was having hot flashes. Just like that, boom, for over a week now there have been these intervals of immediate heat racing over her upper body like a furnace had been turned on. This was a heat that left her sweating. And her heart seemed to be on fast forward while most of these sudden temperature shifts were going on. She was fine, her usual self. Then, wow! What the hell are these?

Day after day, sometimes five a day, at any hour, until, having endured more than a week of this, she was lethargic from erratic sleep. The heat had singed any chance at a complete thought. She was even more stunned by this happening to her because she thought she was too young. She knew there would come a time, but not now. This wasn't right. Five or so times a day she was getting a seriously abrupt rush of heat. Some of them would roll in and last twenty seconds some would go on for five minutes or longer. After five minutes she would be near panting and wondering how it could possibly be called a hot flash. Five or ten minutes of this was no flash.

That's what brought her to Doctor Fryeman's where he took vials of her blood for testing. This man would explain her mammogram or pap smears or blood work to such great lengths that she felt she was taking a biology course with the guy. It always got to the point where you knew more than you wanted to know.

And today was certainly no different. This was classic Fryeman. Fryeman used his easy sincerity and his elongated science speak to assure her that she was in fact pregnant. He knew as well as she did that three years ago John had a vasectomy, which was probably why he began by saying, "You know Kate, vasectomy procedures are considered to be profoundly effective safeguards to unwanted pregnancy, but they are 99 percent effective. Not one hundred percent. There is always the extremely rare chance that the tubes can reconnect. In one case in Vermont…"

"Doctor, please, Vermont isn't helping me. Exactly how long have I been pregnant."

"Four to five weeks."

"I wasn't planning on a baby. You understand, don't you? After all, you did John's vasectomy."

"Actually that surgery was done by a specialist, Doctor Crown. You certainly are in fine physical shape, Kate. Although we do have to monitor these bouts of hot flashes and see what that is telling us. Clearly this is not menopause you are experiencing. Whatever it is, your reaction has a relationship to this early term in your pregnancy. As time moves along we will be keeping an eye on it but for now I don't think it advisable for you to be taking any special medications or hormone therapies. We should just go for a few weeks and see what that tells us. How are you doing with your smoking?"

"God, not now doctor. Smoking? I have just been told I'm

pregnant. I don't know what to think of it or what I feel about it. It's odd. It is not like how I felt the first time. I'm going to really have to think hard on this. The pitiful thing is I came to you because I'm exhausted and I have hot flashes. I don't know if I can deal with having a baby. Not right now. You see, this instant, the only thing I am certain I do want to have is a cigarette."

"We have time Kate. You will be able to work this through in whatever way you think is right. There is adequate time to absorb this information."

"I know you don't need to be told but you know me, I can be a pain in the ass, so I'm telling you, no one, not John, not anybody is to know about this. You and I know and that's it for now anyway. To be totally honest with you I'm not sure I'm pregnant at all. Not in the least."

Fryeman was about to become reassuring and began to dissect the doctor patient relationship, but Kate didn't need that as long as they were both clear on things. Fryeman sounded miffed that she would question such basic professional duty. Kate told him not to be upset; she was the one that was upset and probably overreacting. She just wanted a little clarity. Kate could never recall a time she actually liked Doctor Fryeman. Today's visit didn't change things one iota.

Fryeman was like a bloodhound. Always on her cholesterol level. Didn't like her smoking. Wanted her to drink more water. Wanted her to take calcium, vitamin D, magnesium, and on and on. Wanted her on the fundraising committee for the hospital's new wing. She felt he exercised too much power over her but in the end she trusted him. The fact that she trusted him is what she didn't like most about Doctor Fryeman. For the first time, sharing a primary doctor with Tom felt a little too cozy. From the moment she left Fryeman's office, clarity swam with the fishes deep in desperate tears welling up in her eyes. One time. One single damn time and now this. Dan Bainbridge. Jesus. Now this.

The goddamn diddley stick had a plus sign on it. She was in her own bathroom. She had used one before she went to Fryeman and she was using one again now. She was barefoot sitting on her toilet. Her feet were cold against the polished tile floor.

"Look at you," she said to herself, "look at you. Barefoot and pregnant. Idiot. Idiot. Once, that was it, once?" She was quiet for a long moment. Nothing came to answer her plea. "This little wand is ridiculous, she thought. And Fryeman is ridiculous. And Bainbridge is ridiculous and I'm ridiculous.

"I don't think so. How much can you trust something that costs twenty bucks and was probably made in China for that matter? I don't feel pregnant and for Christ's sake I am not pregnant! There has been a huge mistake! Why me? How can a single time end up like this. Everybody I know has had an affair. Well, not everyone. But the ones who have, they're not all walking around pregnant and neither am I! No. This is bullshit. It has to be. This is all wrong. It is just bullshit."

The smell of urine reminded her to pull herself out of these thoughts. Placing her feet firmly on the cold tile floor, her heart was racing. Her head felt dizzy but she stood up anyway. She wrapped the stick in toilet paper and chucked it into a little trash bucket below her bathroom sink. She caught sight of herself in the mirror. She looked normal, which surprised her very much. Inside she was far from it. Just then another wave of bitter recrimination and futile scheming and boiling self-pity knocked her back into her frenzied mind.

She found herself on her deck. Her eyes were blank. She stood watching the ocean. A heavy blue against her green lawn. It was here even while gulping deep salty crisp breaths where more thoughts piled in. She sat as light as a robin on one of her chairs and thought.

John. John has been in either Paris or Madrid for about a

month and a half and this is the week he has to come home, she thought. No rest for the weary, girl. None, nope, you don't get a break here. It couldn't have worked out that he was just leaving for two months. Oh no, it had to happen when he was home for the first time in a while.

Last night and the night before she felt wonderful having him around the house. Usually they took these first few days to get relaxed with each other. He had crossed a great ocean and she had been alone with Heather for a long stretch. She knew his rhythms. Tonight will be the night he comes on to me, I know it, she thought. Tonight John would be the most attentive man possible and then passionate. This was one of the things she had grown to like about the time apart: the passion. It was a comfortable and lovely way he had about him. For her, tonight was going to be new ground. This little stayover was going to be a strange one. In a matter of weeks John would inevitably be off to the airport and Madrid or wherever. But that wasn't going to be tonight. Or tomorrow night either.

In the past, when he got home, she was repeatedly surprised to realize how much she had missed him. In the beginning, during the early phase of getting his company off the ground, she felt abandoned and resentful. But as the cycle repeated itself she began to see those miserable feelings as a conventional posture and not very positive for her to maintain. And not that genuine either. She chose rather to believe it was a good thing that John was in Europe starting his company and had actually grown to like having the house to herself and Heather.

Kate stood and made her way to her beach. She stopped just where the waves finished. They both expected this pattern to continue. Another year; maybe less. He and Weasel would get their company off the ground. Then Weasel would likely stay in Europe and John would return and assign one of his associates to go over and manage this new side of the business. That was the plan. Expansion. Diversify. Move forward. John always said, "Move forward." That was in fact how it was unfolding up to now, sure, but she had apparently drifted out of her lane hadn't she?

Diversified, oh she diversified but not in the way the plan was set down. What was she doing? What was she thinking? No, this was not John's fault, not at all. Don't even think that way. Whatever happened, this has nothing to do with him. In fact John was the furthest thing from her mind. She can't put this one on him. It isn't the fact he goes away. And it's not that she doesn't love him. Does she? Does she love him? Is that what it's all about here. And what about Dan? Should he be kept in the dark? Of course he should be kept in the dark! Forever? Another week? What?

Kate paced back into her home. She found her couch and curled up on it. She didn't feel a single drop different about John. Not a single drop. What went on in that condo would have happened if he were down the street at the golf course because it had no reason for it to happen in the first place. Oh, my god, what has been done here? It just happened, that's all. And that's the scary part really. There was no planning this. But she came to realize she better get planning whatever is going to come next.

Dominic should never have left her there alone. She was crying now, huge deep moans. Whether or not she loved him, would he love her? She could spin a story, one that made this his baby. Even Fryeman will go down that road. But with his vasectomy, John was bound to slip in a DNA test at some point. She would and she is not the ever-thorough John Tabor. He ends up knowing everything, always. But not yet. He knew nothing then and please god let's keep it that way for a while. Nobody needs to know. She could be the only one for now.

And now with mom in town, she was finally going to Europe with John and Weasel once and a while. And Heather, how would Heather deal with all of this? There was a need to buy some time. Get a handle on this. Let's think, let's think this through.

In the living room she began walking in small circles, thoughts piling up on a single nerve. There was still plenty of time. There was a way forward. There had to be one way better than another. Don't be your own worst enemy, she thought. Move forward. Oh John, how do I do that? How the hell would she move forward from this one?

She had stopped her weeping and was holding her left hand against her belly. She was in the kitchen when she turned and suddenly Heather was no more than two feet in front of her.

"Hi mom, I am totally exhausted."

"Oh poor little one. A hard day at the golf course?"

"Mom, look at me. This is tennis. I was at the tennis club."

"Of course, did I say golf? That was silly of me." She saw that John was coming in the back way.

"It was fun. Buddy Rice and Richie ended up being there, so Shianna and I played doubles for a change. I am so in need of a shower. What's wrong with you?"

"Why, what are you talking about?"

"You are holding your stomach."

"Oh, no, I think I pulled a little something at Zumba class today, I'm not sure. That woman is a slave driver down there." She let her hand slip away from her belly.

"Mom, no one is doing Zumba anymore."

"I'll tell the thirty other women I'm with what your opinion of the class is."

"When are we eating?"

As Heather asked this, John came across the kitchen to give his wife a little hug.

"Yes mom, what are we going to have for supper tonight?" He kissed her on the forehead and remained beside her with a relaxed arm across her shoulder. She was so fragile his arm felt like an oxbow.

"You two only seem to be around when you're hungry. I was just getting into the kitchen myself. What I'm thinking is chicken with pesto, flat noodles and a garden salad. Does that sound like something everybody can enjoy?"

"Sounds perfect to me," Heather said. "When are we eating?"

"Soon enough, why?"

At that instant Heather made a request no one in the house would think to make only a short year from then.

"A bunch of us were thinking it would be great to go to the movies tonight. There's this awesome zombie flick and we all want to see it together."

"Unless I've missed a few days I'm thinking this is a school night."

"Oh, please, please, everybody is going to see it tonight."

John said, "I wish you would define that word everybody a little better and I can't believe you guys are into all that zombie stuff. It seems it would have to be a little senseless and numbingly violent."

"Duh, Dad, that's the point. And really it's not as senseless as you want to think. The movie is a romance story about a zombie falling in love with some governor somewhere."

"Oh really, well then, if I were you I'd have to catch that movie for sure. How many times can one see a governor fall in love with anybody but themselves?"

"Then I can go?"

"Why not? I believe we should let her go. Don't you?" His look and smile held obvious intent to Kate.

Kate leaned against him as if he were a hay wagon. "Yes, Heather, fine," she said.

John added, "Don't think of this as a precedent."

"Dad, I'm going to a movie."

"That's what I mean. This time you're going to a movie, next time probably not."

Kate said, "Alright then, we will be all finished up by 7 and you can be home before 12, does that work?"

"Yes, that's my mom," she said as she left to go upstairs to her room.

John held Kate in both arms and hugged her. They swayed gently. "I'm going upstairs to get out of my suit and then I'll be down to help out," he said. He leaned in and gave her an opened mouthed kiss. She hung on his lips and wondered if he could taste the sweat from her recent hot flash. He broke from the kiss and they were nose to nose. He said, "I'm thinking you could be dessert tonight after Heather leaves the house."

"Yes," she said, "I think that is a delicious idea, mister."

That night they drank Sangria with their pesto. He gave her beautifully delicate Spanish gold earrings. Heather's friends came and she was off. John had her blouse on the floor before the kids were down the driveway. They made love on the couch. John was familiar and she wanted familiar. His hands on her lower back bringing her with him. They knew when and how far to push each other and then they gave into it and let go. Because it was the downstairs couch they quickly gathered their things and went up to bed. They were spooning and sound asleep when Heather returned near two o'clock.

Thursday morning Kate called Dan Bainbridge and got his voicemail. She set up a lunch date and asked that if he could not make it he was to call her. The closing on Lydia's place had taken only four weeks. Those were weeks of many long calls between the two of them. Weeks when even she was unaware of her pregnancy. Last week, a week after the closing she heard nothing from him. Last week was the week she learned she was pregnant, so maybe it was better he didn't call. But still. Why the hell didn't he call?

She had no idea what she would tell him. Maybe it was too early to tell him anything. Maybe she didn't want to tell him at all. She was feeling her way on this. Her thinking had gone choppy. She was moving on impulse. Christ knew if even she would show up for this lunch she was orchestrating. What if she never saw him again? What if he went on with his life never knowing a single thing about what was going on? Her last thought on the issue was: her lunch set up the opportunity to tell him. That is, if she decided she wanted to. Seeing him again might help her make up her mind. So, she called him.

∼

He stood; probably too quickly. There, she appeared there, from behind the glass doors. The sun seemed to stick to everything. The blue café umbrellas, the little tables, each seated person distinct, etched by what seemed individualized back lighting. Even the murmur of everyone at their lunch and the chink of China plates against glass or stainless steel utensils seemed upheld by the light. She was looking for his table and spotted him when he rose. She wore an off-white, chiffon dress with a muted, wine-colored floral pattern. She had on a big straw hat that added mystery. She breezed right up to his side. They both grasped each other's extended hands. There was warmth. A quick release as they proceeded to sit opposite each other. They each extended a hand resting close to the other in the center of the small cafe table. Their eyes were poring into each other's. They both smiled and were enjoying this taking each other in.

"What a beautiful day for lunch," she said. "Really. Look at this place. The sun and the boats. You. And it's so warm and bright. This is good, good stuff. It's all good you know. Good to see you, mister. This makes me very happy, Dan. Am I late?"

"No, not in the least," he said.

"I was driving past the mall and there was such a tie up of police and an ambulance. I saw the police putting a very old lady into the back seat of a cruiser. For just a minute there I thought it was my mother. It took quite a while for them to let us through. That was dramatic, but it put me off my schedule. Being off schedule has been shown to devastate me."

A teenager introduced herself as Sandy. She announced that she would be their waitress this afternoon. They broke from their look to receive small lunch menus. She ordered unsweetened iced tea. He ordered iced coffee. Young Sandy lingered, her pen and pad at the ready.

"What do you think Daniel? The shrimp salad with baby spinach?"

"Yes, well, I don't really know what you like yet but, it seems interesting. It has honey-encrusted walnuts, marinated red peppers, cranberry shavings, dried blueberries. That sounds like something you would like, doesn't it?"

"Yes, exactly, that's it then, and put the balsamic vinegar on a side dish, please," she said.

He ordered the fish sandwich and German potato salad. "Very nice," the waitress assured them. She was so young it was hard to believe her. "I will be back with your drinks."

"I didn't know what possessed me to call you but I do now. It's seeing you. And hearing your voice. That's what I needed. This has the making of a perfect afternoon. Absolutely. Dan, tell me, how do I look?"

"Breathtaking. Stunning. You look great in that hat."

"See, I knew I was going to enjoy this lunch."

"You look absolutely put together. When you were walking across the way I was thinking, man, lunch doesn't get better than this."

"Put together? Really? That's funny, the past few days I have been anything but put together. I've been more like me watching me be me. Right now is a good example, I'm saying to myself, look at this woman. She's out at a beautiful seaside café. It's a sunny day. There is this handsome guy. She is doing good, this woman. Where have you been, mister? We had all those phone calls. And then nothing. God, the phone calls. I looked forward to those. The Daniel Bainbridge voice. We used to talk every day it seemed. After mother's closing, you stopped calling. That wasn't very nice of you, you know."

Feeling scolded Bainbridge raced to his defense, "You know I miss you, Kate. You know that. You must. Please, these last two weeks I have been a complete wreck. I 'm telling myself all the time, don't call her, it is over, the sale is over, I can't keep calling this woman. In the end this was a real estate transaction. She is with her husband. I am a real estate agent. I can't just keep calling and calling and calling. Once your mother was completely moved in, what was there left to talk about? The last time I phoned and we talked I could barely breathe. I didn't know what else to say. I wanted there to be something else to say. I just couldn't figure out what it was."

While listening to Bainbridge spool out his sad predicament, Kate decided not to tell him today. There would be another time. This wasn't it. This should just be lunch. She said, "It was a surprise is all. It seemed so abrupt and final."

Bainbridge pushed on, "I begged my brain for some excuse to keep the thing going. I loved talking to you. We had a month where we talked to each other almost every day. Remember? Using the details of the closing and your mom's big move from Vermont and all the rest we covered so much ground between us. There was always the condominium sale to leverage me in. Don't ever think I didn't pick up that phone a hundred times."

"Well, perhaps we've graduated to lunch dates. The last

thing you said to me was, so we will talk. But you never called back. Men are so cruel. You know that?"

Bainbridge sensed that she might not let this topic go. In a gambit he threw out, "Yes, men can be the most worthless of all worthless creatures. The secret is out I suppose. It is amazing you ladies will have anything to do with even the best of us."

"Don't sell you men too short. They are good at doing a lot of the work that has to be done."

The waitress arrived and placed the drinks on the table saying, "The food will be right along. I just thought you'd like your drinks as soon as possible." She made eye contact with both of them. She learned that establishing eye contact increased her tips dramatically. "Now, I'll be right back with your food. Enjoy."

"Katherine, I am so glad you called and set up this lunch date, I can't tell you."

"She loves the place, by the way."

"Who?"

"My mother. She absolutely loves the place. She's made it her home in a week it seemed. She is curious about everything and especially everybody. Two men in the complex have already taken her out on their boats. I remember the last time I actually saw you we were at the closing. So professional. There was Mr. Daniel Bainbridge at work. You had all the answers and all the correct papers and numbers. Everything went through you. You seemed to know more about it than my husband's real estate lawyer. You're impressive in a tie. But you do know that no one wears one anymore?"

"Go figure, I actually took one off for lunch. I will never wear another tie again."

"Mom told me, 'You make sure you send that man a card. I think he is trying to do his best work for you Kate.'"

"Well, I was. But these closings are really quite simple after you've done a few of them. I don't think your husband's guy was a full time real estate attorney. Truth be told, he did a fine job. What made this one interesting was from the sale to the actual moving in took only about a month. To be honest with you, I was doing the massively efficient real estate professional thing so that I wouldn't have to think about never getting to see you again."

"Business can allow people to be very cold, can't it?"

Their meals arrived. They were perfect. Sandy was very proud of the chef. She asked if there would be anything else and Bainbridge said no. For a few moments they sampled what was on their plates. Bainbridge was thinking, I can't just blurt out I love you. He felt it was too much too early, best keep it to himself. He didn't know how to tell her his feelings were too big. He didn't know where to put them. He was thinking, we know we made love. Is this a time we talk about it or not? People do that don't they? They move on or whatever.

"You are awful quiet over there."

"Let me come out with something Kate, we talked a lot but there was a lot we didn't talk about. Some of this has to be said face to face and we have that moment right now. I don't know where to go with this, this experience. I want to be with you. I want you to be with me. I want everything else to just get out of the way."

"Dan," she said, "That is extremely sweet and I think I've been waiting for you to say those words for weeks and weeks, but you do know we are not there and we probably never will be."

"I can understand it that way. I know you have a life I understand really I do that's not how we are going to happen. We will be friends or maybe over time we don't see each other again. You are married, you have a family. Together we had one day. Only one day. Maybe one day isn't enough to call it love, but what is this feeling then? I have no other word for it. But I want you to know that if that day is all there is then it is enough, it has to be enough."

"I suppose you couldn't very well have said that over the phone now could you?"

"Not really. On the last of those phone calls I tried to work myself up to it but I just could not do it and I hated myself for not saying something."

"I'm going to let you in on a little secret, Mr. Bainbridge. I hated you too. You know, in those talks we covered up so much chit chat we kept away from all the big feelings didn't we? Hardly any of the personal stuff ever got said, amazingly."

"Well, what for example."

"Ok then, I never got to ask you how such a nice guy, a handsome, wonderful man like you ended up divorced.?"

"Suddenly. That is the short answer. Let's not drag all that out today. We can talk it through another time if you like. Connie and I lived a few long, bad years before we got to the point of a divorce, but when it all fell apart it seemed to go down in the blink of an eye. It's been a done deal for a few years now. She's with another guy. He maintains his own place. I know that because I've actually picked the boys up from the guy's house in Newton a few times."

"That must hurt you very much."

"Oh yes, it was a real kick in the pants. The divorce hurt, no doubt. It has been four years or whatever. I've moved on, she's moved on. The kids are holding up. There is a different sense of normalcy I'm finding. There is a new normal. You understand, like I've said to you before, I have the boys every other weekend. Holidays. A stretch of the summer. It works. Things have settled in. It's all good."

"Before me, had you met anyone else? Am I the most recent

conquest in a string of gals? My God I can't believe I just asked you that?"

"No, no, we should always be able to ask each other anything. After all our phone calls I'm surprised you are asking me these questions now. I've been on sort of a four year tailspin and now I found you, beautiful you, but no I'm not seeing anyone, No one is bringing me casseroles."

"Our phone blackout piled up some questions I didn't get to ask. Right now we have this time. We have this lunch. You know what I'm saying so let me ask a few more…"

"Of course. Anything, any time. But this won't be the last we see each other will it? That would just seem wrong somehow, wouldn't it?"

Sandy came up, stood beside him and said," I'll take these plates away for you. Is there anything at all you would like at this point?"

Kate asked, "What do you think your best dessert is today?"

"Well," Sandy answered, "that isn't a very difficult decision but we do have several yummy choices, I'd have to say you must try our three layer orange cake."

"Yes, we will have one of those to share. What do you think Dan?"

"Without a doubt. You had me at cake. And Sandy bring us back refills on our drinks at that point as well. No wait, excuse me, Kate would you like anything else but your iced tea?"

"No. That will be fine."

As Sandy took the dishes away she said she would be right back. In the little vacuum created by Sandy's leaving Kate resorted to her questions for Dan.

"Alright then I'll ask this one, do you remember where you were when you first found out you two were divorcing?'

"Ah yes, it's one of those moments you try the rest of your life to forget but Connie made sure that wasn't likely. I did say suddenly, didn't I? We had this every other month dinner thing with a few of our couple friends around town. They were theme dinners where we would all show up with a part of a Greek meal, that sort of thing. We were at the La Montaine's that night when Connie just stood up and said to everyone at the table that we were through. She had enough, she said. She was sick of me drinking too much, eating too much, talking too much everywhere we went. She said she never had a chance to say anything when I was around. But not this time. This time everyone was going to listen to her. She was divorcing me right then.

"I was stunned. What the hell was she talking about? Everybody at the table was drinking and talking, like we always did. That's half the reason we all got together in the first place. Most everybody had an ouzo in his or her hand, or could care less and was sipping a Seagram's, or whatever else they wanted.

"When Monty tried to laugh it off as some over the top joke she said no, this is real. About then a car pulled up. She said she had a ride home and I should stay and then go somewhere for the night. She said I should come to the house in the morning and all my stuff will be packed and ready to go. I just sat there and watched her go right out the door.

"For a guy accused of talking too much I must say she shut me up that night. I didn't know what to say, nothing came out. I always wonder if that car was a taxi or whether Bob drove her home."

"Oh you poor man. Where did you stay?"

"That night Monty had a spare room for me. The next day I bought a condo."

"Who is Bob?"

"Bob is who she has been with almost the day after she hammered me at La Montaine's. He was in my foyer with her when I arrived home the next day to see all my clothes, my computer and a few other things all boxed just inside the doorway."

"That was cold, really frigid. Poor you. I'm sorry I didn't know. If I knew it was like that I wouldn't have asked."

With energy and fanfare, Sandy returned, displaying the oversized cake. She floated it under their eyes, placing it in the center of the table. Their drinks were also with her. After placing each drink on the table she observed, "Aren't desserts just fun?" She placed a new fork at each setting. "Now is there anything more?"

"Not a thing Sandy, thank you. After a while just bring me the check will you?"

"Certainly," she said. Bainbridge held his fork suspended over the cake and said. "If there is a good way to end a relationship, I don't expect to ever find it. But that bull about drinking and eating and talking too much came undone when I saw helpful old Bob in my house the next morning."

Kate could wait no more. She took up her fork and dove under his to rescue a large piece of cake and take it to her lips

He followed her lead with the fork while continuing. "Of course by then half the town had her version embedded in their head because everybody at that table had someone they just had to tell. For that, and a bunch of other reasons, my listings dropped 35 percent for a long time after that. Not that I was worth a damn at my business during that time anyway. Some of my agents really stepped up when this was going on. I must say, I work with some pretty great people."

"I can see why you always seem just a little tense."

"Do I?"

"A smidge, a tiny little bit."

"I have always basically been like this. Really, whatever smidge I'm showing has nothing to do with the divorce, certainly not now. I've owned my real estate agency for almost seventeen years, seventeen years next month. And that keeps a slight edge on me for sure. My people are great but when you own your own business something or somebody always wants a piece of you every day."

"I imagine especially weekends,"

"Yes, that can be very true Kate. And if it wasn't like that I'd probably get a little edgy about that too. The nature of the game is exactly who I am, so I suppose I'm in the right business for me. That's why I like what I'm doing so much I guess. There is nothing really wrong about that is there?"

"No, you are fine. I care about you that's all. The Italian in me shows a caring feeling as a worry. A worried feeling is epidemic in me lately."

"It is a lovely trait you have there. I want you to worry about me any time you want."

Under the café table she stroked his shin with the arch of her sandaled foot. He only had enough time to recognize the luscious mischief his shin had found down there when it stopped and she said, "What we did, it has become a dream now, yes?"

It took Bainbridge a moment, getting past the feeling of her foot stroking his leg. But he eventually offered up, "Do you think so? I don't know, I know you are John Tabor's wife. That's what I know in my head. In my heart I also know what we did was real. As real as anything I have ever done in my life. We made love that afternoon, not sex. Just maybe for that moment we were perfect. It isn't a dream to me, it is real."

"You are a tender soul, mister."

"So here it is, you are married, you have a sweet teenage daughter, I get it. A lovely family but I need to make you a part of my life on some level. We should make room for each other. With that start we can at least learn to be friends. Friends, simple enough. Check in on each other. Talk, see each other every once and awhile around town, just like we are doing now."

"You're one of the good one's aren't you. I would like that to happen very much. But it won't, will it? We start out as lovers and end up as friends. That really isn't possible, is it? I don't believe I have had a guy friend since my college days. Once I got married it seems like I've gone into another dimension. There is John and his friends and my girlfriends around town and that's it. I wonder what Marc Demarus or Bill what's his name are doing these days. But we don't stay in touch. These days, these days so very far from the old days. I wish we could be friends. I really do but no. We are beyond friendship I think."

"Well I admit you are right Kate. When you took off that biker's helmet and shook your hair free I lost all sense of proportion. You and I are important."

"Yes we are, Let's promise each other right now that we will never feel bad about that day."

At that moment she looked past Bainbridge and spotted her husband almost at the instant he came onto the patio of the café. He was with one of his business partners. He was scanning the tables calculating his chances of getting one during lunch hour. She looked back at Daniel. Her smile widened a bit and froze for a moment. She said through her teeth, "My husband is here for lunch, laugh out loud. Isn't that great. He's coming over now."

John Tabor's voice clapped just above and behind Daniel Bainbridge. "Kate! what an outstanding surprise. I like that hat, I do. If we had talked this morning, you know, we could have all done this lunch together."

"Sweetie, you never, ever call me for lunch. But come on, let's put some chairs around. Join us."

Tabor went around the table, leaned under her hat brim and kissed her on the cheek. "No, that's fine, Jones and I are just grabbing a bite, it is a working lunch and you guys seem well ahead while we would be just getting started." He stood upright and placed his hand on her shoulder and made a point of looking directly into Bainbridge's eyes.

"John, this is Dan Bainbridge." Bainbridge left his seat, reached up and shook Tabor's hand. Their eyes remained on each other even as Bainbridge returned to sitting. "Daniel, sold mom the condo."

Tabor's lips pulled into a thin smile and he said, "You're not buying something else just now are you?"

"No John I am not buying something else," Kate said in exaggerated exasperation. "With all the commission he made on mom's place I felt he owed me a lunch."

"I'd be careful, Bainbridge, Kate eats lunch every day. Strange we've never crossed paths until now. I've certainly seen your real estate sign around town. It is good we met up with each other finally. Dan, let me introduce Weasel Jones, my good partner in all things Europe. A genius in the flesh. Doctor Jones, Dan Bainbridge."

Bainbridge was looking at a small man, balding. Little wisps of hair rose from his skull like smoke from a smoldering fire. Behind black-rimmed glasses his eyes darted from point to point, as if on a compass.

"Yes, I'm Dan, and you are correct, John. I do own Bainbridge Realty. Doctor Jones, how are you." He half stood and shook Weasel's hand. He couldn't believe he felt compelled to say that about himself. It wasn't the first time he'd been in the presence of absolute wealth. What was this sudden need to identify something special about himself. What did owning Bainbridge Realty have to do with anything at this moment? Was it the doctor thing, or the genius thing? "Excuse me did I hear it correctly? Weasel is your first name?"

Weasel smiled back at him, the black frames of his glasses were bigger than the width of his face, he wore a tan suit that was loose hanging over his small thin frame. He put his palm up and said, "No, no, sit down. Nice to meet you. Weasel is not my name. My name is Wesley, and if you can get him to stop calling me Weasel I will be your friend for life."

Kate said, 'Hello Wesley, fantastic to see you here. Look at you. It has been a while but I've heard more about you than you can imagine or want to know. John is very positive about you."

"Coming from you I will believe it. You are as lovely as ever, Kate. Every time I see you it is a delight. I don't know how you can put up with him sometimes, Kate. Your husband can be very severe, well more precisely, I should say focused. There aren't many roaring approvals flying around between us."

"This is a very stressful phase of the operation for both of you. We all know it is just a phase, Wesley. We will all get through it fine, won't we?"

"It's reassuring he has something good to say about me to at least somebody else. That's all I'm saying."

"Oh, poor doctor with the bleeding heart," said Tabor. "You will say or do anything to get a woman to like you, really, you are a bad man."

Wesley continued, "Kate, this company is going to happen. In a matter of weeks we become real. It begins in Spain, but we are prepared to move very quickly. Manufacturing is already underway. We did it John. We did it. We are doing something no one else could do."

Kate said, "John, you have got to stop introducing your business partner as Weasel. It is not a good image, Wesley, don't you want him to stop using that name?"

"You'd have to go back pretty far to hit a time I called you Wesley," said John.

"It's true. Over there I've caught him throwing in the Spanish word, rata, when he's going for my first name."

"Anyhow," John snapped, "you two are doing your lunch

thing. We better shove off and find a table. Daylight is wasting away right in front of us. Doctor Jones, let us leave these two be. Kate, why not ask Dan and his wife to join our dinner party this weekend?"

"I'm sorry. I am divorced," said Bainbridge.

Kate pleaded, "There you go John, embarrassing the poor man."

"No, I'm not embarrassed, it doesn't even seem strange saying it anymore. But what I mean is, it might be difficult, I'm not really with anyone right now."

"Please, pardon me, what do I know? I'm merely saying it would be great to see you again over at my place. Why don't you come? Join us. Single, couple, it doesn't matter. It is a very mixed crowd, interesting people, that's all. I want you there. Good food, wine, music, anything and everything. Please I'm counting on you being there." Before lifting his hand from her shoulder he gave it a gentle squeeze, "Kate, see you at home. Love you."

"Love you," she said as Tabor and Jones left, disappearing behind the glass doors of the interior dining hall.

Kate's and Bainbridge's eyes zipped back onto each other. They stayed locked until the time in silence cracked. "You have to come, you know," she said.

"Of course," he said. "It is the first time I've actually met your husband. This is a day of firsts. He seems, what, he seems, well, really, I don't think I should have an opinion on that right now." He blew a quick burst of air from his lungs causing his cheeks to billow out.

"I'm glad you are coming to the party. Everyone always has such a good time. There are so many people that come, and now you will be one of them. And I'll have another chance to be with you."

The waitress came and asked if there would anything else."

"No, no, I don't think so, but you were to bring the bill," Bainbridge said.

"Mr. Tabor instructed me to put your bill on his tab. I thought there may be something else today?"

Bainbridge was going to quibble over the gesture but Tabor wasn't there to hear his protest so he let it go.

"Isn't that generous of him. Thank him for us." When Sandy went to return to her station near the kitchen Bainbridge said to Kate, "Won't it be strange? Me being in your house?"

"No Daniel, I want you to be at my home. You probably know half the people that will be there. You'll have fun. I'll see to it. No one feels like a stranger at a John Tabor party."

They stood and left their small table. Not before Bainbridge placed a twenty under a pepper mill. One behind the other they wove through the tables and into the dining hall. Kate led them to her husband's table. Tabor and Jones were just receiving plates of food.

"I'll see you at home John. And Wesley, I'm sure John settled you nicely into the guest bedroom. If he didn't you can tell me later tonight."

With his mouth full of his sandwich he pointed at his lips and nodded in agreement.

"It was nice meeting both of you," said Bainbridge from slightly behind Kate.

"We will get a chance to talk soon," Tabor said. "We will see you at our party."

When they were outside near Kate's car they stood close enough to touch. "Thank you for meeting me for lunch, mister. I needed this."

8

LARKY THE DOG

Nothing good came from a phone call to Connie. That's why Bainbridge was not calling her. He was on the road leading to his old house, going up streets that for years were his neighborhood. Now? Nothing like that. He used to know the stories that went on in some of these homes. What the kids were doing, what couples were getting along, where people were going on vacations, who were right-wing nuts, who was having trouble at work. Time had made him an exile on the streets that now just led to where his boys lived when they were with her.

In the settlement, in addition to a hundred other splits, the house became hers and he got to keep his company. He loved that house right up to the day she changed the locks. Today his intentions are to pull into his old driveway and then and only then he would phone Connie to come out for a little chat. He needed to tell her face to face that there had to be a change made this weekend.

On issues like this, being in front of her had more likelihood of generating a positive outcome. Connie found it too easy to hide behind a phone. This was a negotiation he wanted to work itself out in his favor. The boys were expected to be with him but they adapt to change quickly. He was processing a small level of anger towards Connie for making any slight variation to any aspect of the schedule difficult, often needlessly. After all, there was plenty of early notification here, but it was totally up to her. She was the decider on this. If he remembered to keep that in mind he'd have a better chance of things going his way.

She owed him though, for the time she and Bob were delayed in Miami two days. The huge pileup of snow had to be cleared before they could get back. That was the New Year's Eve thing two years ago. That had not been a problem for him. A few extra days was great and he had not made it a problem for her either. He would remind her of that if he had to.

Bainbridge rolled to a stop at the foot of his old driveway and looked at the four bedroom colonial he once called home. Ahead of him, just up the driveway was Connie's parked car. Taylor appeared to be slamming the trunk of the car closed as Bainbridge shut off his own ignition. Taylor turned to wave at his dad and had a sort of shit-eating grin on his face that Bainbridge had never seen before. While getting out of his car Bainbridge said, "Hello Tay. Listen, is your mom home?"

"Hi, dad, yup, she's home."

Bainbridge walked towards Connie's car. "Hey, would you do me a favor and go in and ask your mother to come out? I need to talk to her for a minute."

"Absolutely," and he darted towards the back door.

Bainbridge heard muffled cries from inside the trunk of Connie's car. "Dad, is that you?"

"Russell, is that you in there?"

"Yes, get me out of here!"

"I will. Just relax. I'm going to get you out right now." Bainbridge opened Connie's driver's side door, found the trunk switch and pressed it. Old Larky, the family dog, seized the opportunity to hop into Connie's car. Bainbridge was preoccupied with getting to Russell and when he shut the door the dog was left on the inside, which was perfectly fine with Larky. Russell was crying and blubbering when Bainbridge got to the now opened trunk.

"Poor Russell, let me get you out of there." Dan took him out, holding him against his chest. "What's been going on Rus?"

"Taylor locked me in the trunk, Dad."

"No. Really? That is terrible! Poor guy, you must have been very scared. Why would he do such a thing?"

"He's being mean."

"He shouldn't be doing that. That's not how a big brother should behave. I'll talk to him about that, Russell, I really will. I'll make it real clear he isn't supposed act like that. Listen, look, do you see that little pull handle right there on the inside hood. Car trunks all have them so that if somebody gets caught in the trunk all you have to do is pull that and the trunk opens up."

"Do all cars have those?"

"Yep, they all have them."

"Did they put them in all the cars so that Taylor can never lock me in the trunk ever again?"

"Well, that's true in a way, but lots of people get stuck in the trunk for one reason or another. Enough people so that car manufacturers make sure they put one in every car they make."

"When I'm bigger I'm going to lock Taylor in the trunk so let's not tell him, okay?"

"No, neither one of you is to do that ever again. Guys don't do that to each other. And you are not to be playing around the cars and neither is Taylor. Cars are important tools. When you are older you will learn how to use them. Until then you are to stay away from them. They are not toys. You know all this. I know you do."

Connie came up to where they were standing. In a metallic tone she asked, "What is going on, Daniel? Why is my trunk opened?"

From his perch against his father's chest Russell answered, "Taylor locked me in the trunk." And then he let loose some seriously pathetic sobs while clutching his dad's shoulders.

"What? Daniel what's happening here?"

"I don't know Connie, you tell me. I pulled into the driveway just now and heard Russell crying in the trunk of the car so I got him out. What was going on before that, I have no idea." Bainbridge put Russell down to stand on his own.

"Rus, there is a sandwich in the kitchen. Why don't you go inside. When I'm through talking to your father I'll come in and we will get to the bottom of you being locked in the trunk."

"What kind of a sandwich?"

"It is a good sandwich. A peanut butter and jelly especially for you."

"Is Taylor going to be in there."

"I don't know. Probably."

"What happens if he tries to lock me in a cabinet or something."

"He will never do that and I will be right in to make sure."

Russell walked dramatically towards the kitchen door.

"Has Taylor been doing this a lot lately?" Bainbridge had to ask.

"No, not really. They are boys, that's all. For brothers, they have always played around together quite well. Great actually."

"I know," he said. "Those two guys really do enjoy hanging around with each other. But this trunk thing, that's not good."

"Of course it isn't Daniel."

While they were talking, two unnoticed events happened almost simultaneously. The toy collie, Larky, placed his rear paws on the passenger seat and his front paws on the dashboard so he could stare directly out the windshield. It is possible he was imaging that he was driving the machine. The second event was, Raymond, the family cat, a very large black cat with a full on impression of panther in his eyes jumped onto the hood of the car and slowly paced to a stalking position directly in front of Larky. The separation of an eighth of an inch of glass infuriated the dog. He began frantically pawing the dashboard and barking a single yelp over and over. His front claws were beginning to rip away the plastic coating and were working through the foam back side of the dashboard. Raymond had what Larky could only conclude was the supreme audacity to simply sit and then stretch out five short inches from his snarling teeth. To Raymond there was no better place in the entire yard than right here on this car where a windshield separated him from a helpless, hopelessly enraged little collie.

"Why are you here?" Connie asked in a way that suggested he shouldn't be here. He should be anywhere else but not here.

"Right. I'm hoping we can switch weekends. There is a conference all day Saturday that I should go to if I can. Real estate in a digital space is one of the sessions I'd like to sit through. What do you think?"

"What do I think? I think that from now on you should call me rather than come over to ask me these kinds of questions."

"I hear you. I do. But let's finish this one up right now if we can. What do you say to you taking the boys this weekend and me taking them next?"

Connie was about to respond when she allowed Larky's incessant yelping to turn her attention to the dog growling and yelping like a maniac inside her car. They both leaned towards the passenger window just in time to note the huge gouges taken out of her dashboard and then, bam. The passenger side air bag exploded outwards hurling the dog violently against the inside roof and down onto the back seat where he lay in a pile like an empty sock puppet.

Connie yelled, "Oh my god, what is happening here?" loud enough to be heard in district court.

"Calm down, calm down, let's just take a minute here." Bainbridge opened the rear door of Connie's car, looking at Larky. There was sudden heavy silence. The dog sprawled motionless in the back seat. Larky looked perfect but he wasn't moving and it looked like he wasn't breathing. The cat used the time to right himself on the hood of the car and jump to the side. Raymond went beneath the blue hydrangea bush and quietly observed whatever would transpire with studied indifference.

"Is he dead? He can't be dead," Connie spoke into his ear.

"I don't know, it doesn't look good," Bainbridge rubbed a hand against Larky's ribs, gently but vigorously as if he was trying to wake him from sleep. There was no response of any kind.

"He must be unconscious or something like that. Daniel, please, can you get him out of there."

With his left hand Bainbridge grabbed the forelegs and with the right the back legs. He slid the body along the back seat until he reached the door frame Then he lifted the little dog out of the car. Larky hung there upside down his head rolled towards the ground. Bainbridge held his arms away from himself as if he were holding a turkey roast. There were no signs of breathing. His legs were limp and lifeless.

By this time Taylor and Russell were out of the house. For a few beats no one really spoke until finally Taylor asked, "Mom why is Dad holding Larky that way?"

"There's been an accident. Somehow the air bag went off and it knocked him unconscious."

Bainbridge had been watching the dog closely, "No, it might be worse than that I am afraid he isn't breathing."

Russell yelled "What?" with such emphasis, it was the loudest anyone had ever heard him speak.

Bainbridge marched to the backyard and tenderly lowered Larky to the grass. Both boys knelt beside their dog.

"He could be dead. What do you think, should we touch him Russell?" Taylor asked.

"Yes we should touch him it is what Larky would want. Maybe he isn't dead."

"Let's think about this a minute. If he is dead maybe we should touch him with a stick or with gloves on."

While the boys talked, Connie was on her phone, searching veterinarians.

"Just hold on for a second," Bainbridge said, "Let's give it a minute, I'll try some CPR on him or something."

Connie, in disbelief, waved her phone at him and said, "Really, you are going to do a mouth to mouth resuscitation, are you?"

"Maybe."

Raymond, in his blackness was unseen under a nearby rhododendron. Pacing along the outskirts of the lawn, he had tracked them to the backyard. His pose of indifference had worn thin. He couldn't let these two waste another moment of time. In slow carefully placed steps he emerged from the thick shadows. Suddenly he gained speed. He gave a banshee mad hissing sound and flew through the air, landing on Larky's chest. He stayed motionless on the dog's chest, his four paws close together, his back arched. Like a steam whistle, Raymond released a second frightening hiss causing everyone to draw away from this explosive wild sound. You could see his claws knitting into the dog's chest. He slowly stepped to the grass and darted back becoming unseen in the shadows provided by the bush.

The dog's legs began to twitch. His face swung from side to

side. He yelped and then flipped himself into a standing position like nothing was going to bother him today. Taylor gathered the toy collie up and cradled it in his lap. Both began cheering and petting the dog. Connie came to the boys and huddled with them. Larky had been the family dog for all of them, including Bainbridge. Eventually Taylor handed the dog into Russell's arms. Russell stroked Larky's head, looked up to Bainbridge and said, "Raymond helped Larky a whole lot."

"It is just the most amazing thing isn't it Russ."

"He is not unconscious is he Dad?"

"No, it doesn't look like it. He looks fine."

"But he still likes me petting him doesn't he?"

"He likes it very much," Connie said. "Boys, take him inside and give him water or a little food. Let him go to his bedroll if he wants. If he wants to play, play with him very gently. I'll be in soon. I want to talk to your dad."

She paced directly to the driveway and her car. Bainbridge was carried along in her wake. Granted the passenger side air bag flopped out and the dashboard on that side had chunks of it missing, but the car looked drivable and that is what she wanted to know. She got in and the car started up immediately. She shut it off and got out saying, "I can deal with the rest of this car thing later. You were a big help back there. Thank you."

She looked back at the ruins of her dashboard, "I wonder what could have made Larky so frantic in there. What a shame, oh it is so sad. What would make him go off like that. He has never gotten crazy over anything. He's been with us starting a year after Taylor was born, remember? He's been with us every step of the way."

"Larky has the ability to be with everybody at the same time." She seemed within herself not listening to him. He added, "Talk about crazy, that cat is the strangest creature I ever met. Seriously, I can be afraid of that one. Hey, your car looks pretty bad but I'm thinking, insurance will probably pay to bring the interior back."

"In a way I am glad you are here. I've been wanting to tell you something when we could look at each other. Bob and I are getting married. And we are putting the house up for sale and we are moving to his home in Newton."

"When? When will all this be happening?"

"We tried it here, we did. We can't expect him to be driving from here to Boston every day. It just isn't fair and he has a lovely home in Newton."

"You are going to take the kids out of their hometown? When?"

"Before the school year starts. Newton has wonderful schools. It will be very stimulating for the boys to be near the city."

"This is news, Connie, this is real news."

"I know, but it is going to happen and you need to remember what is best for the boys and not yourself on this one. They will only be about fifty minutes away."

It felt like an avalanche, like the bottom had fallen out of his stomach. "Connie, why move?"

"You know why I am moving. I am starting a new life. Bob and I love each other enough to make this work for all of us. It would be best for the boys if you saw this as a good thing."

The news was too big for Bainbridge to swallow all at once. And it was just as well he didn't go any further with it at the moment because Taylor came to see the damage and report that Larky ate a little, drank a little and now the collie was in his bedroll looking around, with his tongue hanging out, happy as he ever is. Taylor took a look at the front dashboard and was about to inspect the exploded airbag when Bainbridge stopped him.

He said to Taylor, "It is time for me to go. Give me a hug." He hugged his son and said, "It is all good news about Larky isn't it?" After that he led Taylor by the shoulder a few steps away from Connie and said, "Be careful with your little brother. He is your brother for your whole life and he loves you very much. Treat him like you would treat yourself. Do you understand what I'm saying here? Don't go locking your brother in the trunk. You know better than that don't you?"

"Yes."

"And the other thing is, don't be using cars as a play toy. Ever again. And that is final. Remember, you are the big brother and you have to make good choices so he can learn from you. It will make both of you stronger. Can I count on you?"

"Yes."

"Don't just say yes."

"Sometimes I get tired of taking care of him."

"That's alright. When you feel you've helped him enough just let him be. Don't go tricking him anymore. You understand? Just so you know, I had to switch our visit. It won't be this weekend, it will the next one. Okay?"

"Yes."

Bainbridge was two steps into actually leaving when Connie said, "And Dan, it will be all right."

"I know," he said, "that is a lucky dog."

"I mean about this weekend. It will be fine. Go to your conference."

9

THE PARTY

You could imagine the town on a day like this. Not everyone would be going, but that didn't stop everybody from being willingly or begrudgingly aware that on this weekend every year was John Tabor's party. It would be hard to find a person without an opinion around the town as to whether it was too big a party or not big enough. About 400 people would filter through his estate today. Hey, great for Tabor. The event kicked in the high season. There were parties up and down the coastline, as it should be. John Tabor's just happened to be the one going on in this town. Turns out this time Bainbridge was one of the 400.

He arrived around two. He was just into the foyer and could easily see that a very large gathering was underway. He didn't spot Kate immediately but then there she was standing inside the arch from the entrance into the great room. When Bainbridge was out on the driveway he'd placed a text to her letting her know of his arrival.

The text was merely a politeness. Maybe a courtesy to let her know he was here now. Or, as it turned out, it made it possible for Kate to be right there to greet him.

"Daniel, oh I'm so glad to see you mister. Welcome to all things Tabor. Let me show you around this place before you get too lost on me. We will get to this down here and the outside but let me give you a little peek at the upstairs while we have the time."

She took him up her wide staircase. Bainbridge was wondering why she felt the need to show him her house. Admittedly, being a realtor he wanted to see everything about every house he was in.

"We will start at the top and work our way down. Here is your whole house tour. I want to show you the rooms you wouldn't see later tonight. How am I doing, I'm trying to affect the voice of a real estate agent. Did you notice."

"What I am noticing is you know me well enough to understand how curious I am to see as much of one of the town's finest homes as I can see."

She said, "The bedrooms are all upstairs. This is Heather's room."

It came to Bainbridge she could be doing this tour so they could have a little reason to be together alone. At least for a few minutes. He stepped into a large bedroom. In the far corner a short corridor to a private bathroom. "Lots of closet space. Beautiful sunny window. I think the right windows make a room," she said.

Bainbridge fed into her playful role. "As an agent you know how important windows are to the life of a room."

Heather came out from her bathroom and leaned against her wall. Apple red lips. Opal white flawless skin. Pageboy raven hair. A precision nineteen twenties empire cut that looked like it was done by a laser. Her body worked against a tight chocolate brown cotton three quarter length wrap, fishnet stockings, and brown sneakers with orange trim. Bainbridge couldn't tell if she was 14 or 22. She was a gothic crime princess. Among the millions of swampy thoughts he was processing, the main one for Bainbridge was, "Thank god someone else is helping her grow up. She loves drama, this one."

"Mother, please, are people going to be coming into my room all afternoon?"

"I didn't even think you'd be up here. Now, don't be rude. Why aren't you somewhere down at the party? Sweetest, you are not going to stay up here all afternoon, you know that, right? Your father would be boiling. If you don't mingle I'll be very disappointed. Isn't Buddy coming over?"

"Yes," she huffed, her eyes taking the elevator to her eyebrows.

"And Weasel Jones, sorry, Wesley, wants to tell you all about how the business with Daddy is going. Europe is starting to happen. He is leaving next Wednesday. I think. Wesley wants to tell you everything."

"Weasel is your friend mother. And Dad has talked about nothing else since he got home this time."

"It is Wesley. Why am I the only one in this family that wants to use that man's correct name? And Wesley thinks of you as a friend so be nice to him and talk to him. Really talk to him. It wouldn't hurt you to hear what he has to say about all this. It is very big what your father and he are about to do. You could do worse than give up a little time to Wesley. You have to do a little time talking to him anyway so it might as well be about a topic he really cares about. You might as well begin to learn that when you are with men, work is one of the few subjects they are comfortable and articulate talking about."

Heather left her angular support of the wall and went to her bed. She stretched across it and said, "If Wesley says I should visit him in Spain I suppose you will let me then?"

"You are 15 years old. You're not traveling alone even to your grandmother's down by the harbor young lady. And Wesley wouldn't ask you that unless you made him ask you. You be gentle with that man. These are important times for Dad and Mr. Jones."

Heather shifted and said, "Buddy should be here any minute. I hope he is not too boring this time."

Bainbridge had no desire to leave this situation. The longer he was a small part in the conversation the more normal he began to feel with both of them. Kate noted he was in no great hurry so she continued, "Learn to be patient with men. Especially the young ones. And be patient with yourself for that matter. Every minute doesn't have to be a big adventure. Heather this is one of my friends. This is Mr. Bainbridge, and Dan, here we have every mother's dream daughter, Heather."

Heather looked at him for the first time. Her eyes said she was bruised and anxious, probably for all eternity. She had a practiced, pouty atmosphere. "Hello, Heather, how are you? This is a beautiful bedroom and you keep it so neat."

"Today it's neat. Tomorrow we'll see. But of course you won't be able to see it tomorrow will you?"

Kate said, "Heather, I hate to admit it but your room is the neatest room in the house most of the time."

"Is the Buddy you are waiting for Buddy Rice?" Bainbridge asked.

Heather slipped off her bed and stood close enough to Bainbridge that there was heat. "I'm not really waiting for him. He can come over if he wants."

"You know, I coached him for three years in town league soccer. That is when I came to know him, must say he was the best player I ever coached. Nice kid too. He made the whole team better."

"He's a sophomore now and the best player on the varsity team. That's not really what I like about him, but it would do."

"Well, oh really Heather what is it you like about him." Kate asked.

"I don't know. I don't know. Maybe the fact he can get away with keeping a girl waiting."

"That was very funny. But do you have to be so tragic? Go on downstairs now. Be there when he arrives. I certainly don't want him coming up here looking for you. Keep the funny but lose the tragic just for today, will you?"

Heather's cell phone rang inside her small six inch black leather handbag. She put the phone to her ear and slung the bag to her shoulder. "I'll come down silly." She shut it off and said, "Buddy and some friends are down there now so I suppose I'll just get to this party you've got going on mother. Should I call your friend Dan or Mr. Bainbridge?" She was looking at him but talking to her mother.

"I think Dan or Daniel is a lot better than Mr. Bainbridge," he put in. "Why don't you call me one of those. And I'll call you Heather instead of Miss Tabor."

"And that way we will miss the Victorian Age entirely."

"Right, exactly."

"No great loss I suppose. Well here I go mom. Do I look all right?"

"If I were fifteen I'd want to look just like you. Now come on get down to Daddy's party and have some fun. Not too much fun. But fun. You know what I mean."

"Yes, I know what you mean. I already call Mr. Jones, Weasel. Do you have any neat nicknames?"

"No. None that I want to keep alive."

"Daniel then. And I'll see you guys downstairs," she said.

Finally, that was it. She had been standing too close to him, but her cell phone rang again and Heather stepped away to get the phone to her ear, creating an invisible private space. He felt he could move again now that she was distracted. With her a few feet away he felt he could return his attention to Kate. Heather was saying into the phone, "Yes, well why would I want to open it?"

She was heading towards the window when what seemed to Bainbridge to be a fully grown Buddy Rice appeared at the window. Heather and then Kate both shrieked and began to laugh. Heather pulled the window open and Buddy looked through the screen and pleaded, "God Heather, you could have told me your parents were in the room." He was standing on a ladder wearing a wife beater t-shirt and a tri-color baseball cap cocked off to one side. He seemed more annoyed than embarrassed. "Are you going to open the screen and let me in? I'm cratering here."

"Not on your life mister," Kate piped in, "You climb right down and come in the front door like a normal person. And I hope you didn't crush any of the flowers and bushes down there."

"Mrs. Tabor, I've been working as a house painter all spring and I assure you I didn't crush anything down there. And yes, I brought my own ladder. I'm very careful about that sort of thing."

"You're such a bad boy Buddy, I totally don't know why I like you," Heather said.

"Okay, okay, I'll see you downstairs. Where's the drama in that though?"

Heather closed the window as Buddy disappeared below the sill. She said to Bainbridge, "Buddy knows you're not my father. He just couldn't see who you were with the screen down."

"Oh, of course. I coached him, he'd know me, I don't know if I would have recognized him though, I think he's changed a lot more than I have these last few years. He's a big kid now."

"Heather, that was strange." Kate said, "What was he doing?"

"I don't know."

"He hasn't done that before, has he?"

"Mother."

"Well you just, you just tell him to put that ladder away. I don't want that thing leaning against the house all day. Tell him to settle down. That was over the top. Really."

Heather was looking at Bainbridge as she answered, "If he hasn't already, I'll tell him to put the ladder away. We just don't know who is going to pop into my bedroom today do we? I'm off now mom, do I look pretty?"

"You look great. You are great. Now go downstairs and have some fun. And stay downstairs."

"Okay. That's it. I'm gone. Bye Daniel." And she was, before Bainbridge could formulate anything to say.

Kate shook her head in mock resignation, "There is only one Heather. This Buddy Rice phase ought to be something to see."

"I had no idea he was already playing varsity."

"And now Mr. Bainbridge, let us continue our little tour." She brushed past him. He followed behind her. She entered their next room saying, "While we are up here I'd like to show you the lovely guest room and the master." She seemed to have lost that affected real estate voice. Her voice was nervous and edgy.

The guest room provided a king sized bed and its own roomy bath. There was a secretary's table and a magnificent second story view of the ocean. Kate wanted to be alone with him on her own terms. She didn't expect Heather to be upstairs, but that was of no consequence. This was her plan. Her way to test herself and him. Was there still that same need that had been between them weeks and weeks and weeks ago?

There was an area with a yoga mat rolled out. "Wesley is in this room for a few days. He likes to do yoga in the morning.

When he's not here most of the time this is my yoga studio. It is the only thing I have in common with that odd little duck."

"That and the fact you share your husband with him on some massive business venture."

For the first time Kate came close to him. Close enough so that there was no doubt where they had been before. She loosely held his hand and said, "There are only two rules while we are upstairs. One is you never talk business. And the other rule is just for us. Rule two is we have us, just us, for a few wonderful moments." She reached up, kissed him, leaned against him. He pressed her against his chest and sought out more and more kisses. She broke away and said, "There is so much I want to say to you, we will talk later tonight but not now. No words. Is that all right, Dan?"

"Absolutely alright" he said. He jerked toward the open door to close it. "No, not here," she said. She led them out and a few feet down the corridor to the master bedroom. An intimate understanding of silence was between them. Immediately on the right was her oversized walk-in closet. As they entered the closet lights went on. She closed the door, then unbuttoned his shirt, unzipped his pants, and pulled down his underwear. She kissed his erect shaft for a few lush moments then rose up and stood, taking off all her clothes, never taking her eyes off his.

Bainbridge stopped caring that he was in another man's house. He stopped caring she was another man's wife. He stopped caring about anything but reacting to this moment right here. It was easy because he was with a woman he would do anything for. He thought only of Kate every free moment for weeks without end. All that mattered was that she was naked and she wanted him as much as he wanted her. The rest was blocked out by the immensity of this minute right here. This touch. This tongue. These lips. A silken leg raised and held in his right hand. Him finding her and their velvet coupling. The sudden push against him. Her slow drawing back. Hold, hold, not too soon, make this last, swim, swim.

She uncoupled and brought her leg down. She was staring at his chest breathing in deeply. Taking his wrist, she led him to the carpet. He lay down. She straddled him and took him. She was smiling and glorious. They covered each other's mouths with their hands and moaned and roared their climax into the palms of each other's hands.

They lay quiet on their sides, looking for meaning in each other's eyes. The muffled sounds of the party worked through the closed closet door. "I was beginning to think my mind had made us up. That you and I were a mirage. We were so sudden. I have had these ongoing conversations with you in my head for too, too long."

"Don't, no more. We can talk about this, about us and we will. Tonight. We will have time for that I'm sure but it isn't now. I've run out of time. I better be the hostess I'm supposed to be. For now."

"Oh, yes, you are expected downstairs of course."

"You've got to get dressed and go down to that party mister. You get dressed. Go. Mingle. I'll be down in a few minutes. Don't you be surprised, but I am going to pretend we barely know each other and you are going to pretend the same thing. We will talk. We will. Later. Daniel, this is one of those into the long night celebrations. We will find space in it to talk."

He was pulling on his pants, hopping on one leg. She walked to the door and said, "Promise me you will remember I wanted this moment too. Always remember that. There is just no time left to stay here. I'm going to take a quick shower and change into some beach clothes or something. Buckle up mister, there is a party going on."

He pulled on his shirt wondering if she saw the double meaning she left him with.

JOHN TABOR SURVEYED THE CROWD, his crowd, with a compressed gleeful smile. Bainbridge came up to him and it was clear in John's gaze that his party met with his complete satisfaction. Bainbridge began with an easy enough statement to make. "Thanks, John, for inviting me. Really, this is a beautiful house, one of the finest homes in our town. Outstanding views, very nice. And so many people."

"You are very welcome here. I'm glad you came. You know I like to start in the early afternoon so we can all enjoy the ocean. And being outside and inside and all around this place. We will go to the late hours of the night, so don't rush through. Stay as long as you can. There will be limo service when you want to leave. It can get really interesting as we all settle into this party."

"That sounds like a plan. The ocean is beautiful out there."

Bainbridge could not detect any clue Tabor knew that he was in love with his wife. He pushed the conversation, mining it for any evidence. He was disappointed in himself. No matter how he tried, he wasn't feeling a shred of guilt. It freed him actually, so that he could interact with Tabor without giving anything away. Maybe that was it, or maybe he would not allow guilt to be any part of what they had together.

John was saying, "The way water changes is amazing. It is never the same ocean no matter how many times you look at it. Something like how this party generally turns out. Dan, you want to know one of my little business secrets? I make no distinction between my friends and my clients. All the decent ones know how to enjoy a good party. I put them in one place and the games begin. I am pleased to say clients I represented years ago still show up. I tell you, what we have here are my friends, my clients, my associates and their clients and you: a newly minted friend."

Bainbridge joined, "You are hosting a really impressive cross-section of this town today." Left unsaid was the thought Bainbridge held in his head that an event like this must generate some serious business as the year moves along.

"I'm in the people business. We both are," Tabor began nodding at a few people in the area while continuing. "Name recognition is one of the pillars, we both know that. I routinely see your real estate sign and now, finally I've met up with the actual man. Dan, in the end this is a party. If you are going to have a good time it might as well be here, right now."

Bainbridge had to flatten his response. There was no good reason to alter Tabor's belief that he basically just arrived. He went with, "To be honest, I have heard stories about your parties for years."

Tabor's eyes came back and riveted on Bainbridge. "You look hungry. And this certainly is the place to take care of that. Don't miss the shrimp pâté. That, with a few of those kalamata olives, a few slices of tomato, a drizzle of olive oil and basil? It is unbelievable! There is everything over there so please have at it. Oysters, Dan, do you like oysters? I think they are from Chatham this time. It is my job to host this party and your job is to eat and drink to excess. House rules my friend. I'm counting on you doing your part."

"You shouldn't worry about me. I've only been here a few minutes but I'll admit I circled by the buffet table and the raw bar when I came in. My eye is on the chowder and the crab legs. There's cod there too, I think."

"Oh, yes. And some outstanding crab cakes. Outside on the deck are rib-eyes, on the grill all afternoon."

"Then all right, sir. If your goal is to make me hungry you've done it."

"My singular goal tonight is to be in my hometown with a

bunch of happy people. Listen, Dan, before I let you go, have you done any work with commercial properties?"

"Absolutely I'm a broker. I can do anything."

"I like your attitude, Dan. We will talk later. I'm going to need some commercial space around here sometime more sooner than later. I figure you can help me with that."

"Definitely we can talk. I can help you get exactly what you want."

"Wonderful." John slipped his hand into his pocket and handed Bainbridge his business card. "Call me next week. I'll be in Madrid but that doesn't matter. We'll talk. Call me."

"I will."

"Good. Listen, I'm going to grab a drink. Enjoy things."

"Yes. That should be the easy part."

John stepped away, moving towards a ring of people out on the deck. Bainbridge floated in the wake of John's leaving and then set out for the buffet area and the Brazilian men dressed in white shirts, black vests, black pants, and black shoes. They were weaving through the crowd and rooms and stood behind the cloth covered serving stations.

As it would have to be, the La Montaines were hovering near the food. Each was puzzling over what to add to their plates. "You should have more shrimp," said Evelyn.

"No, Sweetie, you should have more shrimp," La Montaine said quickly as if he had used a paddle to bounce her words back to her. "You always tell me to do what it is you really want for yourself. So go ahead, Love, take more from that beautiful pile of shrimp. As for me I'm going for the smoked salmon and Vermont cheese thing he's got going on here."

Evelyn saw Bainbridge first. She sent a calculated smile to her lips, "Good to see you here, Dan."

"Hey Evelyn. Andre. How you guys doing?"

Greeting Bainbridge's arrival as an opportunity to take direct action, La Montaine forked smoked salmon and chunks of cheese onto his plate. "Dan, my god, good to see you here! This your first year here? Tabor's got himself a great home by the sea, wouldn't you say?"

"No doubt about it. One of the best houses in this town. It's a big place but it manages to be homey and spectacular. Not an easy trick."

Evelyn darted back to Andre who was eyeing the chocolate-covered lobster chunks. "Sweetie, wouldn't that just top off your plate if you had any room on it?"

"Sugar, if you are trying to control what goes on my plate you will lose. We have just started. Or at least, I have. The roast beef station or the lamb or the roast turkey. We are still at the raw bar. If I gave it half a thought I'd think you are trying to stop me from eating."

"No, my plum, but chocolate? Chocolate always goes right to the waist, you know that."

"Oh, really, Peaches? You huffed down that cream sauce you had with the scallop dish two minutes ago, and to be honest I can barely make it out on your hips."

"You had eight oysters while I was sampling the scallops I believe. I can only imagine how many calories was in the cocktail sauce you actually shoveled onto them. And you even said it yourself, Honeybun. We can still see my hips while yours have been lost to us for years."

Monty looked at Evelyn and let a moment of absolute silence fill up around them. Then he said to Bainbridge, "I know what you are thinking Dan. You are thinking that every once and a while it isn't bad to be single again, but in this case you'd be wrong. We go back and forth with each other to build up an appetite. Isn't that right Eve?"

Bainbridge said, "I wasn't thinking anything at all actually. I was just listening. It is nice to hear a couple of familiar voices. If

I was thinking anything it was, when did you two start using all that sugar when addressing each other?"

Evelyn said, "We are here for the entire evening and we agreed to play nice with each other. John Tabor's party is like going on a cruise ship. None of the rules at home apply. We will be eating and drinking and dancing and talking the whole night through. And we are trying very hard not to get nasty to each other until much later in the evening."

"I love your strategy Evelyn, I do. I'm going to head outside and grab a scotch on the rocks and warm up to this place a little. Catch you two later on then." He moved away from what was a large dining room into another bigger central room. Small groupings of people stood in close bunches holding drinks, taking hors d'oeuvres from waiters and talking and laughing.

Across the way large double doors were open and a deck stretched out to a view of the ocean. Two people left the couch Weasel and Heather stood near as Bainbridge came up. Heather noticed his approach and said to him, "Daniel, have you met Mr. Jones?" There was more the tone of relief in her voice than the intonations of a question.

"Briefly, one sunny day at a restaurant, but we were barely able to make introductions."

"Then this would be that moment. You two men should get to know each other a little. I have to, like, leave anyway. Bye Wesley, try not to think of work all night. There is a party going on all around you. I'm sure Dad and Mom want you to just let it go tonight. Oh, look at that, Bucky finally texted me to meet him at the boat." She began tapping her phone and made almost a run to the open double doors and the deck outside.

Jones said, "Thanks, I'm too old to have the thoughts she puts in my head. She is way too young to be that hot. Must say, a wonderful dear girl. If I can only find one half as pretty and twenty years older, I'll at least be getting on the right track. You know, Dan, this open couch is a luxury in this crowd. Mind if we sit and have a small chat? We can work through a drink together. Will you?" With that, Jones sat down.

Bainbridge wanted a scotch on the rocks and a chance to fade into the crowd for a few minutes but that wasn't his best choice right now. His way around the coffee table to a remaining empty seat on the couch was blocked by a twenty-something guy. The man was bald and had a wide bandage wrapped around his neck almost resembling a neck brace. He stood in conversation with an Asian man dressed in a crisp golf shirt, pressed khakis and bright brown woven dress shoes. Bainbridge had the impression he had seen the Asian man somewhere but the thought got away from him too quickly. The two of them held drinks and were talking in one of those insular cocktail conversations. This left Bainbridge to inch past Jones and the coffee table to gain the open leather cushion. Bainbridge had a choice to face the seated fellow as he went by or to present his butt to him as he sidled along. Bainbridge was uncomfortable with either option but chose to face him as he crossed laterally to the empty cushion.

"Why didn't you bring her to the party? "Jones asked with a conspiratorial grin. At that moment a waiter leaned across the table and asked if they had a drink order. Bainbridge asked for a double scotch on the rocks and Jones, after a tedious, reflective moment, said he would have a Pinot Grigio.

With that handled Bainbridge said, "I'm sorry what did you say?"

"I said, why didn't you bring her to the party? I know you came to the party alone. I saw you walk in. And I know you were with someone earlier. John would not have minded you bringing an extra person. Believe me this is his massive yearly bash. He'd like to see the entire town here if he could. I think it was last year he had to hire a police detail to direct regular traffic through all the cars parked on the street. I remember when we met you at that lunch spot you said you were divorced, but that should not make you feel awkward about bringing even a casual friend along."

The waiter returned with their drinks and Jones said to the waiter, "My god you guys are quick. Efficient. I hope I can get even close to that level of productivity out of my production line." Having handed them their drinks the waiter smiled and went to other groupings in the room.

Bainbridge said, "Cheers." They clinked glasses and settled back into the cushions. "Wes, I'm sorry but I'm not following you."

"That's OK, I get that a lot. My mind works in probabilities but my nose, my nose my friend, deals in certainty. I have many burdens, too many really and one of them is that I was born with an extremely heightened sense of smell. Not at the level of a bloodhound mind you, but if I wasn't working this science and business gig, I'm always telling myself I should be developing perfumes. If Coco Chanel were alive today I would have gone straight to her. Mere science would not have kept me away from her. It is not intentional. I just have this nose you see. When you stepped past me I smelled, well, you and the bouquet of a recent woman, if you will."

"I don't know what to tell you Wesley. Is it really that pronounced?"

"Absolutely not. There are probably no more than two hundred people in the world with this nose. And don't go getting me wrong here. I know I'm not special. After all, some grapes hanging in clusters out in a field have more genes than I do. And I see now that I have made you a bit uncomfortable. I was just reacting to data. I meant nothing by it."

"Well, your nose is right. This morning I was with a lady friend. Now that you mention it, I probably could have brought her along. I didn't want to press it. We aren't even at the girlfriend stage yet." Bainbridge was making this up as he went along. He had to calm down, admit to the obvious and invent everything else, "She is a very sweet lady, but she hasn't left any of her clothes in my closet. So, what does that tell you? Where does that put us on the chart? I think the rules state pretty clearly that she can only be called a girlfriend after a few clothes start getting hung in the closet. We are not there yet, and she actually had other places to be this afternoon. Sailing is what she said."

Weasel sniffed the rim of his glass, took a sip and said, "Looks like you've been kicked to the curb like me."

"It's not the same when you're divorced. The 'couple' thing is more tenuous. That would be a decent word for it. The women I meet have a definite life of their own going on. The women I've met. Sounds too pumped up. Really, I'm not saying there is a long list of women I have on a string. If anything it is the opposite of that. But I am beginning to meet some ladies, and what I'm seeing is sex does come into it. Must say, it comes into it pretty quickly actually.

"You are killing me, Dan, you know that."

"What kind of women have you been meeting Wesley? Have you ever been married or anything like that?"

"No not me. Corporate bought me a sound lab where I could do testing, experiments, and developments, and that was it. I never really left the lab. No wife, no dates. Just bigger, fancier labs. This last year or so I've mostly been in Madrid. I'm in Spain and I don't really speak Spanish, so you can imagine how that works with the quality ladies in Spain. What you're telling me is my American gals have loosened up a lot since I've been away?"

"Maybe it is a bucket list issue, I don't know. That 'bucket list' comment isn't really fair. It is not that it is completely casual when you get to that, but it's not like it is automatically part of anything bigger either. Then again, what do I know? I'm just out there in the marketplace finding my way like lots of other guys. Including you I guess."

"Really?"

"Obviously, on a lot of levels there is an emotional commitment going on. But that sort of emotion is played out in a very small arena that looks a lot like a queen-sized mattress. And most of the high-stakes emotion seems to stay right there, too. I'm pulling a whole life behind me, and so are the ladies I'm beginning to meet." Dan swigged his drink. "You do realize I basically know shit about women, and haven't got much evidence to back up what I am rambling on about?"

"Of course, that goes without saying. But Dan, that is what I'm talking about here. I've got to get me some of that." Wesley thought that he was sounding like an overripe teenager, but it didn't stop him from rolling on. "Any which way I can find it. I'd take a girlfriend; I'd take marriage if the right somebody came my way; I'd take a holla, even. For the last two years all I have been doing is this work. Far too much work. You know what I'm saying here?"

"You are sounding pretty boxed in."

"Right, but I've got to admit the bulk of it is over now. The launch is in just a few days and I'm telling you right here, I'm retooling my priorities my friend." With an exaggerated waggle of his head, Wesley said, "I'm a catch I tell you. I mean look at me." He scratched the balding crown of his head and looked up from behind his rimmed glasses. "It has been said that love is blind. The odds are in my favor. I am certain of the numbers on this. You've got to figure my chances are pretty good"

"Exactly Wes, it is just a matter of time, certainly."

Jones put his empty wine glass on the table, took off his glasses and wiped his lens on a napkin he pulled from his pocket. "I don't know why I'm saying all this to you Dan, but I'm glad you are willing to listen. It's been quite a while for me, I'm afraid. Why has it been so long between women? I don't know. I'm successful and getting more so, I'm intelligent. I'm young enough. Right?"

"You don't have one foot in the grave, do you Wes? Then you are young enough."

"Yes. And healthy enough." Something was happening to him here. Was it confidence? Was that what Wes felt beginning to override his usual circuitry? "What's not to like here, I don't know. Of all the complex doings in my life the fact that I am alone confuses me the most." Now what little confidence he had manufactured left him. "Probably why I work all the time. The work is complex, very, but it isn't confusing. Trying to catch a woman's eye has way too many variables."

"Wes, what are you and John up to? What is it you are launching?"

"You don't know? Of course you don't know. I'm in the middle of it. But I'm starting to realize that just because I have been thinking about this doesn't mean everybody has. Sure, the work... We can talk about the work. The topic of women, where will that get us anyway?

"I doubt you would know this but before I started my company with John I was with the Bose people. I know more about sound waves than sound waves know about themselves. The headphones that knock out sound when you're on a plane, for example? That's me. Well me and my team at Bose. But Bose didn't want to take the next step with this and I did. So I took my idea with me and eventually met John."

Bainbridge became distracted. His view from the couch through two wide open doors carried across the expansive deck. He could see the patio and deep green lawn trimmed by a ribbon of white sand, waves from the sound coming to rest on the shore. This, in its entirety, stopped his eyes like rivets to this perfect scene. He nodded towards Jones pretending to be keeping up as Jones rambled on.

"I even managed to pull a few of my key people with me. We developed this four-point device you see?"

"Yes, yes I do. But you can't stop there?" Having been called out, Bainbridge thought it was a good counter. A waiter took that moment to replace Bainbridge's scotch without the necessity of being asked. The man with his neck wrapped up and the man in the crisp golf shirt ended their conversation and dissolved into the crowd. A space opened up to his left. He could hear live music being played out on the deck.

"The four points act like an invisible barrier against sound. It eliminates about 98.8 percent of the ambient noise from crossing over. Any noise, car noise, people, jackhammers, every conceivable sound. You put these four points around the perimeter of your room or your home or skyscraper or restaurant or production facility and inside that perimeter it is quiet as a church. Our device identifies, almost anticipates and eliminates noise. One soundwave canceling out another wave."

"Yes, yes, I see," Bainbridge said. "This is huge isn't it?"

"Right now, almost this instant, we are beginning to market it in Europe. For now we are calling it some form of Quietfence. Obviously, our human spectrum of sound is not infinite. Quietfence is a program that can identify an almost complete spectrum of the sound a human can hear and block it from coming into the designated space. And before you ask – inside the space the sounds created there can be heard. But, these are canceled out as the sounds try to pass through the fence from the inside. There is a whole security component to market here as well."

Weasel suddenly shot to his feet nearly shouting, "Well my, my, if it isn't Gurty Klipspringer! There was no one I was more hoping to see than you, here tonight."

Bainbridge stood while Jones was getting that out. "Daniel

Bainbridge, this is the lovely Gurty Klipspringer. Look at you. An author. One of the top five bestselling authors of the year according to the New York Times. That is really something Gurty. But I am sure you know that."

"All the professors at the university are very proud of me." She was at ease and took a glass of white wine as a tray went by. She wore boat shoes, white jeans, a navy blue sweater. She was tall, her arms lanky, her fingers long and delicate. Her hair was going gray and hung straight to her shoulders. She hid a pretty, attentive face between the cleaves of her hair. She seemed to talk from under it most of the time. "The last time I saw you was right here last year. And you had your mind on business the entire night.

"It is nice to meet you Dan. Is Wesley treating you well? Like actually talking and maybe even complete sentences?"

"As a matter of fact, I can say he has been very generous with his thoughts."

"That is very good to hear. Last time was tedious, Wesley. You going to be like that again this time?"

"God you bestselling authors are so hard on the rest of us. I was just at this moment telling Daniel here that if my good friend Gurty would only show up then this party could get started."

"Oh you are so much better already" she said.

Bainbridge pushed in with, "Gurty it is a pleasure to meet you. Listen I'm going to stretch my legs and move about a bit. Wes, I'm glad we had a chance to chat and I wish you the best. The launch, the entire business will be a great success. I'll see you guys again around the party."

With Bainbridge leaving, Jones and Gurty seated themselves comfortably on the couch.

∼

BUCKY AND CHERYL were down on Tabor's part of the beach. They stood together looking at the quiet immensity of the ocean, listening to the slurp of the waves along the shore. They sipped margaritas. Cheryl said, "You should stop scratching under your bandage. It could become infected you keep that up."

"It wouldn't surprise me to survive that woman shooting me only to die because of an infection," he said.

"You do remember you were in her car trying to start it?"

"It is not my fault. I made a mistake. Mistakes happen all the time, Cheryl, all the time! In any given minute, there are tons of mistakes happening. There are more mistakes happening than right moves by a wide margin on some days. ...Hey there, you're not telling me it was okay for her to shoot me are you?"

"No. I am as glad as you are that you're alive. Here's to you dodging a bullet for a change." She clinked her glass against his. They leaned against each other and took in the silver shimmer of the sea.

"Anyway Tabor says I have a great case. And if he says so then I'm not going to overthink it," he said.

"That's good," she said. "Because that is not one of your strong suits. Don't overthink it. You shouldn't try anything new until the bandages come off."

They both noticed a large dark shape washing up on shore not sixty feet from where they stood. A large tangle of seaweed but no, not really, it was too organized a shape to be an isolated bundle of seaweed. Bucky headed towards it. Cheryl not far behind. Eventually, they could both see it was a huge turtle washed up stunned... or dead.

Bucky spoke first. "Oh no! It's about a six, maybe eight-foot turtle. I don't know if it is dead or alive." Cheryl came to his side. They stayed a distance away and finished their margaritas. Then they took a few paces closer to the massive sea creature.

From Tabor's dock, heading along the beach towards them came a waiter in black pants and white shirt and a second guy more lingering at the beach near Tabor's yacht. It didn't seem either had noticed what Cheryl and Bucky were investigating. The waiter said, "Hello folks, my name is Tim. While you're on the beach is there anything I can get you. Anything at all?"

"Wonderful," Cheryl said, holding out her glass. "Would you take these and come back with two more margaritas?"

Bucky handed him his empty glass and said, "Excuse me, what do you see right there. Do you see it?"

"Yes sir, I do now. It looks to be a turtle, sir."

"And the color?"

"A deep blue one. But it looks to be a turtle. It doesn't seem to be moving at all that I can tell."

"When you go back for our drinks would you find Mr. Tabor and tell him what has washed up on his beach? I think he should know."

"Yes sir, I'll tell him directly and be right back with your drinks."

"Tell him how big it is. Tell him it's a giant."

The waiter turned and quick-stepped along the beach towards the big house. Bucky slipped off his loafers and dropped his pants on top of them. Leaving him in his boxer shorts and shirt. He was unbuttoning his shirt when Cheryl blurted, "What are you doing? No! Not this time. This is a massive party, with the entire town here. Why would Mr. Tabor even want to represent you if you can't keep your pants on? Stay out of this, please Bucky? You can scratch your neck all you want. Just put your pants back on and we'll call it even."

But he was already in the water, coming up behind the turtle, only inches from its back flippers. To him they looked like a man's snorkel fins. The turtle had hulking, reptilian shoulder muscles, and long front flippers the size of Bucky's legs. They remained motionless. The last of each wave thinned and murmured along its body, its head resting at the water's edge. The eyes were closed. As Bucky rounded the far side of the shell, Cheryl came to within four feet of it, took out her phone and clicked a few quick photos.

"Oh god almighty, it's eye just opened and it raised its head for a second. It is alive! Be careful. In fact, get away from it, will you?"

Instead, midway between the front and back flipper he knelt in the water beside the creature and placed one hand on the crown of its shell. He craned his head over the shell, his eyes taking quiet inventory. "Oh Cheryl this isn't good. This isn't good at all. The poor thing has at least three very deep slices through this rubbery shell of his. Deep enough to cut into his back. It looks festered and filled with pus below the shell casing."

"Bucky, get away from him. Come over here right now."

He looked into her eyes and said, "This is incredibly sad, very sad."

The inky blue turtle did not attempt to move. Barnacles and white dots streaked across its dark blue body. From its leathery head, a single stern eye stared into Cheryl's worried gaze.

Behind her appeared the waiter, balancing two glasses, their rims caked in salt. Next to them was a capped silver shaker, presumably filled with margaritas. He stood a little way back from her and said, "Ma'am, Sir, I wish you would come away from that turtle. Please."

Bucky stood up from the few inches of water he was in and slowly followed his path around the back of the turtle. When he reached Cheryl, they both retreated the few steps it took to reach the waiter. While they moved toward him the waiter carefully lowered his tray to the sand, opened his silver cocktail shaker and poured the strawberry-colored liquid into each glass. He stood, holding out each glass, and said, "There is at least as much remaining in the shaker. Should you wish for more."

"Pretty, pretty damn likely. Thank you. Man that is very considerate of you," Bucky said, taking his drink.

With their drinks in hand, Cheryl and Bucky turned their backs to the shore and took in Tabor's sprawling lawn. There was a large white tent to the right, and to the left, Tabor's big house. They seemed to hammer their attention to the distant meandering groups standing, sitting in lawn chairs, eating from little plates, laughing. Bucky and Cheryl had their backs to the turtle, as if they too were as oblivious to the sad state of affairs here on the beach. Cheryl clinked her glass to his and they worked through their drinks without once looking back at the ocean.

Just then, they noticed the waiter from the beach was busy directing eight other waiters. Each was carrying white Adirondack chairs. The beach waiter was arranging the chairs in groupings of two behind the high water mark, not too far from where the shaker of drinks stood on its round serving tray.

"Excuse me. Come here, would you?" Bucky said. The headwaiter was taking a small parcel from the seat of one of the chairs. He quickly turned.

"Absolutely. Another margarita?"

"These are delicious" Cheryl said. "And it's very kind of you to bring them."

"No such thing, miss. Mr. Tabor assigned me to the beach today." As he said this he placed his parcel beside Bucky's boat shoes and pants, then stepped to the shaker and poured its contents into their glasses, snapping off the pour when each drink was at its brim. Bucky and Cheryl sipped this time.

"You do see the turtle right there?" Bucky asked.

"Yes sir. It is very big and it hasn't moved since I left."

"Did you tell Mr. Tabor about this?"

"Yes sir I did."

"Well, what did he say?" Cheryl wanted to push him along.

"Mr. Tabor would like you to leave the turtle alone. He will deal with it in the morning. It would make him very happy if you would come back to the party. In the bag are dry socks, underwear, linen pants and a shirt if you'd like to change out of any of your wet things."

"That is just too much. How did he even think of it?"

"Binoculars. From the porch, sir. Though he does have cameras on the beach, he did not feel he needed to step away to view the screens."

"That is so sweet of him, Bucky."

"Yes it is. I suppose I will need those clothes by the time this is over." Bucky finished his drink and handed his glass back to the waiter. "What color do you see?"

"Where sir?"

"Behind me, the turtle."

"As I said before, it appears blue to me. Dark blue like the sea in Greece. It has white spots and stripes."

Bucky scratched under his bandage and said, "What else?"

"I see it hasn't moved since we last talked about it." Bucky turned to the turtle and walked into the water. "Sir, Mr. Tabor would very much like you to not go near it. Please. There is his wonderful party to enjoy."

Before continuing towards the turtle, Bucky said, "You didn't say you saw them but there are three deep gashes on his back. It is a very sick creature and needs help now, not tomorrow. Cheryl, use your phone and call 911. Get an ambulance down here."

"I don't think ambulances handle turtles, just saying. And 911... I think that's for people emergencies," she said.

Bucky threw both arms above his head and pleaded, "God Cheryl, please just call 911. They are in the emergency business.

They will get in touch with the medics that deal with big fish. Just do it please? 911. Just do it."

Cheryl knew he wasn't going to give up on this. He wasn't just going to let this thing die while he returned to the party. She looked at the waiter who seemed to be hopping from one foot to the other. "Don't blow a gasket," she said. "I'm going to get a fish medic."

"It is not a fish, miss, it is a reptile."

"Right, of course, a reptile medic," she said. "Could you get us another round on these margaritas and some sandwiches and maybe a salad of some kind?" She headed to the nearest Adirondack chair pressing, 911 into her phone.

∼

JOHN TABOR WAS FINISHING the last line of his current scotch, chasing the vapors and bits of ice and water into his mouth. He was talking to the young musician unclipping the latches on her guitar case. They were beside a small stage inside the white lawn tent. "I'm grateful you could do some music here this afternoon. It means a lot to me. You know it's a privilege to hear you again. Two summers ago you were in college when you played here."

"Now I'm out in the world full time. And believe me, I consider it an honor to be back playing at your garden party again. We'll be set up by three and we plan on playing three 20-minute sets with about twenty minutes between sets. That will bring us to about 5. I believe that is what you'd like us to do this time, Mr. Tabor?"

"Allison, please, you've graduated from college. I insist you begin calling me John. I've known you since what, you were in middle school? And now you have your band and are out as a full-time musician. Outstanding! Just what you should be doing.

Impressive, young lady. Call me John. You're making me feel old with the 'Mr. Tabor' business."

"John, you're not old. You look like you are just getting started."

"There is top notch food of all kinds and beverages all day and all night. Make sure you and your band don't go away hungry. In fact, stick around, please. Make my home your home tonight."

At that moment, two people arrived; Allison's backup singer and Doctor Fryeman. Fryeman appeared intent on talking to him. Tabor gave a quick wave to Allison's co-writer, said to be a really fine guitarist, before stepping towards Fryeman. Staring intently at him, he said, "Well, there goes the neighborhood." Because he was trying to be funny they both chuckled. Tabor continued, "The esteemed Irwin Fryeman is in the house tonight, ladies and gentlemen."

"I can't tell you how glad I am to see you back from Spain for a while. John, could I take a few of your minutes to talk to you privately?"

"Well you've come to the right place, Doc. It is at a big party where you have the best chance of talking privately. Conventions and conferences are the same way really. Listen, seems like what you have to say will require a little stiffening." Tabor led Fryeman to a small bar stationed under a corner of the tent nearest his garden and lawn and view of the beach. With a clink of their glasses they stood looking far out to sea.

Eventually Fryeman began, "Is there anything new in your life?

"No, Irwin, nothing beyond the obvious. I'm not stressing out if that is what you mean. We are finally going to launch. If anything I'm breathing easier now than I have in about a year. You are off duty Doc. I'm as fine as fine can be."

"From the start I want you to know the why of it. Why I am

talking to you. It is because I believe it is in the best interest of my patient. The short version of what is happening here is, Katherine insists she is not pregnant, but your wife is pregnant, John, by any medical standard."

"Kate? Pregnant? I have to tell you, Irwin, when you said you needed to talk to me, I didn't see this one coming. Katherine is pregnant. Is that what I am hearing? When did Kate start thinking she is pregnant?"

"Katherine refuses to believe she is pregnant. That is the problem we are having here."

"But she is pregnant?"

"Yes."

"Really?"

"Just a little over a week ago we had our second appointment on this issue. Our office became involved four weeks ago. It was at that point I made it clear to her she was pregnant. She came back to the office for a re-examination, this time with my female associate, Martha. When that test also came back positive, Katherine refused to believe any of it, would not listen to anything about counseling, and called us all morons. She has been pregnant now for six weeks but she continues to be wrong headed all this time."

"She hasn't mentioned one whit about being pregnant. I can't think of a single suggestion she made on having another kid. Not a clue she even wanted one for that matter. She can't keep denying it when she starts showing now will she."

"John, this is about Katherine. We both know if your wife finds out I am talking to you without her permission she will sue to have my license to practice burned at the state house."

"Without a doubt. That's my Kate. It is not certain she would win Irwin. I've been your lawyer for fifteen years. We have something of a firewall here."

"Again, I'm doing this because I believe it is in the best

interest of my patient, I am doing this because I believe Katherine may need you more than she has ever needed you.

"She is apparently in a huge stage of denial. That's not a healthy place for her to be. She may never tell you, look at me John, remember that. But in this case it is not the pregnancy that is the issue, but the denial of it. Because she is refusing to accept the reality of her condition, it is best for her in the long run that you know the facts. I expect that by you knowing the facts you can manage this situation better. And get her the help she needs without going off target and actually believing her pregnancy is not real.

"I know you. You love her. She is going through something very dramatic, and for her benefit, I need you on the right side of this issue."

"She'll tell me. It is possible. We made love before I left for Spain. I've been in Spain a good month and a half. And Irwin, you know as well as I do that I had a vasectomy with that guy you sent me to."

"Doctor Crown. I knew this, and Doctor Crown concurs. And there are rare but statistically significant instances where the vasectomy doesn't work out as expected."

"Well given the odds, statistically significant is a tiny probability. I suppose at some point a DNA test is on order. I've been shooting blanks for a few years, which means the operation has worked for a good while now. There should be no reason to think it stopped working." Tabor was shaking his head, puzzling the thought. "Clearly I have to account for another man."

"Don't get ahead of yourself. We don't know that yet. Act carefully with what you do know. You should make an appointment. We'll see how active your sperm are and see if the vasectomy has been reversed.

"But the point to keep in mind here is that Kate is pregnant. That should be very good news, regardless of anything else.

Also, try very hard to let her be the one to tell you. Or are you not as good a lawyer as I think you are? How do you feel about what I am saying to you?"

"This needs to sit awhile. Basically having another child would be good, it would be fine. But I don't need to tell you the odds of this being a miracle baby. Most likely there is another man in the picture. You and I both know that."

Inside his head, he heard the loud rasp of a steam whistle blowing a hell of a note. His eyes narrowed and his right hand tightened into a fist. He slugged down the last of his drink and put the glass on the small table. Then, as an afterthought, he pushed the empty glass off the table. It came to rest in the bottom folds of the tent at the grass line. "I don't think today is the day for doing much about this," he said. "I think it best to do what she thinks is best at the moment. Tomorrow is a better space than today to work out this information."

"Exactly."

"If she doesn't want to talk about it, we won't. In a few days, she will. I'm sure of it. She could be thinking, 'a day or so after the party we will have a talk.'"

Fryeman leveled his eyes on Tabor and said, "Good, excellent. Give this whole thing a little time to settle in. I'll see you in my office tomorrow or the next day regardless of whether she tells you during that time period or not. We will do the test and talk some more. When do you return to Spain?"

"In five days"

"Can that be extended at all?"

"Usually, but not this time."

"Ah yes, the official opening of your company is very soon, isn't it? Well then, I'll see you Monday or Tuesday certainly.

"John, you both are to be commended for having this grand event. Hosting an amazing party like this. The entire town counts on this party to get the season started. I'm telling you, we're all so glad you've kept the tradition of this party for what now, 16 or 17 years?"

"This is the seventeenth," John said. "Can't believe it myself."

"So let that be what today is. You're alright. I know you are. Today you just be our timeless host. You're a good man. It is best you know what is going on in your family. I know you'll deal with the information when it's the right time." Irwin left his empty glass on the same little round table.

Tabor said, "My old man told me a thousand times, 'If you don't know where you are going you are likely not to get there.' I appreciate what you did here, Doc." Fryeman stepped onto the bright lawn and went in the direction of his wife. She rose from her lawn chair. Arm in arm they walked to the patio steps and up towards the interior of the house and the banquet tables.

Kate came out to the deck, telling Senator Roberts about organic cucumbers at the farmers' market. She was actually talking through him to Irene his wife. She noticed jolly couples all along the deck. Some turned to look at them. Several couples migrated nearer to where Roberts and Irene stood. Kate began to feel foolish about what she was saying now that a small crowd had gathered. "And the tomatoes. Remember when tomatoes tasted like tomatoes."

"Tomatoes," Irene said by plucking every syllable. "They have tasted like nothing for years. And very good of you to let me know or rather, remind me, about the wonderful farmers' market."

Roberts, sensing folks gathering around him, piped in, "A free market tends to correct itself much more quickly than a regulated market. You see, you found your better tomato because we in Washington have kept our hands off the industry. The less we do the better the market can respond." Several in the group nodded in sage agreement. What they didn't care to know was, the Tomato Growers Association in Washington had been, over the last few years, delinquent in contributions to Senator Roberts' party. The result of that was an easing at the border for Mexican tomatoes, which were universally noted to possess a very robust flavor.

Within the little bubble of people around the Senator, not everyone was agreeable to his point. Paul Roullard quietly hissed to an Asian man standing near him, "The problem is, until tomatoes can talk they can't tell us what has been done to them."

"I don't understand. Is America developing tomatoes that can talk?" asked the Asian.

"No. If anyone was going to come up with talking tomatoes it would be you guys. Sorry, I didn't mean anything by that. Talking tomatoes would be stupid for any country to make. Anyway. No, I'm just saying men like Roberts have this big idea that less government is good government. Their type doesn't get it. They don't understand that if they aren't going to do anything, well then, we don't need him either."

Waiters swarmed through the clutch of people around Kate and down through the patio, taking drink orders, offering fried oysters and scallops wrapped in bacon. A waiter presented a tray of fresh fruit and sliced vegetables, and another, trays of smoked salmon and cheese.

In this sudden swarm also came marinated steak tips skewered to bamboo slivers. Kate took a large strawberry that was tipped in a creamy white chocolate sauce. She let her gaze focus on the ocean for a breath, then spotted Chelsea Fryeman. Then of course, the Doctor. As they reached the last step to the deck Kate called out, "Chelsea and Irwin, come meet Irene and Senator Roberts."

Roberts broke out of the group with a bold step saying, "I have known the Fry Man since college. Irwin, you don't look much different than you did in Thatcher Hall."

Roberts' hulking body blocked an immediate look at Katherine – Irwin was grateful.

"Well, well, Anton Roberts, the Gazer himself. I'll have you know, I have been voting for you for years, even though, even though you never did return my English 101 textbook. You borrowed it and never gave it back. And at mid semester to boot."

As a reply, Roberts offered, "I thank you for your vote. There are never enough of those, even with this grudge you are holding. Oh the ties that bind. As to the book, my story on this hasn't changed. I borrowed that textbook for Irene and somehow she managed to lose that one along with her own. The big point here is, I didn't know anything about all this till after Christmas break. By then we were in second semester and who cares about a useless book from the first semester? If it had been of any use, I would have bought you a replacement. You know that. We talked this through about a hundred years ago."

"Ant, you are stunningly consistent. Always holding to the party line."

"In troubled times consistency is something we can hold on to."

Irwin batted back, "Even if the party line is the very thing causing the trouble. I'll tell you how you can solve this Gazer, buy me a copy and send it to me next week."

"Irene!" Roberts called out. Getting her attention, he dramatically pointed at himself, then Fryeman, then to the bar at the far end of the expansive deck. She nodded and went back to chatting with Katherine and Chelsea. Roberts placed an arm across Fryeman's nearest shoulder and said, "Irwin I got lucky with her. She seems to misplace everything she puts her hands on but me. Come on I'll buy you a free drink in honor of your long lost book."

"It will be a start, Ant, a very decent start."

A LARGE CABIN cruiser could be seen coming in from the south east. It altered its course and headed towards Tabor's dock. Kate knew as it made its turn that the yacht must be carrying the trade minister from the Spanish consulate.

She said, "Well, gals, there is a party going on."

Everyone around her watched as the 80-foot craft expertly coasted along the vacant side of the dock. Two young deckhands jumped to the dock and quickly tied the vessel to the pilings. Kate noted that many of her own quests were watching the skillful docking in admiration. Kate broke from the scene to say, "I suppose it would be good to find my husband. Irene, Chelsea, we will catch up later won't we? John and I had best welcome the Spanish minister to our slice of America. I'll introduce the both of you to him in just a bit, right gals?"

In a delighted voice, Irene said, "Yes, I insist you do."

Kate left her deck to cross the brick patio in search of John. The first notes of a beautiful voice singing Scarborough Fair carried in the air from under the tent.

Kate searched the patio, the lawn, the tent, and along the beach. After texting John and getting nothing, she made a pass through her busy kitchen and found him. He sat on a stool near the butcher's block table. He had a glass to his mouth and he gave a little wave when he saw her.

She said, "You better pace yourself, mister."

"That is what I am doing. This is ice water," he said as he tipped the glass in her direction. "Is everything all right?" he asked.

"Yes, of course, why do you ask?"

"Because while you are standing there you are rubbing your stomach."

"Now don't you go worrying about me John Tabor," she said

as she dropped her hand to the side, leaned closer and kissed him on the cheek. "We have the makings for a great, big night. This could be our best party ever," she said.

He put his empty glass down, stood and hugged her in a rocking embrace. He said, "Remember five years ago we were dancing on the beach at sunrise. And we weren't alone. General Hurly and what's her name, his date, they were singing some fool song and marching up and down the beach."

She said, "Yes. I think it is all changing for us now."

"Really," he said. "What could possibly have changed in only five years?"

"For one, she still comes to our parties but our general has not been seen since his parade."

"No, I mean with us. What's changed?"

"We are involved in your huge, wonderful project with Wesley."

"And?"

"And for another, I'm telling you right now, John Tabor, I'll be lucky to see a minute past midnight. It is time to stop with your questions and it is time for you to stop hiding in the kitchen. Your Spanish Trade Minister has arrived by sea. We will go now and welcome him. Make sure he gets a good start at our party don't think?"

"Pretty damn cool way to arrive, must say."

"The kids," Kate framed the term in air quotes, "have taken over our boat right there at the dock beside the minister's yacht."

"That's fine. It's all good. They can hang out on ours all they want. Text Heather will you and tell her everyone is to absolutely stay off the minister's boat."

Kate began texting that message while saying, "I'm sure Heather would know that on her own."

∼

IN A SPOT of shade on the patio sat Aubrey and Bainbridge. Bainbridge watched Kate glance at him, but she was obviously in search of someone else. She left the patio and moved about on the lawn and garden.

Aubrey asked, "Do you know her very well?"

Bainbridge didn't know if she was attempting a trap. After all, when you talk to Aubrey, you're with a lady who reads the future for a living. He hoped she wasn't as good on the immediate present. "No, not really. She recently arranged for me to sell her mother a very fine condo on the harbor. She is a very special woman. I can tell you that."

"We are all special women. I'm surprised you don't know that by now."

"Oh I know you are. I'm sorry, I didn't mean it that way."

"Then why haven't you called me. I clearly saw a date. It even sounded like it on my voice mail. I can't tell why it got sidelined, but I'm thinking you can fill me in."

"The truth would be something like the last couple of months just got away from me. It certainly isn't you. I came over to your shop hoping it would eventually get me a date with you. But time keeps getting away from me. I have my boys every other weekend, I'm running my business after basically being an absentee owner for a couple of years. These are not excuses. I should have called. But I didn't. That's the fact of it and I'm sorry. I'm trying to figure out myself why so much of me is on hold."

"It is on hold because you haven't yet learned to let go" Aubrey said.

Her ex-husband, Paul, came up to them, holding a plate of food in one hand and a drink in the other. He asked, "Mind if I join you?"

"Not at all," Bainbridge offered.

He found space and slid his plate onto the little table, "Great, this is better. I've been on my feet since I got here. Aubrey, did you know that Senator Roberts is here?"

"I know," she said. "There was a little rush to the deck a while ago. He looks fatter than his pictures make him out to be. Paul, you've met Dan Bainbridge before, do you remember? I should make it clear, Dan, I'm here as the designated date of my ex-husband. How pathetic is that?"

The two men seemed quieted by the thought. Bainbridge broke through with, "Aubrey, if you are pathetic, what am I? I showed up here alone."

Paul stopped eating along the bone of his dry-rubbed rib to say, "Yes that is more pathetic. You see, Aubrey, how easy it is to find someone worse off than you?"

Aubrey said, "I insisted he take me. I've heard about these parties for years. He wasn't planning on going. And I knew it. I told him I would go with him and here we are."

Paul began poking the air with the rib bone. "It is not that I'm Tabor's buddy or anything. Sure, I've done some plumbing in that house and his firm is representing my family in a lawsuit, but he doesn't know me from Adam really."

Bainbridge asked, "Who is the lawsuit against?"

"Monsanto and others."

"Don't you go into all that," Aubrey said. "This is a party, remember?" She stood, saying, "I'm going to wander around the main house and chat up some of my gals. You have to dance with me later tonight Dan Bainbridge."

In turn, Bainbridge stood, "That sounds perfect. I warn you though, I won't dance if we are the only ones on the floor."

"No excuses. Find me and dance with me."

"Paul, good seeing you again. I'm going to check out that monster cabin cruiser that just came in."

"Cabin cruiser, funny. Before you go, you in real estate?"

"Yes, yes. That's what I do." Mechanically and seamlessly he pulled a card from his wallet and handed it off to Paul.

"I might give you a call. I'm always looking at stuff. But that's not why I asked if you were in real estate. I asked because I'm wondering how much you think Tabor's house is worth?"

"Off the top of my head I have no clue. This is a unique house. Masterpieces are harder to price. I wouldn't want to guess. I'd rather do the research and give you a figure that is accurate to the market at this time."

"You sound like me when I'm doing up a plumbing contract. I'll keep your card. I'm always looking for a deal around town."

"I know you are. You own several fine rental buildings around town."

"How did you know that?"

"You know your plumbing, am I right? I know my real estate area. We are professionals at what we do."

"Oh, we're pros, right down to when the interior pipe blows a leak for the second time or a closing falls apart. Then we're just the dopes that have to take the blame."

"Yup, if you're a professional you are in it. In for the good, the bad, and the ugly. Listen, Paul, I'm going to walk around a little. Catch up to you again later, maybe."

More guests were arriving with each passing moment. There was a buzzy chatter from the edge of the lawn right up through the house. Couples grouped in small temporary circles, laughter often breaking above the din. A quiet zone seemed to exist along the beach. It was there Bucky and Cheryl still held fast.

∼

THE SIGHT of an all-terrain vehicle passing along the edge of the property roused Bucky from a brooding, silent study of the blue turtle inert at the water's edge. A few minutes earlier Cheryl took a beach towel offered by the waiter, spread it on the sand and stretched out on it. She was snoring, big stuttering bursts from the back of her throat.

At first Bucky thought the vehicle carried the animal rescue team, but it was clear there was only a single man driving a vehicle that was pulling a small trailer stacked with split firewood. The driver turned a sharp right and motored behind Bucky where the grass gave way to the sand. The man was huge. His paisley shirt turned out to be not a shirt at all. Instead, the driver was shirtless, his neck, arms, chest and back completely covered in tattoos. The tattooed man did a double and then a triple take at the large turtle a few feet from where Bucky sat.

The wagon stopped two-thirds of the way up the beach. The driver swung his legs to the sand, then used a hydraulic lift on the wagon. The bed angled up and a pile of firewood tumbled to the ground, producing a rumble like bears fighting, for a loud second or two.

Bucky stood and draped his own beach towel over Cheryl to protect her from too much sun while she puttered on. He was curious by nature and this man with tattoos, well that was a hand he needed to shake. Bucky walked towards the garden tractor. He could see a short conga line of waiters, each carrying a ceramic tile in either hand. They walked behind their leader who held out a shovel like a dead fish. Not far from the wood pile the waiter began to shovel a shallow circular pit. Each waiter placed his two tiles within the circle and just as fast as it took to realize what Bucky had seen, they were finished and the line of waiters was marching back to the main house and other duties.

At that point Bucky reached the driver. "Looks like you guys have done this before" Bucky said. He was sorely tempted by the hundreds of symbols and faces and animals etched onto every inch of skin, given that Bucky was talking mostly to the man's torso. The guy appeared to be about Bucky's age, though all that ink made it hard to tell. His height reached to Bucky's chin and he had more muscle than two guys put together.

"What can I do you for?" said the guy.

"Nothing really. I'm sort of stuck at the beach waiting for somebody. Not you, though. He extended his hand. "Hey, name's Buckland, but I'm called Bucky."

"I'm Nick Cuomo. Kate's cousin. Do you know Kate?"

"No. Not so much. Though I know she's Mr. Tabor's wife. Mr. Tabor's my attorney on something I've got going against an 80-year-old woman, if you can believe that." He pointed to the neck bandage. "She shot me."

Nick looked very closely at the wrap but said in practiced indifference, "Every year my cousin, she insists there'll be a fire on the beach. The two of them have been doing this party thing for a ton of years. I'm the guy that gets the wood to the beach. No problem. No questions asked." He retrieved a tin from along the dashboard of the ATV and pulled out a joint. Had a bit of a problem lighting it in the sea breeze, but once it caught, he inhaled and extended it to Bucky.

Bucky tapped off the ash, put it to his mouth and gave a steady pull. He released his breath in stuttering bursts while asking, "You see that turtle over there?"

"Of course I see it. Being about the size of this rig it is hard to miss. John texted me about that turtle, said to just leave it be. If it is there tomorrow he'll deal with it," Bucky returned the joint to Nick who took another hit and offered it again to Bucky.

Bucky's brain began to blossom just as he drew in a second toke. "For a minute there I thought you were the Animal Rescue people. But then... You know, I forgot what I was going to say next."

"Look," Nick said. "On my back right shoulder." And there Bucky saw a well-defined blue turtle in his skin. It seemed to be swimming towards his neck. "You called for a rescue did you. John's not going to love that. You think it's alive or what?"

Bucky returned the stub of the joint, which Nick flicked into the sand. "Oh its alive. I've been watching it for a while now. It's in big time trouble but it moves its head a little and opens his eyes every once in a long while. There are gashes, pretty deep on its back, though."

Nick was in swimming trunks. He slid out of his flip flops, telling Bucky, "Dude, I'm gonna jump in before I bring back the machinery and get into my party clothes. Probably see you later on then."

"You bet. Nice meeting you, Nick Cuomo." Bucky watched him march directly into the waves. Just then, Bucky's bladder decided to call out to him. It took a heartbeat or two, but it did dawn on him. He needn't go all the way to the main house. He could relieve himself by following Nick into the surf. He angled away from Nick and more toward Cheryl. He judged the thought as stunningly efficient on so many levels. He could keep one eye on the turtle another eye on Cheryl and empty himself all by taking one simple action.

The first waves broke against him and he pushed off into the crisp water, which served to intensify his buzz. Four people in bright red vests came from where Nick had driven his rig onto the beach. Behind them a truck followed in their lead. Bucky saw all this as his head came up for air and he hung suspended in the water bobbing with the waves. It was at that moment he realized the bandage stuck to his shoulder and neck had gotten soaked, then loosened and was now floating some sixteen feet to his left.

The sound of a truck nearby and an intuitive sense of a commotion shook Cheryl from a deep rest. The first thing she noticed as she propped herself on her elbow was that the daylight had gone soft. She guessed it was nearing six. Sundown was coming in an hour or so. She wrapped a towel around her shoulder as if it were a shawl. Bucky broke out of the water and stood above her, dripping cold splats on her toasty leg. She stood.

"There's something different here. You're not wearing your bandage. Stay right there let me look at that," Cheryl peered at his wound. "Oh. It looks fine. It looks like it is beginning to heal really well. It's not leaky or dripping or any of that. I don't think you need that huge bandage anymore."

He held the wrapping crushed up in his fist and said, "Well this won't do me any good, that's for sure." He gently stroked the point on his shoulder where an entry wound existed, an eighth of an inch above his clavicle bone. "The salt water probably did it some good."

"Maybe you should air it out a little. That could be good for it. But you can't be touching it. At least when it was wrapped you couldn't put your hands all over it.

"Take those dry clothes Mr. Tabor sent you. We'll go up to the house where there is bound to be a band-aid we can use. I think a simple band-aid will do just as good as all that wrapping. You'll definitely blend in better when you have your neck back and some dry clothes."

"Fine. We have to report to those folks over there first though."

In a rare instance of public affection, he held her hand as they went to where the rescue party was figuring an access point.

Paul Roullard, along with several other party goers, was drawn away from the main house by the activity going on beach side. He got close enough to identify a large turtle stranded right there on the shoreline. He also spotted two people hovering near it. When it became clear to him it was that girl Cheryl and that hammerhead boyfriend of hers, Roullard spun around. He needed a lot more time before he wanted another go around with them.

Bainbridge was also part of the small group of curiosity seekers pulled to the beach by the sight of a team of uniformed people. He walked past the dock, where he observed Tabor and Kate talking to a man in a blue blazer and cream-colored pants. Tabor's own boat seemed small in comparison to the craft they were standing on. Bainbridge could see Heather and Buddy and about ten other teenagers lounging on Tabor's boat. Rap music thumped from speakers in the cabin. Clearly those were not Coke cans in their hands. The smell of skunk cabbage hung near Tabor's boat. Kids were cannonballing off the bow. Others leaning against each other.

At least two of the green-shirted crew of the minister's boat were chatting it up on Tabor's. Bainbridge pretended not to be interested in what was going on in either boat. He kept a steady casual pace until he found one of the Adirondack chairs vacant and far enough away from the kids on the boat that he couldn't hear their music. But he was picking up the group playing under the white tent.

He pulled the chair close enough to sit and have a clear view of whatever was happening with that poor turtle. The moment he sat down a waiter was at his side asking him if he wanted anything. Bainbridge weighed the offer, decided to back off the whiskey for a while, and ordered orange juice on the rocks with a cherry.

∽

WHEN THE FOLK band broke off at dusk, a general quiet rested on the party, except for the idling sound of the truck down at the beach. Its spotlights illuminated men hoisting the large turtle by means of a sling onto the bed of the truck. The dark of night settled in. Under the tent a stand-up comic began what turned out to be a generous and wonderfully funny routine. This drew more people to set up in and around the tent.

Eventually the big lights on the truck went dark and the beach returned to the stars in the night sky. The comedian introduced a rhythm and blues band known for its blend of great covers and original music. Couples were flocking to the dance floor. Bainbridge listened to his second song while threading through the back edge of the crowd, standing at the perimeter watching those actually out on the dance floor. Not far away he spotted Aubrey talking to an Asian couple familiar to Bainbridge, familiar in that he remembered them from Aubrey's shop. Aubrey waved him closer. "Dan, how are you?"

"I've been down at the beach, caught the sunset, absolutely great."

"It can be like a painting, can't it? Dan, this is Holly, Holly Chung and her equally spectacular husband, Tim."

"I am learning Aubrey has high expectations for us all, Dan. It is very nice to meet you. I believe I saw you at Aubrey's shop a while ago."

"Yes, I remember. And now we get a chance to say hello. How is that for a close knit town? Do you guys live in the area?"

"Tim and Holly are seriously looking to buy something." Aubrey said.

"Almost ready aren't we Tim?" Holly looked into Tim's eyes with intent.

"Tim, if you don't mind, here is my card. I may be of help to you. I am usually very good with real estate. Call me tomorrow and let me join your team for the hunt."

"That was fast," Tim was smiling, "Did Holly talk to you before the party or something?"

Holly said, "No don't be silly, Things just happen. We could use the help don't you think Timothy?

"We are seriously looking, Dan. I can promise you that. The area seems to have everything we want but we just haven't found the right house yet."

"I'll go through everything and get right back to you, absolutely"

"Tomorrow, Tim. Dan will help tomorrow," Aubrey said. "Right now, this guy promised me a dance. So let's do it!" With that the two of them broke off from Tim and Holly.

When she put her left hand in his, she said, "Well, imagine that. The world works."

Bainbridge wasn't so sure of that. He hadn't danced with a lady in years. Actually to begin with, one of the only women he had ever danced with was Connie. They reached a space on the floor and as a couple, faced each other. Sound filled in around them; "Down on the Corner," an ancient classic. One of the songs his father turned up so loud on his CD player you couldn't think straight until it was over. For a few chords they were awkward and jerky. Then the rhythm pushed them in the right direction.

Bainbridge let his arms lurch one way and a leg take a half step the other way. Aubrey swayed and used her hands as if drumming the beat. Another song followed, a slower song. Leaning into each other, they let their feet shuffle through the corners of an imaginary box. That one ended just as they had worked out a comfortable closeness. A fast tune hurled them into some leaning this way, leaning that way motion. Bainbridge felt the phone in his pocket vibrate. When the song came to a halt he led Aubrey towards a little bar tucked into a corner of the tent. "I'd say we have some moves wouldn't you?"

"It was real fun," Aubrey said. "You at least seem to dance along with me. Some guys that ask me to dance just seem to be dancing with themselves once they get out on the floor."

Bainbridge pointed his index finger into the air and put the phone to his ear and heard his voice mail. It was Kate. "Alrighty mister, I told you we would get a chance to talk. Meet me between the tent and the firepit. I'll be seated at one of those little tables arranged on the lawn."

"My guess is we won't be having that drink just now," Aubrey said.

"No, not just at this moment anyway. I'm sorry, but I had to take that call. A real estate guy is a slave to his phone. That was Kate Tabor. Something about the property I sold to her mother a few months ago."

"I'm glad you're at least giving me a half truth. It is Kate, but that is pure bull about her mother's house. I can't tell exactly what's going on, but I can plainly see it isn't about her mother."

"You know, there is a lot to like about you Aubrey, but that ability you have to see into the future is a mixed blessing, I've got to tell you."

"Oh, so you think it would be better if men could just flat out lie to me?"

"No, not necessarily. It's just that honesty is shared. You can't just take it from me. It can be messy."

"You little duck, the whole world happens faster than you can think. Honesty is usually a luxury"

"True, I see your point. I'll hunt you up after I take care of business, what about that?"

"That could happen. It is early at this party, isn't it? So find me."

"And on that note, I'd better get moving and find out what Mrs. Katherine Tabor wants from me so much it had to be right now. Thank you for dancing with me Aubrey. It was a lot of fun out there."

"Catch you later, Dan."

"Is that what's going to happen? I'll be back after the talk?'

"No. We never see each other again."

"That sounds horribly extreme."

"See? See how easy it is to set up a lie? They are so easily set up."

As Dan left he added, "And so hard to live by."

∽

BEFORE KATE CALLED Bainbridge she placed a call to John, who was laughing it up with the minister somewhere in the main house. She told him to come and talk to her in ten minutes. "I'll be between the house and the firepit. I'll be seated at one of those little tables arranged on the lawn. No, it is nothing really, I just need to talk to you. Just for a few minutes."

When she knew that John would be here, she worried the chairs into adjusted positions around the cast iron table. The scraping noise helped her think. A waiter patrolled past and she ordered a red wine, telling him it would be the first drink she'd had in a month. She took this time to convince herself that this was the way it had to be. It had been a mountain in her brain for weeks. Enough was enough. The final part of the trail, the part with Dan maybe two hours ago, taught her all she needed to know about herself. She worked on her phone. She called Dan and got his voice mail. Finally, he texted that he was on his way.

John arrived first. He came out of the shadows and they gave each other a little peck. She noticed the second button on his white shirt was undone. His collar seemed to fly out from his sports jacket. He looked happy. Or was it amused? The way he presented himself she could tell that everything in the main house was humming along nicely.

John quickly found a chair, saying it felt like he had been standing at attention for an hour weaving Carlos into the party. He left him to La Montaine and Senator Roberts and a little cloud of women. "It's about midpoint in this party we're spinning. I'd like you with me," he said. "When you left us, Chelsea and Irene seemed to attack Carlos. And of course Carlos enjoys the attention. Why did you come out here? You have to tell me what is going on Kate. Now what is this all about?"

From somewhere in the dark they both heard a man's voice say, "Kate, there you are." As he came closer, it was apparent that Bainbridge was intent on joining them.

"Dan, please, sit. Join us." Kate said. She pointed to the chair at the other corner, leaving an empty chair between the two men.

A sudden understanding gripped Tabor's expression. "How's the party going from your point of view, Dan?"

"John, we're not here to talk about how the party is going," Kate said. "We're not here to get mean or even angry, really. It is what it is. It is time you both know that. John, nothing I'm going to say requires you to do a single thing but listen. And it's going to be very hard for you to do that, but I'm counting on you John. Can you just listen tonight? Then we move on any way you want."

"You've never been like this. Kate? What is this? Of course, I always listen."

"This has to be said. Dan has to hear it and you need to hear it. Both of you sit and hear me out." The waiter returned with her red wine. She sipped into it. Her eyes closed. She said, "This is the first drink I've had in a month-and-a-half. John, you ready? The both of you listen to me. I'm finally able to tell the world and me, and especially you two men, that I am pregnant, I am pregnant, I am pregnant."

Tabor held back. Several long heartbeats passed with nothing said. He needed her to tell it. Every possible detail should come from her.

Bainbridge stood, rubbing both eyes. The news exploded

any sense of composure he was trying to sustain when this close to Tabor. Why was she telling him now?

"What?" He blurted. "You must be sure of this, of course, but what? That's wonderful news. Right Kate? Really." His voice climbed an octave higher. "I'm happy for the both of you."

It crystalized in Tabor's mind. The reason Bainbridge was here. A question roared out at him as to how long the affair had been going on. He remained in his seat partly because if he stood he would throw a punch. This moment was Kate's. He remained seated but fired out, "You prick, not even the decency to wear a rubber."

When Kate could see that John was about to leap up, she stood in front of him and said, "I want you to control yourself and I want you to listen more than anything else you do tonight." Tabor simmered and chose to remain quiet.

She saw that he was going to let her have her say. "Dan, sit back down and listen. This won't take long. Now John, this isn't because of you or anything like that, but I did something I knew could hurt us. It could. Hurt us maybe a little, maybe a lot. You need to know, I've slept with Dan, yes that's true. I did that. It wasn't planned but it did happen."

"Why?" John hissed.

"I can't find a 'why,' John. There is no 'why.' There is me telling you I love you, John Tabor, but it did happen. I want our life together John. I don't want our marriage to end. That's very clear to me. You need to know I want our marriage. But it's up to you, though, it really is. To be completely honest John I just don't want you to hate me. If you just won't hate me that would be enough really."

"I'd never hate you. Hate will never be part of who we are."

"That is good John, I am so glad to hear that. There is one more thing, one extremely important thing. This... this situation is happening in my body and I decide what goes on in my body.

I'm being out front with both of you when I tell you my mind is made up. That's one of the reasons you are both here right now. I've been working with this for so long. My answer finally got to me. I don't play fair but I can't do wheels within wheels and secrets. I'm through. I can't hold it anymore. Not with you two."

Bainbridge was knocked on his heels by the fact Kate was telling her husband about their affair right here, flat out, right now. He was shuffling slowly through his connection to her pregnancy. But he was thinking, how could this baby possibly be my doing?

Kate continued. "I could have just said nothing. If I were stronger or a different person. Oh yes, this could have been done without either of you knowing much of anything. Clearly I'm struggling, you can see that. But I don't feel guilty or miserable about any of it.

"Dan you're here because until this very minute you had no more idea I was pregnant than John did. I can't go through this twice. You both should know that about me. I'm struggling, but I will not feel sad and I won't feel guilty. So be the men I know you are and listen.

"I don't want any discussion or input from either of you. Fact one: I'm pregnant. Fact two: I've decided it is best to end this pregnancy. Fact three: I make the decisions about my body. I'll admit to both of you that I have had a great sense of relief since the minute I decided to end this. I'm not supposed to be a mother again, I am not that woman."

Tabor didn't want her to stop. Not now. He wanted her to get it all out if she could. "Go on Kate. We're paying attention. It's okay. Is there anymore?"

"I just don't see me as a mother to a new baby. I really don't. Or ever again. And I tried, believe me. I tried to see me with a newborn baby and I just can't see it. You both may hate me now. Probably do, and I'm sorry. But in the end I won't allow myself to really care what either of you has to say. This is my decision. There you have it men. I am not hiding this pregnancy anymore from myself or you and I'm not hiding my decision."

Words were the hardest to find around the group. Beyond them, at the beach, the firepit was taking flame. Bainbridge got a sight line angled off from actually looking at Tabor and said, "You're right I should have used protection. It's not an excuse. But about two years ago I had a vasectomy. So I don't really think about it as much as I should. Kate, I haven't even told you this, why would I up to now? But on the day my divorce became final I had a vasectomy. For me, I thought I needed to focus what remained of my fatherhood on those two sons of mine. This pregnancy you have, isn't this more between you and John?"

"You what? What am I hearing? What are you telling me? You two, each one of you, has had a vasectomy? This doesn't seem right on a thousand levels. Every week some state is shutting down abortion clinics and you guys can just wander in off the street and get yourself clipped as easy as pulling weeds from a flowerpot?"

John said, "We talked about it a hundred times before I went in."

"Yes, we did, but you know what I'm saying. Believe me, I've had a hard time admitting I'm pregnant. Both of you with a vasectomy just kicks it up a notch."

John stood, looked at his watch and noted the time he and Kate were spending away from the other guests. "Are there others, Kate?"

"Are there others? No, don't either of you even think there is anyone else involved."

Bainbridge said, "So, John, you've had the operation as well. That makes it a puzzle doesn't it. Either way we have a miracle baby here."

"Didn't you hear my *wife*, Bainbridge? We don't need a

whiteboard do we? There will be no baby. I think we are done with this topic for tonight aren't we? I am, or I won't get through the rest of tonight. We need tomorrow to work through some of this. Agreed? Now that I think on it, tomorrow is Sunday."

"It will take through Monday for the doctor to confirm. You two know that." She continued looking from one to the other. "It doesn't matter whether it is you or you. It doesn't change my decision."

"Right, no question. But it does mean we need to get to Monday for any reliable information. There's nothing more we can do now is there?" He felt compelled to close this up like some acrimonious office meeting. "There is something whacked about this."

"Look at me John, I'm telling you, and Dan must hear it too, I want our marriage. I see myself with you. Am I wrong to see it that way?"

"Alright Kate. I hear you loud and clear."

"If you will still have me say so."

"You don't have to ask that," he said. "That thought never crossed my mind. And I won't ever let the thought cross my mind. You are home Kate. This is your place. I am your home."

Bainbridge found himself nodding his head, his eyes squinting, his lips pressed into a slit of smile. He was following all this but that did not mean he had a handle on any of it. The further this went the less he could say. He basically was just leaning into it, nodding his head in an attempt to emote an understanding of things.

"There is a promise I want from you John. Dan lives in this town he has a business and a life here, and he has this decision of mine to digest just like you and I do."

Bainbridge began to recognize that she was lobbying on his behalf. He eventually grasped the obvious, that Tabor was a very powerful, very rich man.

"Promise you will not just tolerate Dan. Accept him. See him as only one part of this situation. He lives in this town, just like we do. Let him be, promise me."

"Anything Kate, say it all, ask for anything. There are plenty of people in town I don't talk to. Bainbridge just became another one of those."

"I'm not this foolish am I, John?" Kate's eyes widened and began to water. She pulled her hands into a prayer like gesture.

"We will make this all work. You know we will. Now, though, we put this on a shelf right? We move forward. Bainbridge, you hear me? That's the end of it for tonight."

"John I want you to know I respect Kate's decision and always will."

"Bainbridge, if you really take a look at yourself, you'll find you have no respect at all for anything. You heard. I promised. You are nothing to me." Tabor wrapped an arm around Kate's shoulder. "Let's move on to the house, and Carlos, and make sure everyone else around here is having a good time."

Bainbridge numbed up. He felt heavy enough to fall through his shoes. Tabor and Kate were headed for the main house. He turned and entered the darkness that led to the amber lights under the big lawn tent. Kate seemed so driven and yet built of nothing more substantial than nerves. She was so quick with such huge information. Without a hint of a clue from her, he had been called out. And yeah, he might be the father. Too, too much was going on. How to handle any of it, well that answer was beyond his reach.

He swatted flies that weren't there. He punched out a little groan that only the thick darkness absorbed. He had nothing. The brain had blocked up. An acoustic band was registering in the lowest part of his hearing. A great female voice led the sound. Bainbridge started puzzling out whether this was the same band he'd heard at four. His brain, knowing it was incapable of dealing with any big stuff, jumped all over the question.

He could hear laughter and chatter and see little groups of people and clutches of Heather's friends, probably all that Spanish ship's crew podding around the circular tables radiating out from the dance floor and stage. Kate's words were crackling around in his skull. He let in all the noise, leaving no room for thought to breathe.

∼

LA MONTAINE SPRAWLED at a table nearest the bar kiosk, the one furthest from the stage yet still under the roof. He had his left arm across the table and his head propped up by his forearm. The mass of his chest, shoulders, and the glass of rum he held extended in the other direction made it pretty clear he and his drink needed the entire table. La Montaine was listening to his own woes. Listening to his head rattle on about the stunt Eveyln pulled off tonight. He was somewhat muttering out loud the words Evelyn said to him: "I want to have some real fun tonight. Every year it is the same old thing." The rest of it went directly into the boozy confines of his head.

La Montaine answered her. "What, I'll be goddamned Evelyn! Come on! You've been dancing up a storm. And a lot of those have been with Carlos, if we're counting. Dancing all night with the Spanish trade minister, that's something new, isn't it?"

"It is not enough," she said.

Even now, forty minutes and two rums, later he couldn't believe his ears.

"He wants me to have a night cap and give me a tour of his yacht! Can you believe it? Me! Carlos told me we danced so much he needs to sit in a quiet place and just relax for a few moments."

"Evelyn, Jesus! Why don't I go hit on Senator Roberts' wife? She's pretty hot and seems alone."

"Carlos actually said he doesn't want our night to end so abruptly. Me! Can you imagine? This has to be a different night for me, Monty. I've never known you to act out of spite, but you are fine. This is your party too. I love you, you love me, every other night before and after. But not this one though. This one is going to be different. I am taking this adventure."

Monty could see in her eyes that as sure as there was rain, she was determined to do this. "It may not be any more than a cocktail and a chat on a couch in his stateroom Evelyn. It *might* be just what he said it would be. Remember, the Spanish government owns that boat out there not Carlos."

"That's why I'm telling you. It probably will be just a chat, but it will be nice, different."

"Why don't I come along with you then.?"

"Monty this isn't about you. You are too far along on your rum to hang out with the trade minister, don't you think?"

"Alright Evelyn, I've got to say, you could have just slipped away. Do you want me to stop you? Is that why you are telling me?"

"Well, are you going to stop me?"

"You never fight fair, Evelyn, ever. Tell you what. It's 11 something. At one I'll be at the fire pit. If you aren't there by one, I suppose you can find your own way home. Tabor has limo service from his front door all night long."

"Thank you for not making this something it isn't. And by the way, be sure to take your own advice when you're going home. Make sure you use John's limo service."

This was the scene playing in loops around what remained tonight of La Montaine's mind. It rode like a boat up and down the waves of his rum-soaked brain. He set himself as almost a pile across the table.

Bainbridge stood at the kiosk. With an Irish whiskey on the rocks in hand, he spotted Monty all alone, his head in his hand. Bainbridge went to the table and said, "Permission to come aboard captain?" Monty looked up and blinked away his thoughts. "Dan, of course. Sit. If you don't mind that this table is wallowing in some heavy seas."

"Too much food?"

"No, too little rum. But I'm catching up on it now. What's it like out there in the single world, Dan? Let's have a report from the single life, me Matey, arghh!"

"Monty, come on. I don't know. We live with the situation we find ourselves in. Every day is a new day."

"Danny, we both remember you being married. We both shared the being married thing. You are out there now. Boom, somewhere else. What's it like out there?"

"Ah, god, Monty there is a single world, that's for sure. And it is a life that is absolutely different on one level and the same on another, if that makes any sense. Maybe what I can say is, you are never really alone, even in the single life, though there are long stretches of time where you'd swear I was wrong about that."

And with those words, Bainbridge and La Montaine raised their cups and drank as if they had been on a dusty trail.

"Speaking of marriage, where is Evelyn?"

"She's on an adventure."

"Really, what do you mean by that?"

"It gets damn complicated if I tried to explain it out. At this point I'll just let the rum do the talking for me."

"Well, what's the rum saying about Evelyn?"

"Evelyn who, that's what its saying."

They said nothing more. For an entire song they let their separate minds buffer and they drank from their glasses, quiet as sod.

Aubrey made an appearance at the bar. She spotted them. Bainbridge waved her over. When she arrived she said, "Well look what is hanging out at this corner. It is past 11. Should I even sit with you guys? You both look like you need another drink. Or maybe a rescue dog."

Bainbridge said, "Sit down. I'll be right back. Monty and I could use some more fire power. I'll get us a rescue drink." He jiggled the empty glasses at her, stood and left. Aubrey used the opportunity to talk directly to La Montaine. It was clear he was sinking into the bottom of his glass. She said, "Monty put the sadness away. Don't let it take root. This isn't about you. She is doing something for herself that is all it is."

"How do you know about the damn trade minister? Oh yes, of course. You'd know if you wanted to know. You'd know. I get it but why, why are you telling me this? And by the way, thank you for telling me. Whatever. Always good to see you, always."

"I'm telling you because we are neighbors and friends and have known a little bit about each other for years. I'm also telling you because I don't want you to stress out. Stress is real. Remember that. Stress has to be recognized and managed. Give her tonight. Let it go and you, yes you, will be much happier. I can see it. It can work fine if you let it. Deep down you know they are only going to talk and flirt. I don't have to tell you that."

Monty was handed another rum on the rocks. He settled back to propping his head up and staring out at the two of them. If you could see his eyes you would see a fog rolling in.

To Aubrey, Bainbridge said, "Let's walk to the fire pit, what do you say? Monty, Aubrey and I are going to move around a bit."

"You're going to abandon me are you? That seems really, really popular tonight."

Before leaving Aubrey rested a hand on his shoulder. "You don't have to, so why go there? Ask yourself that." Bainbridge and Aubrey ducked under the tent roof and went into the darkness toward the beach.

Bainbridge said to her, "I can't have you in my head right now. I can feel you in there rummaging around and it is not a good time. If we are going to be friends then you have to give me space that is just mine, that you don't know anything about unless I tell you. Can you do that?"

"Of course I can," she said.

They stood outside the wobbling glow of the fire. There was a bush that marked the end of the lawn and the start of the beach. They sat right there. He saw many other couples sitting on blankets pocketed around the fire pit. He took a pull on his whiskey and that is exactly the last thing he could remember about the night, no matter how hard he pushed against his noggin.

10

THE BACK NINE

Bainbridge woke near a bush at the end of the lawn up against the sand of the shoreline. Morning dew rested on his face and hair. Someone had dropped a wool blanket over him. He lay there and remembered Aubrey and the chip chip of laughter from people lounging in a circle nearer to the fire than he was. He remembered the murmur and slushy sound of the waves along the beach. He remembered Venus hanging in the night sky like a lantern. He tugged the blanket tighter to his shoulders and he lay still, watching the morning sun spread light across the sky. He remembered he could be, just might be, a father again. He remembered Tabor closing in around Kate. Bainbridge pulled himself to a seated position. He used the warm inside part of his blanket to rub the dew from his hair and face. Nearer to the fire a few others lay asleep, each with a large blanket.

Buddy Rice was standing, folding his blanket when he noticed Bainbridge pull himself to a seated position. He said, "Well Coach. Morning. Nothing better than starting a day off at the beach."

"Buddy, you are growing up right in front of me. Stop that will you?"

"No can do Coach. High school isn't as easy as everyone thinks it is. I've got to get out of there as soon as I can. By the way, my soccer has gotten a whole lot more serious."

"Impressive, Bud, I'm glad you work hard at what you are good at. Not everybody does. You are one of the good ones. Remember that."

"Nice of you to say, coach."

"Hey, you were coming in through Heather's bedroom window. I'm going to make a leap and think you two must be dating?"

"Coach, that was more a joke than anything. Come on. I'm not sure dating is the word but we are friends. She told me that was you up there. Not her father."

"Right, Mrs. Tabor was showing me the house. You being friends with Heather, that's a good way to be. Have fun. Do each other no harm."

"That does sound about right. You know, if I leave now I can get home before my parents even get up. Not that it matters. They know where I am, but I can get some points here if they don't know I'm coming in at dawn."

"Off with you then," said Bainbridge. "Stop wasting time here."

He stood and shook himself loose. He needed to get to his car. He needed to get to his condo and a shower. After that he would shoot back here and see Kate if only for a few minutes. Or at the very, very least, talk to her as early as possible. He really had to go over this thing one more time. But right now, he needed his car.

From the lawn he took the stairs. Reaching the deck, he went into the big room and dropped his woolen blanket carefully on the couch. The same couch where he had chatted up Wesley

Jones. Two women were moving about the downstairs rooms. One was picking up bottles and glasses. She was hawking the little tables and bookcase shelves. Another was vacuuming the large room where the buffet stations once stood. The power in Bainbridge's phone was dissolved to nothing. A clock in the hall claimed it was 6:15.

Bainbridge left by the front door. A valet waiting at the driveway asked him his name and drove him to his own car. The car was located at the Mariners junior high school parking lot not two blocks from Tabor's home. When the valet came to a stop beside his Volvo he was given his keys. Bainbridge sealed himself in his own car, breathed in the warm confines. He imagined a child's car seat strapped in the back. He could almost make it out in the rearview mirror. This figment bounced around his mind the entire drive to his home.

A hot shower washed the dull cold of the ground off his body, but not Kate's emphatic decision to have an abortion. It couldn't wash through the fact Tabor knew of his affair or that yesterday was the last time he would make love to Kate Tabor. Showers don't do all that and never could.

Bainbridge kicked over how little he knew about himself. He was in a zone where he didn't know the rules. He did know Kate shared herself with him. Both times. They had been as close and true as two people can be. He knew that and also knew he would believe that for the rest of his life. To see her rip it up so suddenly, what was he expecting? No, he would not allow himself to believe he was simply used. He knew better. He had been there. Did it even really matter if he were used?

He charged his phone while he showered and dressed. When he picked it back up, he was able to see there was a voicemail from Tim Chung, who was wondering if today would be good to research some properties around town. Tim said he'd just jogged past a for sale sign on 12 Shore Road and wanted to know more. 12 Shore Road, the house Bainbridge used to call home. Now only Connie did that. Really? It must have just come on the market. Bainbridge duly noted she didn't list it with him.

Eight o'clock. The thing he wanted to do most was drive over to Doctor Crown's office and find out what he could about his vasectomy. But that isn't going to happen on a Sunday. All that sort of thinking had to be pushed down the pike straight into tomorrow. What did Tabor call it? Put it on a shelf. There was no response to a voicemail left for Kate when he borrowed the valet's phone on the way to his car earlier this morning. He put in his second voicemail now that his own phone was up.

"Kate it is really important for me to get to see you today. Even for a few minutes. There was a lot left unsaid, I'm sure you'd agree. I'd like to go over some of it with you just one more time, please Kate. Call me, at least call me. I'm coming over in an hour if I don't hear from you. Maybe we can see each other then. I really do feel like I need to see you if I can. It doesn't have to be at your house. It can be anywhere. Just a few minutes that's all I ask. Call me."

After ten minutes, Bainbridge was working his car into Tabor's driveway.

Just a bit from the front steps a valet remained on duty. Bainbridge noted it wasn't his valet from just over an hour ago but another one, standing with his arm's clasped behind his back. Bainbridge parked to the side. He went past the valet and waved his hand, showing a firm grasp of his own keys. He rang the doorbell. One of the two heavy plate glass doors was opened by the lady who collected bottles and glasses. He explained that he wanted to see Kate and was told there were people in the kitchen.

Jones leaned against a butcher block table peeling a hard-boiled egg. The smell of bacon was rich in the air. "Dan, you are looking put together and ready for the day."

Gurty was also in a pair of men's pajamas. She was spooning her tea and bringing it to her nose. She said, "Don't talk a lot if you don't have to. Either of you."

"Have you seen Kate? Is she up?"

Jones answered under a stage whisper in deference to Gurty, "We haven't seen her this morning."

"And why would we," Gurty added. "After last night, this is what early morning has become. Want some tomato juice?"

"No. But thank you."

Jones said, "We haven't seen Kate but I think John is out on the deck."

Bainbridge looked at his phone. There was no message of any kind from Kate. He pocketed the phone and took a side door from the kitchen to the deck. A few feet away Tabor sat at a table in the sun chomping on a slice of bacon. Kate's cousin, Nick was seated across from Tabor sipping coffee from an oversized mug. Bainbridge approached.

"John, is Kate up? I'd like to talk to her. I need to talk to her just once more and that will be it."

John remained seated, turned and took him in focus and said, "Dan. Dan the Man. You are a pushy bastard, aren't you? This may be interesting to you. I know you've met Nick. Just now he's telling me about taking Kate to that listing of yours. The one Lydia ended up buying. Nick, you remember Dan, right?"

"Sure I do. Yes. I remember Mr. Mushface. I'll tell you something Dan. I'm being told things that make me wish I never left you alone with my cousin for a single second. You know what I'm saying? You shouldn't be here." Nick was getting to his feet when Tabor stood bolt upright and shouted, "You sit down, just sit there Nick, please."

Heather, cradling a bowl of cereal, padded further down the deck. She seemed in her own world, disinterested in anything except staring off into the horizon. Her spoon knew its way to her mouth. Several men were taking down the large tent. The trade minister and two of his crew emerged from his yacht, crossed to the dock and began walking to the main house.

"You give me a listen, Bainbridge. Your party is over. I don't want to see you within a mile of this house ever again. You straight on that? If Kate wants to get in touch with you she will. Got it? But if you put another foot on this property I will slap you with a stalking charge that will keep you locked up for two weeks. And in court for two years."

"This isn't over John. You know that right?" He pulled out his phone and called her again. No pick-up. Just voicemail. "It will be over but it isn't right now. How could it be John? We just heard about this a few hours ago."

"Put the phone down and get the fuck off my deck."

Bainbridge couldn't stay any longer, he knew he had no choice but to leave. He made a point of leaving by going down the deck, passing Heather. When he was close he asked, "Have you seen your mom this morning?"

"You should talk to Grandma Lydia, if you want to talk to anybody."

"Will you tell your mother I was here?"

She gave him a sudden glance. "Disappointing isn't it?" she said. "I don't suppose you dare visit the upstairs bedrooms again to find out for yourself."

"Heather, I'm just trying to say a few words to your mom, is all." He began walking to the stairs, then down along the side of the house to his car. His mind boiled and steamed with uncertainty. She was there, right there in that house. He knew it.

His office was an oversized shop in the village along main street. He warmed up the computer, took to his phone and said into her voicemail, "Hello Lydia. This is the realtor, Dan Bainbridge. I've got something I'd like to ask you about. I'd like to come over for a few minutes if I could. Alright, I hope to hear from you real soon."

He turned to the computer. The screen displayed the most recent listings in his area. One of them was his old house, now on the market for $825,000. Listed by Kelly Realty. Bainbridge lowered his head and tried to breath deeper into what had become shallow breaths. The gravity in his brain was heavy enough to crush a soup can. He shot his eyes up to the ceiling and gave himself to the silence of his empty office.

∼

THAT SAME MORNING came up quick for Kate. An hour before dawn she had her bags packed and at the foot of the stairs. The valet was putting them in the black Suburban. John had a good hour before he would get up completely. When she was ready, she leaned into the bed, kissed him on the cheek and rumpled his hair. It was enough to get John to open one eye. She reminded him she'd be gone a few days and that the story was that she was visiting a very sick friend. They would talk later in the day.

"But for now, rest up and be ready for breakfast with the trade minister," she said softly.

She sat at the edge of Heather's bed taking in the rhythm of her daughter's soft breathing. She gave her shoulder a little shake.

"No, sweetie, don't get up. Just listen for a few minutes. I have to tell you something, and it really can't wait. Last night at the party, I can't believe it. It's so sad. I got a call from a college roommate I had a long time ago. She and I were even sorority sisters. Agnes Chapman is such a dear friend. Well, she called me right out of the blue. I had to take the call but I learned some very sad news. She has cancer. Agnes wants to be sure to see me before she dies. It's terrible, terrible news. I didn't let on that she was calling me in the middle of the party. But now I have to deal with it."

"Oh mom, that is horrible!"

"I'm leaving to see her for a few days of course. I wanted you to know from me and tell you I'm leaving this morning for Denver, where she is."

"That's fine, mom. Like, I'll be fine. You have to go. It will help her a lot. We both know that."

"I knew you would be my Little Miss Fine. Once daddy leaves for Spain, you will spend your nights at Grandma Lydia's. You have to promise or I will worry the entire time I am there. Or I just won't go at all."

"No worries mom, honestly, I will do exactly that. When does dad leave this time?"

"He has today and all of tomorrow. He flies out the next morning. So, you two will have some time together. That will be a bonus. Big stuff happening all over the place. I need your support Heather and so does Dad. We really do. No missing school, no late nights with your friends. And you help Grandma pick up around her house."

"I love being with Grandma Lydia, you know that. I stayed with her so much I had my own room. That was a great place, her Vermont farmhouse. This will be fun, being with her in the new place for a few days instead of just dropping by."

"And you'll keep your grades up?"

"Of course I will. It is what I do best. How long you going to be gone for, anyway?"

Kate drew her into a hug. She said, "You are my little trooper."

"I am 15 mom. I'm your big trooper."

"It is too early now, but I will call Grandma later this morning. Thank you, thank you, Heather. We will talk when I'm in Colorado."

"Okay, mom, go. Check your room. Make sure you didn't forget your brushes. Love you mom."

"Oh, looking out for mom, that's sweet. Get back under the sheets, catch some more sleep. It is very early."

∽

BAINBRIDGE GOT JITTERY. Something needed to get done. Actually done. He called Bridgit Daliwal of Kelly Realty. Bridgit was their top agent. He knew she would answer her phone and she did. They had worked together on four or five sales over the years. She would be happy to show him and his client the house at 12 Shore Road. They agreed on eleven o'clock.

Next he put in his call to Tim. As expected, Holly wanted to join in the showing. This was good. He printed out fact sheets on two other properties, the two he knew to be the best houses on the market in this area. Turns out he'd been in all three of these houses. Of the three, he thought the Tudor with the corner yard and slight views of the bay was the best of the choices at hand.

The crunching sound of car tires against sand came up from the office parking lot. They were early, but Dan had to admit Tim and Holly seemed serious about a sale. "It will give me more time to talk about their financials now that I can take them around the area instead of just to the house," Dan thought. "It will give time so they will see each one in its setting and its relationship to the village."

The office door opened and closed almost with no sound at all. Nick Cuomo stood there in full steam. He was wearing a surgical mask and a watch cap pulled over his ears. He hissed, "This ain't about John. John doesn't want me to touch you."

Bainbridge tried to stand but Nick stepped forward and

threw a fist that hit him like a shotgun blast, just below his solar plexus. Nick followed that by sending a blow to the side of his head that knocked him to the floor. The bottom part of his cheekbone began throbbing. He could hear muscles snapping back into alignment along the jawbone.

Nick stood over him, one of his work boots only an inch from his nose. Bainbridge was choking and gulping for air. Nick's eyes could be seen above the mask inspecting the different parts that made up Dan's office. Nick's boot moved away but it was back before Bainbridge could even finish his next spasm for air. Nick took a putter that rested against a bookcase and directed its handle to point above Bainbridge's eye lashes. "I figured I had some skin in this game. You deserve worse."

Bainbridge shut his eyes, in anticipation of the putter handle going right through his eye. Instead, Nick raised the club and smashed it down onto Bainbridge's computer screen. The screen crinkled and fizzed. Nick stormed out, slamming the door hard enough it skipped the latch.

Bainbridge stayed down. He had short little breaths without the spasms now. From his chest to the back of his head he wasn't sure what was working any more. Tenderly he touched his cheek bone. He could feel it swell to the size of an egg. Lurching upright, he staggered and coughed, which sent lightning bolts of pain through his head.

Holding the edge of his office desk, then staggering towards the bathroom he got a look at the damage. A red welt was forming under his cheekbone, and there was a fleck of blood in the white just where the green of his iris ended. This was new. The other eye was normal. Bloodshot maybe, but fine. The swollen cheek made his face misshapen. It was going to be hard to ignore. He filled the sink with cold water and pressed his face into the bowl. The cold seemed to suck some of the fury away. Time had spun out on him.

In only eleven minutes Tim and Holly would be in the office. That couldn't happen now. He went for his phone. "Listen Tim, I've been thinking. You haven't left yet, good. I'll come by and pick you both up at ten minutes to 10. Save you a ride and we can get started. Alright sir, there we have it. See you then."

He couldn't cancel. Aubrey would eventually find out and he didn't want anyone to know about what just happened. He didn't want this around town. Hell, his own boys had taken some real hits out on the field. He had to tough it out because that's what he expected in his kids. Nobody in town was going to know about this one. Not Aubrey, not the cops. Just tighten up and tough it out. It was a showing. How hard was that?

He used the half hour to drive to CVS. He'd spotted a trickle of blood coming from his nose and was glad he got to it before he went into the drugstore. A short while later, he carried out a bottle of ibuprofen, a six-pack of cold bottled water, a box of tissues, and facial makeup in two different flesh tones. He placed two bottles of water into the rear seat divide, one in his cup holder, the other three went into his trunk. He gingerly placed three pills into his mouth, took a slug of water and swallowed. He drank again, testing whether his stomach could hold a liquid. Using the rear-view mirror, he was able to glide the flesh tone cream across his swollen cheek. It looked a little like his cheek was made of clay, but the redness and whatever color was to follow was hidden for a few hours.

Bainbridge waited curbside. The two rear doors of his car were open wide. When Tim and Holly came out, he ushered them into the back seats. His tinted prescription glasses hid his eyes some. By placing the couple in the back, there would be less to see of his patched-up face. While taking them to 12 Shore Road, he found out they were prepared to offer twenty to forty percent down on whatever they wanted. Tim was an attorney representing a wide range of American firms doing business in

Japan and the Asian market in general. Holly laughed and said her job was to make a father out of Tim.

Bainbridge said, "Today's strategy is to visit three properties. Take as long as you like in each. Take as many pictures as you want, ask as many questions as you want. At the end of the tour, I'll take you home so you can talk it over. In the morning, give me a call and we'll go from there. Or, if you see one you'd like to buy right on the spot just tell me and we will talk about a price that suits you and we will go that way." There was a sudden painful deep chest cough, a gulp of air. He chopped through it. "And if none of these work for you, tomorrow I'll start looking again. There aren't a lot of rooftops, but I can find the ones that are out there. We will find what you want to call home. It is a process more than a science."

While Tim and Holly looked at each other in happy anticipation they didn't notice Dan brush a trickle of blood away from the nose with his index finger. He saw no advantage in telling the Chungs that 12 Shore Road had once been his mailing address. That wasn't the point right now. It might play in later. Bridgit waited for them in the driveway. Bainbridge introduced her to Tim and Holly saying, "This lady is the best agent Kelly has had in ten years."

"Welcome you two. It's a great house I'm glad you've come to take a look at it. Dan this is awkward, I hope you don't mind. The owner insists that I show your clients around by myself. You can stay with the car and I'll take them in."

It wasn't wasted on Dan that Bridgit had been careful to say 'owner' rather than 'your ex-wife Connie.'

"It's odd," he said. "But that will have to do now won't it. You guys go ahead with Ms. Daliwal. She's great. Take your time. I'll be right here."

When they disappeared through the front door, Bainbridge came to realize the day was getting bright. Heat was radiating up from the cobblestones. Humidity began to stand on his shoulders. He checked the mirror when he returned to his car and sat down. He looked worn out and desperate, the makeup sitting on his cheeks like a plasma that would turn and slide down his neck if he moved his head too fast. He turned on the car and punched up the air conditioning. The white of his left eye held a bright red blood spot. The only good news was the nose had apparently stopped leaking. He checked his voicemail. There was a message from Lydia. She was out sailing with a neighbor. Tomorrow, she would love to see him for a visit. Any time would work for her. Just call tomorrow and let her know.

Bainbridge adjusted the mirror back to its appropriate angle and saw that Connie's Buick was parked directly behind him. He was startled to see Taylor standing beside his door. Lowering his window allowed heat to push into his car. "Taylor, what's up? How are you?"

"Mom says that if you want, after you get through selling the house, if you'd like to take Russel and me to the beach for the rest of the day that would be okay with her. It is really hot Dad, what do you say?"

There were two other houses to show after this but it didn't matter. He could see a way to accomplish this as Taylor finished the request. The sudden gifting of the boys must be coming from her budding awareness he would be seeing less of them when they pulled out to live in Newton. That's how Bainbridge saw and felt it.

"Wow, yes, I hadn't thought about that, but yes. That sounds great. Tell her we will head to Chapaquoit Beach. How does that sound? When these folks are finished looking at the house, you and Russell zoom right in and get your beach gear on. Let's do it. And point of fact, Taylor, your mom is selling the house, I'm just helping her make that happen. Go back to the car and wait it out, won't take too much longer."

When Taylor got in the Buick, Connie rolled it back out to the street. They parked discreetly in a shady spot a block down from the house. He realized they must have been there to begin with. Time ground to a halt. You could push against it but there was no movement to it. It sat on its haunches. Holly was the first one out. Bridgit, being the seasoned professional, made sure she was the last to leave the house.

At the first sight of Holly, Bainbridge blew out from his car to greet them. The Chungs were leaning into each other and smiling. Bainbridge went directly to Bridgit.

"Could you two wait just right here for a moment? I'd like to have a few words with Bridgit if I could." He walked Bridgit to the side and said, "How did they like the place?"

"They liked everything about the place or it would seem so."

"All right. Do you have some time today?"

"Yes, I have some free time right now. And by the way, are you all right, you look like you're coming down with something."

"You are so right, I picked something up this morning and I'm feeling miserable. A touch of the flu. Or maybe allergies. I don't know what the hell it is. But the timing couldn't be worse. I've come to realize I don't want to expose the Chungs to whatever this is. Could you take the Chungs to their next listings? Here are two more homes they are set up to see today. Daliwal, I'm asking you to do this as a favor. If they buy any one of the three I will split my end of the commission right down the middle with you. What that means to me is, if they buy this house under normal terms you'd get three percent and I'd get three, But not this time. You'd end up with 4.5 percent on this house or either of the other two I have remaining to show them. That's got to be worth your while, don't you think?"

"I'll do it. And I'm holding you to these numbers. But I've got to tell you, I would have done it just as a favor. You should not be out looking like this."

"They are going to buy one of these, I just know it"

"You're right about that. These are the three best houses on the market right now. I'll sell them one of these, but I have to make it clear: if they don't like any and if we have the time to see some of my other listings, well that's *my* commission. But I won't push them off any of the three because I agree these are the best out there"

"Fair enough Bridgit."

"I'll take it from here then."

As soon as Bridgit's Mercedes rolled down Shore Road, Connie was pulling up. Connie and the boys hustled into the house. Connie made sure she had no eye contact with Dan.

Now in flip-flops, sunglasses and bathing suits, bath towels hanging from each neck, his boys came out of the garage carrying folding chairs, headed for his car.

Russell was the first into the water when they reached the beach. He dropped his towel and chair, kicked off his flip-flops and was in the ocean up to his shoulders. Meanwhile, Bainbridge and Taylor set up an empire in the sand. They were comfortable with each other and the duties each had in the routine of setting up the umbrella and chairs. Taylor screwed the base into the sand while Bainbridge slipped the casing off each chair. When Taylor brought the base snug against the sand, he was given the pole, which he guided in and screwed secure. Bainbridge snapped the umbrella open and slipped it atop the pole. He was adjusting chairs around the newfound shade when Taylor bolted to the water's edge, marched in and dove into a small breaking wave.

For a long time they swam and bobbed, using boogie boards to ride some of the waves, Taylor had a skimboard he was practicing with. A small foam football became a game of choice. They stood waist high and passed the ball around the triangle made by the three of them. Bainbridge could feel the protective shield the boys were building between them. The usual carping at a wild throw became "Nice dive Russell, almost brought that one in."

Bainbridge went to sit in the shade. The cool ocean water was an unexpected healing touch for his chest, but he was starting to feel dizzy and it might be that he had a pinch of a migraine starting up in his head. Taylor did a quick methodical search of the wrack line along the beach and came back under the umbrella, handing Bainbridge three brown and two green pieces of sea glass. Eventually both boys came up spread towels on either side of the umbrella and stretched out to dry. As they relaxed, the late afternoon sun became golden. Bainbridge had a moment he could chew on later. A moment where everything was fine, exactly as it was supposed to be. He gained strength from his boys there with him. Strength enough to know that this day would work out.

Around five they packed up and went to Putters for an early dinner. They were hungry and relaxed. Russell had Francis's monster peanut butter sandwich, thick cut Texas toast, pan grilled in lots of butter, a thick slice of tomato and a heavy slather of Putter's home-ground peanut butter. It came with fries or coleslaw. Francis included both on Russell's plate. Taylor had a salad and fish and chips. The moment Francis could get a look at him, he became quite chatty with the boys, to the point of almost ignoring Bainbridge.

Bainbridge ordered a salad and a bowl of lobster bisque. Francis insisted he slurp down four oysters, telling Dan it was part of the meal. When they finished eating, Francis took the dishes away and slid a slice of seven-layer chocolate cake in front of each boy and a cup of coffee in front of Bainbridge.

"Don't you dare even think you are paying for this," Francis said. "By the way that eye looks, you already paid."

As the boys worked their way through the cake Bainbridge

said, "You guys will be moving to Newton pretty soon. Taylor, how do you feel about that?"

"I don't really want to go Dad. All my friends are here."

Russell piped in, "I won't have any friends either. Why can't we just stay with you at the condo?"

"And let mom go to Newton with Bob." Taylor added.

"I wish you could, you both know that, right? You have to remember that your mom needs you just as much as I do. We will all just stick to what we have been doing, okay? Every other weekend, a month in the summer, just like always. Don't think anything between the three of us is going to change.

"You know, when I was about nine like you Russell, I had to move. I came here from Dorchester. Your Grandma and Grandpa just drove me to an entirely new town one Saturday morning. Grandpa changed jobs and began working in Woods Hole. They hadn't told me about any of it before that and there I was in a new town and a new bedroom. Sure, I left some friends in Dorchester. But it turned out I met some great friends right here. Francis, for one, went to high school with me, you know. We played varsity baseball together. Listen, Newton has one of the best schools in the entire state."

"So?"

"It means the kids that go there are very nice and you both will meet wonderful friends. You guys will do very well in Newton."

"I like where I am, Dad. Can't we live with you?" There was a flat tone to Taylor's voice as if he already knew.

"It is not how this works. You go with your mom. Stay together and you keep an eye out for each other. I'll always be there. Not much will change between us. You guys will be just an hour away. That's not far at all."

He drove them back to the house on Shore Road. Russell left the car, saying "I love you" and asking Taylor to bring his wet towel and beach chair in. Taylor appeared to stay put a moment.

"Is there anything else, Taylor? Tell me anything, ask me anything."

"What is that blood on your eye?"

"That? Oh, that's just a fleck of blood. It is nothing really. It is like a fever blister, a little fleck that will get absorbed back into the body in a few days."

"Could I get something like that?"

"What? No. You're not going to inherit the spot of blood in my eye. And it isn't contagious in any other way either. But thanks for asking though."

∽

MONDAY MORNING BEGAN WITH AN INVENTORY. His chest loosened considerably. He could draw his shoulders back. Oddly, the left side of his neck was stiff. It hadn't been an issue yesterday. The spot in his eye actually had gone down a little bit. His jaw worked without snapping. There was no blood on the pillow from a leaky nose. The sun he took in yesterday brightened his face up a bit. That's what he had to work with today. And the work was to find Crown and demand some immediate answers.

Right now, Dan had no proof Kate's baby was his. Until he knew better, the child could just as easily be Tabor's. He could feel all he wanted and guess all he could, but it would be science that will throw the most light on the situation.

Crown's office was on a side road very near the hospital complex. A woman sat at a laminate desk behind a little sliding glass panel that was only partially opened. She told Bainbridge, "Doctor Crown is no longer active at this office. What I can tell you is, he has temporarily stepped away from his practice."

"I was a patient of Doctor Crown," Bainbridge pushed. "I

need to know some specific details about an operation he performed on me. It was a couple of years ago."

"Any questions of that nature, then here," she began writing on a notepad as she continued talking. "There are two contact points listed, one is a Dr. Fryeman and the other is an attorney at Tabor Associates. Her name is Meghan Polatano. There, these are the two names and phone numbers."

"When did Doctor Crown leave this office?"

"Over a year now. Anything more and you should contact one of those names. Would you like to schedule an appointment with Doctor Ziebert?"

"No, no. Not right now. But maybe. Can Ziebert give me my sperm count?" He whispered that so low he could barely hear himself. "Alright then, yes I would like an appointment."

She studied a large screen on her desk. There is an opening this Friday, the 12th."

"No, no, no. I have to know my sperm count as soon as possible." Bainbridge heard himself saying this and it sounded almost like shouting to him. The woman behind the glass looked at him, then back at her screen and said in a conspiratorial tone, "If that is all you need at the moment then it is possible the doctor can see you tomorrow morning. It is even possible there will be time today at 4. Would you be able to make a 4 o'clock appointment?"

"Yes, yes absolutely."

"Then I will check with Doctor Ziebert and call you within an hour or two at the most. Fill out this patient questionnaire. Make absolutely sure the contact information is accurate and I'll call you as soon as I know. How's that? Is that okay?"

He took coffee at Starbucks, sat on a square little red cushion and placed his coffee and phone on a knee-high table. This was his very public temporary office. It was here he called Meghan

Polatano. He didn't want to think or feel. He just wanted to do. It was only 10:47. A lot could be done.

Polatano's secretary picked up. He asked if he could have an appointment. The secretary recognized him. Five years ago he worked with her and her husband. Once he learned that it was the three-bedroom Cape on Briarwood Road he knew exactly who she was. That in itself did nothing to secure a meeting any earlier than three days from now. Bainbridge said in a confessional manner, "This is about some work done on me by a Dr. Crown."

"Oh. I see, Dan. That is an entirely different situation. Tell you what, I'm putting you on hold for just a minute." His phone began playing indifferent music that sounded like his speaker was made of crinkled aluminum foil. He sipped his coffee and heard the phone go into a second melody that may have been carried by a sax but you would never be sure of that.

"Dan," he heard.

"Yes"

"Tell you what. In an hour you can have a brief consultation with Meghan. How about that. We got lucky here."

"I am impressed Lynne, and grateful. Thank you so much."

"Not at all, we make rainbows here. See you in a bit."

A bit meant that in less than an hour he was in Meghan Polatano's downtown office at Tabor Associates. She sat behind a desk twice as long as normal and stood as he entered but did not go around the desk to greet him. She pointed to a cushioned leather chair he was to sit in.

"Mr. Bainbridge, welcome," she said. "Sit. Let's talk for a few minutes and see if I can be any help to you. Lynne tells me you have some involvement with Dr. Crown. If that is true then I think you are in the right place, very much so. So, tell me, what's going on with you?"

"I'm divorced. It happened about four years ago. That's what started this off."

"Sorry to hear it, there are few more painful transitions in life than divorce. I hope you had good representation."

"Absolutely, Jimmy Morgan represented me very well I thought."

"That is good. I know Jimmy, he does some very fine divorce work."

"Yes. I got into a divorce situation and found out within hours I needed someone on my side. The whole thing was a mess, but he did fine, I was lucky to have him. Anyway, about a year later, I decided, a life's decision, that I wasn't going to have any more kids no matter what happened, no matter who I may meet in my life going forward. The two I had with my ex, Connie, were enough for me. Taylor and Russell, I am their father. Those are my sons, that's it. And that is what brought me to Crown's office and a vasectomy."

"Is there a reason for this sudden concern? You said it has been about two years. What is it about today that brought you to my office. Something predictive of a botched operation?"

"Meghan, this is all coming at me. You could say I'm in a discovery phase since I started out this morning."

"Yes I can see you've been having a rough time of it. That red blotch in your left eye looks painful. You have gorgeous green eyes. They draw you in. I'm sorry. It's hard not to catch the red blotch."

"No. It isn't painful. But I must be terrible to stare at, I'm sorry. I was wrestling my son and got a finger poke right in the eye. It doesn't hurt but it must be awful to look at."

"Relax, it isn't horrible to look at. It just makes you look like you're having a hard time that's all. Tell you what, you are here, you are in the right place, we can help. There is light at the end of the tunnel."

"That's good to know, but I've got to tell you, I can't even find the tunnel yet."

"This office represents the interests of several clients in a legal action against Doctor Crown. We seek significant damages and charge intentional malpractice. There are eight men. Perhaps you will be the ninth to discover that Doctor Crown – I am going to be very specific here – slit a quarter inch opening in the sack and then simply stitched up the incision. He told each one of my clients that the vasectomy was a success. He did this at least eight times. Another odd behavior we researched is that Crown, during this time performed many more than eight. In fact, there were 54 surgeries of this kind that Doctor Crown performed. We haven't been able to assign a specific reason why eight men, maybe nine, were singled out to suffer from malpractice."

"Why? Why would he do such a thing? Of course I want to be a part of this. I strongly believe he did the exact same thing to me. But why? Really. Have you any ideas on this?"

"Since you stated you want us to represent you, I will tell you a few more things. First, we don't have to prove motive. That doesn't mean we aren't looking into it."

"I'm stunned. You have to help me here. I could very well be one of these guys. What was that man doing? What was that man thinking?"

"One line of reasoning we are working is that Doctor Crown married a woman who, over the years, has been very public with her donations to conservative Catholic charities. Crown himself is Jewish. At one point, four years ago, they went on record filing for divorce. About a month later they pulled the filing."

"You're telling me a conservative Catholic and a Jewish doctor married each other."

"And I'm telling you they are still married. It is not a leap to conclude Doctor Crown began thinking about his practice differently. He may have been trying to appease her, or he simply got lazy and went a little crazy, it doesn't matter. My clients have endured severe bodily injury at his hands. We have no doubt we will win against him. And we will win soon and we will win big. He won't get away with this."

"I'm glad I'm here. This is exactly where I'm supposed to be right now. Thank you, Meghan, so much."

"Alright Mr. Bainbridge. This is what happens next: while you are here, you'll sign our contract. Then you have to get to a urologist as soon as possible and find out everything you can."

"I am actually."

"What?"

"Seeing a urologist. I have an appointment with one later today."

"Who would that be?"

"Doctor Ziebert. I pushed for an appointment with him just this morning."

"Good. Excellent. And he's very good. Interesting fact, he is in Crown's old office complex. Get the evaluation as soon as you can. If there is any delay we can recommend several other very fine doctors."

She stood and walked around her desk. He was up. A large bottle of hand sanitizer stood at the corner of her desk. She stopped about five feet from him and said, "This is a little ritual I do with all my first-time clients. It is a handshake, used to do good business for thousands of years. The problem is that I'm starting to hear from relatives in the old country about something contagious. But I like to keep good things going."

She squirted sanitizer onto her palm, rubbed it in and said, "Alright Dan your turn." He did the same. "You have to agree our agency takes every precaution." He really didn't get exactly what she was saying or any of this hand sanitizer rigmarole, but they did shake hands. A robust shake. It felt tribal.

"Alright, while you're here then, what you should do is sign on as a conditional member of our class action. When we find out from the doctor what we believe to be true, your signature automatically transfers to a direct member of the class action. Lynne will take you through the rest of it for today. She is out there at her office. She is great. She will take you through everything."

In the lobby, directly across from Lynne's desk was a small conference room. Lynne took him in saying, "We have some papers to sign. How did it go? Isn't Meghan terrific?"

Bainbridge was handed one page for a signature and another and another. He glanced at each but it might as well have been Greek.

"I wonder if there are any personal tests, like there are for pregnancy tests?" He said. Then he realized he was asking Lynne, a person he'd sold a house to. That's all he knows about her and he's asking her if there are over the counter sperm tests.

"You mean sperm count? Yes, there are tests like that at CVS. And a lot of other places, too."

"It stands to reason doesn't it?" he said.

"Yes of course it does, but we need a doctor's evaluation for the court. Are you able to see a doctor today or tomorrow even?"

"Yes. I'm trying to see a Dr. Ziebert as soon as possible."

"Call us by tomorrow afternoon. Let the office know what's happening – okay? Remember, you're not billed for a single dollar. All those papers you signed say we get paid a contingency fee. If we win we take fifteen percent of the gross amount."

"It sounds more than fair to me" he said.

"The last thing I'm going to ask you to do is, I'm going to leave you in here for a few minutes with a pen and this pad of paper. You can take some notes on your visit to Dr. Crown. Write down whatever you remember, whatever comes back to you. Then I'll come in and turn on that camera over there and I'll leave you to give an official record of your statement regarding what you remember during your visit and surgery. Okay? Don't worry. It doesn't have to be a Hollywood job. You'll just be telling the camera what you remember about Dr. Crown and what was going on from your perspective."

"Who uses this recording?"

"No one without your permission. It only is used by Meghan to prepare for your case. It is used in no other way without your permission and the consent of council."

"Okay, okay. I'll take a walk through that day. Let's keep the ball in play."

~

Dan sat and recalled that fateful day. He'd taken a very late lunch of steaming noodles and cabbage, a clear dumpling soup at a Thai restaurant located in a strip mall not far from Meghan's law office. It was there he realized he was going through this damn thing all day long. He'd just finished telling his story to the camera at the law office. Very soon, he'd be in Ziebert's office going through this again in one form or another. He brought out his phone. There was nothing from Kate. Nothing. He had Ziebert's office announcing the doctor would see him at four, and Tim Chung wanting to talk to him about the houses he'd gone through yesterday.

Obviously, he returned that call. He was a sales agent. If he wasn't on the phone, he should be.

"Tim, oh yeah, yes there is a lot to love about that Tudor, three garages, ocean views. It is beautiful around the inground pool, isn't it? Listen though, how was Bridgit? That's right she does know her stuff, listen I want you to work with her now. Yes, I know I didn't tell you Shore Road was my old home. I didn't want that sort of information to get in the way of your own tour of the place. No, there was no problem, really. Just an opportunity for me to catch up with my boys. It was just that simple. It was a situation that I saw could work out for the both of us, you know. I am certain Bridgit is waiting for your call, I'd appreciate it if you would work through Bridgit on the Tudor or any of the others. She's great and she'll work really hard for you.

"How's Holly? She loves the place too right? I know. To be honest with you, I thought the Tudor was going to be the best of what you were going to see and it turns out you two have good eyes. Give Bridgit a jingle right now she can make things happen for you. And if anything comes up, my company listed the house so I can keep an eye on the progress if you move forward on the Tudor. Yes, personally I think it is a great house. One of the top houses in town."

Lydia recorded a voice mail on his phone during the time he had been with Attorney Polatano. Lydia said she had been out Sunday sailing along the Sound on a boat owned by one of her neighbors. It was planned that it would be a sleepover on the boat with a dinner in Tisbury. She would be back today.

He put in a call. "Lydia, hello. Please call me Dan. I'd love to come over for a brief visit if I'm not intruding. No, no, nothing like that, I just have a question you might have the answer to. Also, I'd like to see how you are settling in. Apparently pretty well if you were out sailing yesterday. No, I don't believe I do know him. How does six o'clock sound? Wonderful. It's not too late? We can open that cabernet I gave you. That was part of your welcoming gift. I would have thought you had opened that months ago. Well, with your neighbor the captain I suppose. Then it will be perfect for our visit. Thank you Lydia, see you at six."

He fought off his body's cry for sleep by looking for facial patterns on the ceiling tiles. He felt no good at all. She hadn't called, she hadn't reached out in any way. Oh Dan, I'm pregnant, and by the way you'll never see me again after I tell you. How could he live with that? That couldn't be the way things worked. I could be the father in all this. For Christ's sake, call me, talk to me, Dan thought. Tabor may or may not know that Nick knocked him into next Tuesday. But, knowing that Kate's affair was with him, Tabor might have something of his own to throw at him.

His mind felt jellied up with too many unknowns. He straightened himself out and headed to the urologist, pushing hard to knock down some of the unknowns he had to deal with.

∽

THE RECEPTIONIST WORE a clear plastic shield attached by loops to each of her ears. She said, "I am going to ask you to put on one of those paper surgical masks. Please and fill out this form."

He was handed a clipboard with a checklist and a pen. He put on the mask, prompting ten minutes of claustrophobic breathing and fogged up sunglasses. How can anyone function with this thing on, Dan wondered. He wondered if he had missed the news. Was there an outbreak somewhere? He sat and filled out the long, tedious list of medical details. Eventually everything had been checked off and signed. He took the clipboard back to the lady behind her Plexiglas mask. With purple rubber gloves protecting her hands, she took his clipboard and studied it.

"I know you filled out our form but just to confirm, you haven't had any alcohol today is that right?"

"No, nothing, only coffee."

"And you're not on any medications, is that right?"

"None."

"Are you taking any supplements or smoked any marijuana?"

"No none of that business, though I think I should."

"Should what?"

"Never mind, nothing, I haven't taken anything."

She held his gaze for an uncomfortable moment and said, "No Tylenol or Ibuprofen for the swelling perhaps."

"Jesus, yes. I'm sorry I've been taking Advil for a couple of days now. I didn't even think of it."

"Well it is important we do these lists correctly; wouldn't you say? I'll put those down on the chart. Those should have no influence on the tests. All right then, we are going to put you in that little privacy room. Try to get as much of your ejaculation as possible into this plastic cup. The more the merrier. On the counter you will notice a folder with pictures that may help you achieve an erection. When you are finished place the cup back on the counter and then wash your hands using the sanitizer lotion. Then come back out and we'll get you in to see the doctor."

Alone in the little windowless room Bainbridge flipped through glossy, laminated, four-by-six-inch photos of naked women and others that were naked men. He shuffled through as if it were a deck of cards, pulling out the men and turning them over on the counter. What remained were naked women stretched out, long legs open, firm breasts, some with nipples the size of saucers, some with nipples as small as a bullet. There were several women on their knees and hands, their firm round butts to the camera, their breasts hanging down like jugs.

Even though he was seated in a tiny room that had an overwhelming smell of antiseptic, it took Bainbridge no time at all to grow large in his hand. He managed to hold the cup just above the head of his penis with his left hand while his right stroked his shaft up into a frenzied release which did in fact mostly land in the mouth of the cup, with a few spurts coming to rest on his wrist.

A thought rocketed out of his head. This is not what he expected he would be doing on a Monday afternoon. What the hell is going on here? One minute you're going to a party and the next you're masturbating into a plastic cup. Snapping the lid, he washed his hands and was done with it.

He stood in the open doorway of his little chamber. The nurse came over, saying, "Okay, Mr. Bainbridge, terrific. I see the cup is on the counter. Why don't you follow me down to the examination room. Doctor Ziebert will be with you in just a minute, and please return to wearing the mask if you would."

Bainbridge almost zonked out while waiting infinite minutes for Ziebert. Eventually the door popped open. Behind a Plexiglas face shield was a bald man with a close-clipped beard and moustache intended to look like a two day growth of hair. He was dressed in a white lab coat, was thin, sparse, and had short, quick motions. He was surprisingly young, perhaps in his early thirties, and was light and quick like a sparrow.

"Mr. Bainbridge, very nice to meet you. Welcome to my practice. I'm told you need more than just a sperm count. You'd like an evaluation of an earlier vasectomy performed, I believe, by a Dr. Crown, yes?"

Ziebert tended to talk in a whisper of a voice, which made Bainbridge lean into what he was hearing.

"Yes, yes indeed, that is exactly what I need."

"And how long ago was the operation performed?

"Nearly three years ago now."

"Fine, I can do a physical inspection and then we will move on to the sonogram. How does that sound? Several other patients of Doctor Crown have been here to be evaluated, as well."

"Of course, yes. Anything you can do to help me understand this situation I find myself in will be a godsend."

"Certainly, yes, why don't we get started then."

He asked Bainbridge to drop his trousers and underwear and sit on a cushioned bench with a wide sheet of white paper stretched across it from end to end.

"Now, we are going to put this paper sheet, what we call a bib or a donut, over your penis, leaving the scrotum to hang out as well, very good. Now I am going to spray the scrotum with a warm disinfectant. I don't believe we will need anything to numb the area. Yes I see the scar of a quarter-inch incision into the skin of your scrotum. It healed very nicely; probably dissolvable stitches were used. Do you know Mr. Bainbridge?"

"I don't, Doctor, not for certain. But they probably were dissolvable. I can't recall going back to him. Could you just speak up a bit, I'm having a hard time hearing everything you are saying."

"Certainly, Mr. Bainbridge I can speak up a bit. As you know, there is a tube running up from each teste. These are called the vas deferens. Your scrotum would have been shaved and washed with antiseptic. Next, local anesthesia would have been injected. You would still have been aware of touch, tension and movement. After the incision, the tubes would be snipped and usually stitched."

"Yes, that is how it went, very close to the way Dr. Crown explained it. But to be honest it was nearly three years ago. What I remember most is lying in bed with an ice pack on my balls. I don't much like to replay the operation. Not to put too fine a point to it but this will be about the third replay of this operation I've been through just in this one day."

"Of course. With your permission I'm going to use my fingers to feel around and see if I can find one of these vas cords. Yes, there's one. Can you feel any tension as I slightly pull the cord? Yes. Now the one on your left side you feel that yes?"

He felt that his nuts were pulled just a tweak, like tight little puppet strings. "What is that telling you Doc?"

"It is an indication your tubes were never cut."

Next, the doctor rubbed a warm lubricant on either side of his ball sack. He held a warm hand towel on the left side, then used a device that produced a sonogram image displayed on the screen of his laptop, which was stationed at his side. He switched to the other side.

"Yes you can see it clearly can't you? Both tubes appear connected."

Bainbridge took his word for it. The screen was off to the side and what it showed him was a slightly pulsing blob, a smudge of blacks and grays, and some sort of dull white streaks curling through.

Ziebert put the probe down on his little stand. He took away the paper bib, crushed it into a ball and tossed it into a metal trash bin.

"That is about all that can be done with this part of the exam. You can put your clothes back on and wait right here. I am going to get the results of your sperm test."

"Excellent, very good. Let's push this down field. Thanks Doctor Ziebert, really. It will be nice to be in a place where I had some answers instead of just a long line of questions. The results will tell us a whole lot of what I need answered, I would think. I can't thank you enough for taking me in."

"Of course. You can make yourself more comfortable by sitting in that chair. There will be a few minutes as I review the results and then I will be back and tell you what we know."

Bainbridge dressed himself, immediately feeling warmer. He paced the little room between the doctor's swivel chair, the door, and the supposedly comfortable chair, until the chair won. Eventually the door flew open and there was Doctor Ziebert. His small, foxlike eyes bounced across his oversized cellphone.

"Yes, Mr. Bainbridge we measured your volume and it was very good at over half a teaspoon. The PH levels were good and your sperm count is well over 15 million per milliliter. Mr. Bainbridge, it does not appear you had a vasectomy."

"Well that settles it. This is on me. It is hard to hear something like this and not get a little angry."

"Yes that can be a healthy natural reaction up to a point."

"I'm angry, but it's weird. I'm happy knowing it was me rather than the other guy."

"There is a lot to think over. You'll have to take time with what you're learning. We studied how active your sperm are. Sixty five percent are moving, which rates it as active."

"I know so much more now. I can't believe this really. Why would Doctor Crown or anyone else on this earth do this. Why? Why do this at all? And why me?"

"I really can't say. There are over 500,000 vasectomies a year in this country. It is hard to argue that a mistake could happen, but it is an overwhelmingly safe procedure."

Bainbridge's phone came alive. He instinctively answered it, effectively putting Doctor Ziebert on hold.

"Hello Meghan. Yes, I am with a urologist right now." Dan held the phone toward Ziebert. "She wants to talk to you. Would that be alright Doctor?"

Ziebert corralled the phone to his ear.

"Yes, of course, I'll send it all to you, not a problem, good to talk with you again."

The phone went back to Bainbridge. He could hear Meghan telling him, "Listen, Dan. It is very smart of you to follow up and find out. You have to stay strong now. I wanted to make sure the good doctor had taken the sonograms. You don't want to come back twice, now do you? Remember, you're not alone on this. We will deal with Crown, you deal with the rest of your life, okay?"

"That sounds just fine, thank you Meghan." He hung up, turned to the doctor and said, "And thank you Doctor Ziebert, thank you so much for getting me in and so late in the day. Very, very helpful of you."

"That's what we are all here for, isn't it?"

Holy mother of god what am I into here? Dan thought. Jesus jumping Christ. I got another woman pregnant. He suddenly wondered if Kate or John had pursued the DNA quest. It was doubtful. Kate didn't even seem to care whose baby it was. Tabor would move on this, but probably not today. He felt compelled to call her. Again, he got her voicemail. Because he could not connect to her directly or at all his voice was sharpened to a bright edge when he said, "I deserve better than this." And nothing more.

11

THE BROWN PALACE

Bainbridge wheeled his car into one of the several empty parking slots that looked directly down through the harbor and its many beautiful boats. The Island Queen was slowly pulling into its berth. He was thinking that the odd thing was there wasn't that much of a surprise to it. This insight is what struck him the hardest. Somehow he knew it. Before Kate announced she was pregnant, he knew it. He remained in that parking spot for almost an hour. He was in a quiet guest's spot in Lydia's condo complex.

He breathed in deep volumes of crisp, briny air and let it out slow, washing out the interior of his head a little. The phone had nothing from Kate. Eventually he pulled himself out of the car and he stepped into the bronze sun of a late afternoon.

Lydia came smiling to her glass door. She was sharp, compact, and quick, like a beautiful sea tern.

"Lydia the place looks absolutely stunning. You feel like home the minute you come through the door."

"Dan Bainbridge, I knew I liked you. Come. We will sit in the great room." As they headed the way she intended she continued. "I want to clear something up, but first pour us a glass of wine, will you? It is already open. Just pour us a glass and come sit right there on that couch."

She settled into an easy chair and he handed her the crystal glass of deep red wine. They clinked glasses.

"Here's to the good people," he said. He drew a big sip of rich Spanish wine and he found his spot on the couch. There were many views of the harbor through her windows. You could hear the ding, ding, ding of a shroud in the wind against an aluminum mast. A charming sound like wind chimes.

Lydia was studying him as he took in the room. She said, "The very first thing I want you to know, Mr. Bainbridge, is that I did not sleep with my neighbor. Captain Joyce has a wonderful sloop with two bedrooms. We slept soundly, but in separate quarters. My voicemail to you may have started you thinking in the wrong direction. Now that I'm here I have a reputation to protect." She was being playful. "I'm living with a very chatty bunch in this complex."

"Mrs. Cuomo, I don't allow myself to judge people. I think we can both agree, Lydia, everybody is their own worst critic. Who needs another judge?"

"I am so glad we are past that 'Mr. Bainbridge' and 'Mrs. Cuomo' phase and back to Lydia. Now, Dan, why are you here?"

He blew air from his lungs. It sounded like steam. "I need your help. There is no other way to say it. There is no one else I can turn to. I haven't seen or heard from Kate. She's disappeared. She brought something up at the party, something very important, and I really need to talk to her about it even if it's only for a few minutes. But I have nothing. I don't know how to do this, she's just disappeared."

"It's alright, Dan, calm yourself. Kate talked to me before she left. Heather will be staying with me for a few days, which will be lovely. She also said you might call me."

"Kate has gone somewhere?" Bainbridge blurted.

"That's right. I don't know everything of course. She is visiting her college roommate who is now dying of cancer, poor soul. That is sad duty I am sure."

"Please help me, Lydia. Can you tell me where she is?"

"Actually I can. We had a very detailed talk before she left. In part of it she said that if Dan Bainbridge contacted me, I could give him the address of where she was staying. She also said there would be no calls. Show up or not, but no calls. It is very strange to me. Do you know Kate's college roommate?"

"No. I just need to see her about something entirely different."

"Well, she has shut off her phone to quiet herself and be able to help with her sick friend while she is there. Isn't that just like her, to be focused on the care of others? She has the biggest heart, my daughter. If you have to talk to her I suppose you will have to go see her. Her roommate also became her sorority sister so it is all quite sad. Kate tells me she was a mathematics professor at the Air Force Academy, right up to her illness, bless her heart."

"She's in Colorado or something?"

"Pour us more wine, will you? I'll get the paper with her address on it. I'll be right back."

Bainbridge sat there in a stew. Colorado, a sick friend, no calls. Inside his head, a blacksmith was hammering these key words into his skull. He managed to move towards pouring the wine just as Lydia was returning.

"I've got to tell you, Lydia, in this profession I have been able to meet some of the most wonderful people in the world."

"Stop it. I will tell you either way. You don't have to butter me up."

"But it never hurts," he said and they laughed a little.

"Now, I don't know how you got connected to her visit to her friend in Denver, but she did say that if you showed up, I should give you the address. Here it is. The Brown Palace Hotel in Denver. There you have it. And I don't expect you are going to tell me why you need to know this, are you?"

"I would, really, I would. But I need to talk to Kate first, you understand? After that I can tell you anything I know. You have been too kind. If you ask I will tell you what I know. I can't thank you enough Lydia."

"Yes, you can thank me by going home now and getting a good night's sleep. You look all in pieces."

"Do I? I'm sorry."

"It just looks like you've had a long day. But it ended well, didn't it? You got what you needed?"

"Yes, indeed. It has been a huge day and with the help you have given me I can settle the accounts of the day on the plus side."

"Nothing wrong with that, now is there young man?"

∼

AT HIS OWN condo he got the coffee machine up and running. Bainbridge gave himself a hard look in his mirror. He did have the look of someone pulled apart then carelessly put back together. His eyes had been sand-papered and that red blotch was still sitting in its place just beside the cornea of his left eye, even though it was smaller. Once you saw it, though, you couldn't un-see it.

He took the longest, most satisfying shower of his life. He found new slacks and a dress shirt, spent time with his coffee and laptop. He booked a three-night minimum at her hotel in Denver. Next there was the plane ticket, a United round trip leaving at 10:35 a.m. Four-and-a-half hours on a plane and he'd be in Denver. He said to himself, "You've got to be somewhere.

If that is where she is, then that's where I want to be right now."

He spent the rest of that night sleeping in his clothes beside an open travel bag containing a few pairs of pants and a few shirts, loosely folded beside a handful of socks and underwear. When he awoke, he drove himself to the airport and left his car in long-term parking. By four in the afternoon he was getting into an Über lift along the curbside at Denver airport, his suitcase in the empty seat beside him.

"The Brown Palace Hotel? You can get me there?"

"Yes of course on 17th Street. It is a very fine hotel. You picked a good spot, sir. The theater district, the museums, many wonderful restaurants all around that hotel. It is in a great, great part of town." While raving about the place the driver was putting his Kia through turns and twists along a busy path from the airport and towards the Brown Palace.

"You seem to know the city really well. Tell me, in that part of town what's a good restaurant?"

"To be honest, I stopped answering that question. And you know why? It isn't fair to the others. The hotel itself has I think something like three bars and at least two really good restaurants. One of its lounges is a big place for music in Denver. I love that place myself. I tell you, I've brought people to this hotel who say to me, when I'm bringing them back to the airport, that they basically never left the place."

∽

KATE'S hot flashes had given way, replaced by sudden nausea. It seemed to Kate she had no breathing space between one pain leaving and the other one coming on board. Picky little nausea. Last night any entrée on the extensive menu even remotely connected to seafood made her stomach take a small jump.

Seafood, something she loved up to last night. Especially the oysters and sushi. Now? No raw bar. Oh my god, no. Even as she thought on it, she was one breath away from a gag reflex.

She knew thoughts like this kept her brain from enacting the plans for her abortion. She saw that she welcomes the complaints from the body because her brain was free to process something other than its constant loop about her appointment at the clinic on Friday. Yesterday she and a yoga instructor had a session in one of the private stretching rooms at the Fitness Center. For two blessed hours the session took her mind off the chatter that snapped around in her brain like lightning strikes. While in this hotel, a routine was developing.

For the third day in a row, she was craving what she called her 'soup and salad dinner.' There was her favorite table by a window looking out at the street. She felt comfortable and she took her time when she ate. The bread, the beet salad and the chef's soup would be just perfect. Seems I'm finding change difficult, she thought. Well, hold on. It isn't exactly the same meal every night now is it? Last night was an Italian salad with thick slices of mozzarella and tomato on the top. Not the same you see? She was talking to herself while she rested at the hotel spa with warm black stones placed along her chest, arms and legs. A toasty blanket was added and placed over her and the stones. She was to lie there quietly and zone out for a while.

She had never been to Denver, or Colorado for that matter. More importantly, no one she knew had ever mentioned the state. She chose a place far enough away where she was on her own. A place she or John or his company were effectively unknown. Texas and a zoo of other states were martialing against the actual decision she had made. Denver was north of all that, and as far as she could tell, women's rights were not a political football, at least not yet. Though that could explode into something – or not. Mostly she needed to put actual distance between her and everything and everyone else.

The unborn in her stomach used the opportunity to come back and begin talking to her again. At this point, a sonogram would show little more than a black dot within a bigger black dot. But she could hear it saying, 'Why would you even consider that I'd want to be born into a dying planet? And why this one? What's so special about this one? I think we need to go through that one a few more times. This planet is in trouble and you know it. And you really don't want to be a mother. Let's not underplay that one. Really. Even now with Heather you don't see yourself as that great a mother. That's another big thing. That's no small matter. And of course, Heather's labor really hurt you. It put you through something pretty frightening didn't it? Right now, you're a wreck already with your nausea and exhaustion. And we aren't even into the real game are we? Why would I want to be born to that pain. You think that would be doing me a favor. And if this went bad and you really got hurt, do you think I want that on me. The timing is not right for either of us. Admit it. This is not right for either of us.'

Kate could admit no such thing. A few breaths later and Kate was completely swayed by the logic. The discussion rattled around in her head like a pan lid falling to the floor. They have had many discussions over the last two days. It was this one now. The spa had done some good today, no doubt, but it had run its course. Now, Kate was trying very hard to find an empty moment.

It was time to go back, read her book for a little bit, then freshen up and go down for her soup and salad. That was, if she could stay awake long enough to change for dinner. She said to herself, "You don't have to, you could just stay in bed until Friday." That idea sounded good to her right then. In fact, she believed it to be her best original decision since the whole thing started.

∼

A HUGE, tall, maybe ten-story triangle of brick came into view. The Kia pulled up to the curb midway along one of the sides of the massive brown wedge. Dan went into the lobby pulling his own travel bag. The place was impressive. A wonderful main lobby, the walls done in mahogany and walnut and gold and copper. He registered at the dark granite counter and took in the many seating arrangements in this beautiful hall. A woman took his credit card and returned shortly with his card and the key to his room. She asked if there was anything else.

He said, "Katherine Tabor is registered here as well, am I right?"

She looked at her screen. "Yes, she is with us."

"I'd like for you to give her a message. Do you have a card for that?"

To her credit she pulled out a small card and envelope from the drawer below the counter.

"Wonderful, thank you. I'll write this out over there and be right back. Then I'll be out of your hair."

Bainbridge wasn't supposed to call. She hadn't answered a single call of his in days. He wasn't going to blow that now. So, he wrote, 'Kate, I am here. We can talk now. If I don't hear from you, I'll be at a table at seven in the main restaurant here at the hotel. Let me buy you dinner. We can talk a little. I'm in room 305, or you can call me. Whatever it takes, let's just talk, okay? Daniel.' He wanted to write 'love you' but he hadn't talked to her in days and she hadn't made any effort to contact him. He didn't want that love word to spook her.

Returning to the counter, the attendant drew near. Bainbridge said, "I know you wouldn't tell me Katherine Tabor's room number so I haven't asked. But please make sure she gets this note."

"Yes, absolutely, of course. Enjoy your stay sir."

∼

HE STOOD; probably too quickly. There, she appeared, while the sound and bustle of the room went stone quiet. She was looking for his table and eventually spotted him as he made to stand. She wore a crème colored sweater, olive green slacks, leather half boots. A pearl the size of a dime hung from each ear by gold rings. Her dark hair was now clipped above the ears. Bainbridge was taking her all in as she moved towards his table. So much about her had changed in so few days. He reached over to touch, but the way she stood with her hands held together in front of her made him save the gesture by pointing to a seat at his table. They sat down while she held his gaze and said, "I thought I'd put you off the scent. But here you are mister. We can talk, but a few facts. I get tired pretty quickly these days. And I'm very cranky. I'm not very good company. And I've made up my mind. Believe me when I tell you, I'm where I should be on this Daniel. I have my own plan. It needs to be my decision. And I've made it. You understand that don't you?"

To Kate, Bainbridge looked like he had come out of the trenches. It was apparent to her he had been wrung out since she threw down the news of her pregnancy. She frightened herself a little, feeling that in only a few days her picture of him had dissolved to the point she might not be able to identify him in a lineup. She looked closer. No it was him. It looked like the rest of him hung like rags on his green eyes. Kate held out his little note card and tossed it happily on the table.

"Well, well, you have taken a room in this hotel. I guess over the next few days we can have that talk you were asking for in so many of my voicemails. We have time. A little, I admit I didn't do the best job letting you know what was what. Also, you do deserve more than you got that night. But where do we begin?"

"I have a million beginnings, but let's go with, it's good to see you. Honestly, it went down so fast that night, I just needed some time with it, a chance to talk it out some." Bainbridge could see she was listening as she gently toyed with one of her pearl earrings. "We probably both knew, but I needed to be in front of you when I tell you, Kate, I am the one responsible for your pregnancy. It is a fact. I'm here because I am part of this deal. I'm here to support any decision you make. But I'm part of this deal. I'm supporting anything you want to do, but I have to see it through. I'm thinking maybe you don't want to be alone. I don't want to be alone in this either. When we made love I thought it would be perfectly safe for us but I was wrong. Way wrong."

Kate had already scrolled through all of this, very early in her thinking process, and was becoming impatient with his soulful explanation.

Her favorite waiter arrived. She ordered her salad and tonight's mushroom soup. He selected a steak, baked potato, green beans, and another house merlot. She asked for sparkling water, a splash of cranberry, a twist of mint in a glass full of ice.

"Dan, can you see from my perspective? I know John had a vasectomy, if I'm pregnant it had to be you. A DNA test seemed pointless and as for responsibility between you and me there is plenty of that to go around. Of course it is you."

"Yes, it turns out you are right." He sensed she was becoming impatient. He plowed along. "You might want to know that I was a victim of an intentionally botched vasectomy. I know that now. I did not know that when we made love. Even if I had known I don't think it would have been enough to stop me from being with you at that time, if I am honest about it."

She was becoming grateful for the way he was sharing these hours and the way he was processing his involvement. "I'm going to tell you something, mister. My decision is not based on you being the father. Listen, even if John were the father I would still be here tonight. The only difference is there would be no one on the other side of this table."

"If we are going to talk about perspective, you have been processing this event for how many months?"

"About nine weeks. But in dog years it could be forever," she answered.

"I've known about this for about four days. You have to see that I need to talk through some of this. It is all happening faster for me."

She could tell he couldn't comprehend the pressure time put on you when you learn you're pregnant but she wasn't going to hold that against him. He was obviously catching on to how fast things can feel.

"In two days, John will launch his company in Madrid." She stopped herself right there. She wasn't going to get into the fact it was the same week she chose for her appointment. In the early days, before all this, she was making arrangements to be in Madrid. As her weeks rolled on, the notion of being in Madrid, producing endless pictures of her with John out in the world, was a lot. Her pregnant self convinced her the time would better be used to arrange for this appointment right here. John could see that as well. They agreed. In the long run it was the launch that mattered most. It was business that couldn't wait, after all.

The drinks arrived first, then her salad and warm crusty bread on a wooden platter. His wine came in an oversized goblet. He worked his nose into the chasm then looked up and said, "There were nine weeks or so where you kept this to yourself."

Her soup came to the table, as did his steak plate. They just took a few minutes while they ate and looked at each other in silence.

Kate experienced a sense of impatience, which served to cover any shallow feelings of guilt that she kept the news of her pregnancy private. Now that she had said her piece, and in exactly the way she wanted it to happen, tonight she was willing to say more.

"Yes I've had a lot more time with this than I allowed either of you men to have. With this 'deal,' I heard you call it. You see, you were both there. You can imagine, can't you, I didn't want to go through my little speech twice. I knew the party had a few hours to go. It would contain John's reaction a little. The poor man has a public persona he has to keep intact. The party would keep him occupied while he processed a little of this. And it would make the next day with him much easier."

"And me? What did you think was going to happen to me at that point in the party?" He began to understand that he was talking to someone who was more comfortable talking to herself than anyone else just now. He watched her pull herself out from her thoughts.

"Daniel, I am going to tell you something very mean. I didn't think about you at all after that. You heard what I had to say. I told you everything I needed to tell you. That was it. That was all I had. You were on your own. I outed you to John so you would understand completely that we were through. It was up to you to figure out how you were going to handle it. I wanted John to stay with me and he has. But that night it was up to him."

From the night of the party on, Bainbridge knew she'd had enough of him. 'Why' would be a question never to be asked because it would never be answered to anyone's satisfaction.

"I hear you. I really do. If you will let me, what I want to know is, where do you place what we had together?"

"I don't know, Daniel, I'm not there yet. I'm not placing things on some sort of counting table. I have what I am doing right now to deal with. I have already given birth once. The very nature of it is life changing. You understand me? I can't, I don't want to change my life any more than it is. I can't, I can barely keep up with who I am now. At this point I would be a horrible mother and I know it up front. I can't ask a child...."

"Kate, Kate..." he tried to interject.

"I would be a confused, resistant mother. There is nothing worse and I don't want to become that. I believe it is wrong to start a child's life that way."

"Kate, Kate, that's enough."

"To be honest, in some ways I wish you hadn't come to Denver. You make me more, not less, conflicted. Let's use that word. But that doesn't mean much. I'm conflicted about almost everything these last few days. One thing I am not conflicted about, though, is that I'm with John. I'm staying with John."

"I watched you two walk right past me. I get it, I was there to see it."

"Good. It is very clear in your head. I get unbelievably tired these days Daniel. It's been a good talk, yes?"

Bainbridge realized she was breaking off the conversation. His brain flopped around in the empty air she was creating. "Alright, absolutely. But this doesn't have to be the end, does it? What do you say I meet you tomorrow morning at ten in the lobby and we go for a little walk around the city?"

Kate took a long pause. Silence times three. He was part of this. Tomorrow would be another long day. There was no good reason to be completely alone. "Well yes, that sounds, refreshing," She gathered her things and stood. "I'll see you in the morning, mister. If you are in the lobby at ten, call me and I'll come down."

He chewed a steamed green bean, paid the bill, went down

the corridor, and found a chair at the bar. A jazz ensemble was quietly playing in the far corner. He ordered a Jameson on the rocks to celebrate the fact Kate was taking his calls again. A blonde in a black evening dress came to the microphone. The band picked up again and her smoky voice filled the room, leaving just enough air to breathe.

He noticed his Über driver at a table closer to the little stage. He was leaning in, talking quietly into the ear of his gal, who was gently nodding her head in rhythm to the song. Or was it in agreement to what his driver was telling her? Bainbridge made no effort to connect with them. He stayed at the bar and let the race he has been on settle out a few beats. He had tonight to slow it down and walk it off.

There was a song that featured a saxophone and another with a major clarinet part. And then the blonde bombshell torched a few songs. The Irish on the rocks and the music filled his head right up until the elevator took him up to level three, where a corridor led to his room and his bed. He took off his shoes and slept on the bed in his clothes. He was proud of himself. Proud he hadn't thought about a damn thing since she walked away. See, he wasn't drunk. He was medicated.

The next morning, Bainbridge sat in a wide, deep cushioned seat in the great hall near the coffee station. Little piles of the local morning paper added a quaint touch. It was Denver's answer to 8:30 in the morning. He planned to have a few coffees and sink in a bit after yesterday's plane from Boston. He picked up the paper because he thought it would give him the appearance of a purpose while he sat sipping his brew and being part of the moment. He could have used his phone for the same purpose but the papers were there. Whatever the pages had to say would be more local. His eyes scanned this column and then another. He slowly turned the sheet of print on its crease and there he read that the city museum was hosting a Monet exhibit, including one of the artist's wall-sized masterworks. His google map told him it was very close to the hotel. He called and bought two tickets, which would be waiting at Will Call. He used the map on his phone again, this time to figure out a good walking loop. Something that put the museum at one end of the loop and the hotel at the other. He was about to get up for his second cup of coffee when he realized ten o'clock had come up on him. He put in a call, a number he had entered, it seemed, a thousand times with no answer. Boom, not this time.

"Hey how you doing? Yes that's right. I am. I am downstairs, yes. In the lobby, right, in fact I am sitting near the coffee station. Yes, tell me, are you ready to go on that walk we talked about, what do you think? Outstanding. Come on down then, it looks like a beautiful day out there."

An elevator opened. Kate stepped into the lobby. She was behind Bainbridge, who was seated some distance away with his back to her. She looked closely and saw the handsome man she had brought into this mess. This man thinks he loves you. I wish he wasn't here, really. But he has a part in this. It's just that it's another thing for me to deal with. I have plenty of that already. By then Kate's thoughts had carried her to Bainbridge's side.

"I don't believe we have ever taken a walk together. This is good."

"Everything has a first time," he blurted in surprise at seeing her at his side.

She remained standing. He stood, as well.

"Would you like some coffee or tea before we head out?"

"No, I don't think so I tell you what, we'll walk and have a nice lunch somewhere and come back. That would be a good way to do this don't you think?"

"Yes, that's the way to do this. We will get going then."

In a little cluster, they went through the lobby out onto the sidewalk and came to a complete halt. He said, "What about we take a walk towards the art museum? They are having what could be a great exhibit. We can take it in as part of our tour."

"You sweet thing. You planned it all out didn't you? Well, well. Which way then mister?"

"Okay. All right. We're going to that corner, crossing over, and we will be on our way."

The intention of the artist, obviously, was to create a life-sized view of a lily pond, not the usual portrait-sized painting. When you stood at the masterwork you were standing beside a pond. It was when the two of them were standing beside the painted canvas, the lily pads and the mirrored reflections on the quiet black water of the pond, that Kate wanted to get down to something. Thought it best to push for something that ought to be said, if there was any of that around today. She said, "Ask me a hard question?"

"Kate, I have a fist full of them."

"Start with one and that will probably answer it."

"Why the second time? What was that for you, Kate? Knowing what we know, why that second time?"

"There's a lot that goes on with me. I'm not always the best judge of me. Some of it I do, some of it is done to me. Our first time was us. Neither one of us knew that was going to happen. No one pushed us into that first time, we did that together. It was there so fast. And then it existed in such isolation. I suppose I wanted you again so I could remember you. I needed to know you more. It sounds ridiculous doesn't it?"

"No, it isn't sounding ridiculous. It is sweet of you to say on so many levels but what does it mean exactly? Once you knew more about me, your decision became have an abortion?"

"Daniel! Don't be cruel and don't be stupid. I told you already, my decision is not about you, it is about me. You have to get that."

"You said there was an 'us' just now. Those were your exact words."

"Yes there is an us and it is going on right now. I don't think we found love in those two instances. I think we found us. And if we need to call it love then yes, on some level, we loved each other. The word love covers a lot of ground, so it can cover us. I'm glad I loved you and I'm glad you loved me and I'm glad that it is almost over. All of it."

They were walking now along a sidewalk warmed by the sunlight directly overhead.

"It's tomorrow, isn't it? You'll be fine Kate. It is a very common procedure. Though I really don't know how common. I'm just making that up."

"Not me, I've studied up on it. Close to a third of American women elect to have an abortion," she said.

"Well there you have it."

"In many countries in Europe it is much higher than that." She added.

"My point is Kate, there will be no surprises. There is nothing to worry about here."

They sat outside at a small round table. She asked for hot tea and chicken tacos. Bainbridge ordered the chili and a draught beer. They remained mostly quiet. After brunching, they ambled some side streets and found a park very close to the hotel. They sat at a bench. She thanked him for Monet and the museum. She thanked him for the café and this lovely park, and she told him again about her lack of energy and the low grade nausea. Sleep, she had found, was nearly impossible last night.

He told her about the great jazz he'd listened to last night at the hotel, a ploy to see if she would say maybe she wanted to hear some good music tonight. She seemed to ignore his commentary.

"It is time I get back. This whole meeting thing was wonderful."

They walked towards the corner with the hotel across the way. Bainbridge rattled on. "Kate you used the words 'it will all be over, all of it,' but let's be real. You will forever be a part of my life story. I am sure of it. Yes, tomorrow ends a chapter in your life. Mine too. I don't think either of us is going to forget. And I don't think either of us should. It was wonderful to be with you.

"Listen, I know it is over between us. At the party when you made it clear you were staying with John, to be honest, I agreed with you. It is best for you to be with him. It is who you are."

They were waiting patiently at the curb for the light to change. Bainbridge noted a bicyclist flying along the gutter space very close to where they stood.

"Don't you go getting soft on me mister," Kate had become fidgety listening to what Bainbridge had to say. She made a quick, short, impatient move towards the street. The helmeted full-gear cyclist was coming up fast, leaving no time for Bainbridge to do anything but scream, "Kate!" and grab her arm and pull her against him.

A slip of color flew by and the two of them heard tires screeching and plastic crunching. Twenty feet up ahead they saw a red Kia very familiar to Bainbridge. The cyclist was sprawled on the asphalt. Horrified, they held each other's arm and ran the twenty feet it took to get to the man on the street. Bainbridge dialed 911. There were several other couples on the hotel side of the street doing the same. The driver's door opened on the Kia and yes, it was the Über driver. He stood against his open car door running both his hands through his hair.

"The dude just pulled right out! He pulled out!"

Two passengers opened the rear doors of his car and without looking back continued across the street and into the hotel.

Kate was on her knees beside the cyclist, quietly weeping.

"Come on, oh, come on."

Bainbridge knelt beside her. "Don't touch anything Kate."

He could see a two-inch dent on the front end passenger side of the Kia. The impact of that glancing blow spun the bike into a pirouette, sending the rider turning in the air before coming down on his head. Bainbridge could not detect a single movement, not a flicker of the eye, not a noticeable breath. He saw no blood. He yelled, "How you doing, man? Can you hear me?"

"Oh god, Daniel! He is so young!" Kate sobbed. "He wasn't supposed to die today! He has red hair and freckles. Look at him, he isn't moving." Sirens were screaming from not far away. A small cluster of people began edging closer to the scene from all sides. "Do you know CPR?" she asked.

"No, Kate, not on your life are we touching that guy." Bainbridge pulled himself and Kate to a standing position. "We don't know anything. We could do him more harm than good. Let's move from here right now."

Kate considered, "He could still be alive. We don't know."

"We should move from here right now," he said.

"Yes. We shouldn't be here."

They walked back to the corner where it all began for them.

"Did you see the car coming?"

"No, I didn't even see the bike. I was looking at you and all of a sudden you yelled at me."

"Yes, yes I did. I yelled. I saw this guy pumping his bike and you were way too close to the edge so I yelled and I grabbed you."

"I think I'm going to be sick. Daniel this is terrible. I can't take any more of this right now."

"We're going back to the Brown Palace. How does that sound?"

She was huffing and holding her stomach, "That is the best thing to do right now, yes."

At the elevator he asked, "I'll see you tonight won't I?"

"No," she said without hesitation.

"I'll take you up to your room."

"I just want to be left alone. I'll be fine."

"Well, I'll be with you to go to the clinic tomorrow?"

"Oh god, Daniel, stop! Just stop! What did we just see out there?" Having the protection of the lobby and a small ripple of time, she'd changed her tone. "Daniel, we will do this last thing together won't we? I think I'd like that"

"When?"

"Nine."

"So we should leave here by?"

"It is a short ride. No more than 15 minutes from here. Be ready to join me by 8:30 mister."

"8:30 then. And you're sure you want to be alone right now after what we have seen? Isn't it a good idea we at least have dinner together later on, like last night?"

"No, I can't find a place for that right now. Last night is a long time ago. I doubt you can understand this, but with all I'm dealing with I better stay pretty close to myself tonight."

Still holding her stomach, she entered the elevator alone.

"I can understand. But it could be a long night," Bainbridge pointed out. "You can use the phone, call me any time."

Bainbridge was left with nothing to do until morning. Out he went, back through the lobby and outside. Blue, red, ultra-white light flickered and blurred. An ambulance was at the curb where they had been standing. The police had cordoned off a wide patch of road with yellow tape and orange barrels. Officers were directing traffic around the red Kia. The body was turned on its back. EMT's on either side of the body were putting equipment back into their plastic cases. Each stood and headed back to the ambulance. A man was taking notes while talking to the driver, who squatted against his car.

Bainbridge's phone buzzed. It was a text from the police, a notice they were at the scene. If needed, please dial a second time. No, thought Bainbridge. He had nothing he wanted to add to this. No good can come of getting any closer. A woman began taking pictures of the body, the bike and the Kia, as well as the intersection and the road surface. Bainbridge waited with his hands stuffed in his pockets, near enough but still on the hotel side, with several other folks gawking at the commotion. He watched as a blanket was placed over the body.

More beefy cops arrived in cruisers that added more flashing lights. A purple hue covered the area. He noticed a second man with a notebook talking to a couple that stood in space fenced off by the yellow tape. He watched the EMTs return to the body and lift him quickly to a thin gurney. They slid the gurney into the bright interior of the truck. A policewoman opened the tape allowing the ambulance to move out.

Bainbridge had a brain that stopped in its tracks. He wasn't trying to put meaning on it anymore. He wasn't coping with it so much as it was simply getting it on file. He saw the Über driver standing to the side as his Kia was being pulled onto the flatbed. The driver was pawing at his phone when an officer wearing a bullet proof vest came and escorted him to the backseat of a cruiser. Bainbridge had enough of it. He took himself inside and toward the hotel bar. If he was going to be alone tonight he was going to start it off in the company of a good drink. It was getting cold outside. This he knew above all else.

∾

WHEN THE BROWN PALACE takes you in, there is the immediate warmth and quiet, the insular world of the lobby just beyond the door, and its arc of ultraviolet disinfecting light. He found the bar. He was asking himself, 'Is it good the bartender knows your name after only one night?' His first Jameson on rocks lit a candle in his dark brain. What he needed were some clean clothes. There had to be a men's store around here. By the time he finished a bar burger and a Coors draft it was around six and shopping still seemed like a good idea. He asked the barkeep, Chuck, not Charles, and yes, there was a good shop two blocks north of the hotel.

Everything outside all was gone, the street and the corner returned to what they always were. Dark shades of evening took over from the daylight. He found the shop easily and went in. He swept through the men's section and bought more socks, grey slacks, one white and one light blue dress shirt. The thought visited him that he was here in this store because he was afraid to go back and be alone in his room. No, he said to himself. It is too early to call it a day, that's all. He draped a heavy knit dark blue sweater across his arm and then went to the conga line at the checkout. Before reaching the register he had to pass a gauntlet of impulse items. By the time Bainbridge arrived at the counter, he was carrying the clothes, a jar of green olives, a small bag of chia seeds, a larger bag of caramel-coated popcorn, and an oversized bar of chocolate with a German name on it.

Room 305 helped out with a shower and spacious bathroom. The TV was on. It was attached to the wall across from the king-sized bed, breaking news about some Senator accused of insider trading scrolling below the talking heads of an anchor and three correspondents, sharing space in small panels along the side of the screen. They were discussing whether nine supreme court justices was enough, weighing the issue from all angles. They were going on about it when he went in for his shower and they were still at it when he came out. I'm a salesman and I can't produce that much wind, he thought. There is nothing here but the TV. There is no need to be here. Not yet anyway.

Bainbridge put on his new clothes and went back down to

where it was likely the first set of the group playing on the little stage would happen. Chuck, not Charles, gave him time to settle in. "A Jameson on the rocks, Mr. Bainbridge."

"Absolutely. It looks like I'm going to be my own best company two nights in a row."

"There are worse ways to spend the time."

The whiskey arrived. "True enough," Bainbridge said, tipping his glass to his lips.

A thin, angular man was sitting at the piano. He was college age. Young. But his set was full of ancient music. There were stretches where it was just the piano. Then he'd pull down a Billy Joel song, Tracy Chapman, John Lennon, then out into pure instrumental. With every song more and more people came into the bar. Eventually Dan's view was blocked by people standing behind him. The songs remained clear. He couldn't shake his father's music. Wasn't there anything his own generation had written that was worth some bar band learning?

This was a quiet crowd. Barely a hush disturbed the air between pauses between songs. Bainbridge managed to get the bartender's attention. "Chuck, I'll pay the butcher's bill now," he said, handing him his credit card.

He rolled into his room around 11, slipped onto his bed and began eating caramel popcorn until his fingers and lips became sticky. Abruptly he stopped and pushed the bag to one side. He was proud of himself. Since he left the street he hadn't allowed the mind to connect anything to anything. No dots to no dots. But now that he was alone, it was like somebody tapped the play button. He could hear it deep in his ears. The Über guy yelling. He saw the cyclist again, inert, one eye closed, the other against the road, half open, staring out from nowhere land. Then, for Bainbridge there was sleep.

It was sleep that ended when he could feel his phone vibrate and ring out, waking him from the deep. While slipping the phone to his ear he saw that it was Kate.

"I was wondering if you would open your door?" She said.

When the door opened, she gave him an appraisal. "Oh really? It's 12:30 a.m. and you open the door in your dress clothes?"

"Well you have yours on too. So what does that tell us?

"I don't know if it's a good idea or not, but can I come in?"

"Of course you can come in."

She saw that the TV was on and noted that the sound was muted. She could clearly make out that the top blankets to his bed were not pulled down.

"Do you suppose there is a way we could do the rest of the night together?" she said. "I can't take any more of this night alone, I really can't."

"Yes, yes, yes, of course, please, stay with me. We can order up some food or tea or coffee or drinks, anything. In a place like this, 12:30 isn't very late at all."

She took the bag of popcorn from the bed. "I see you are the gourmet of hotel food, "she said. She tossed several pieces into her mouth, groaning with exaggerated pleasure.

"Daniel, what I need most is to find a space where I can shut the lights off, go to bed, and get some sleep. Even a little would be good. I am so bad. I know I woke you. But I can't find sleep in my own room tonight."

"It's all good Kate. You made the right move. It's a huge bed. Way more than one person needs. You have a friend here, Kate. You're not alone. You know that, right?"

"Even for an hour or two. The clinic is at nine... I am becoming such a wreck," she confessed. "That settles it. But... one last particular... we are under the covers."

"Listen, anything at all. There is a nice, thick robe in the bathroom. You can hang your clothes right in this closet here. I'll get down to my t-shirt and boxer shorts and meet you under the covers."

They spooned and witnessed the darkness without words. They found the pause button. Bainbridge understood the experience for what it is. He was to protect her and give her comfort. She gave him these hours to share. He thought of them as being gifted something. He would have been his usual alone self, just like most every other night. Instead, his arm draped across her ribs and his nose in a little nest of hair at the back of her neck. It smelled like sweet grass.

He knew that on this night there were three of them. He had more he wanted to say, but Kate's warm body against his and her complete repose made him quiet. He was giving out wordless goodbyes as if down a well until sleep took him. Later, when what remained of the dark laced the early light, Kate was heard whispering.

"There was a freckle-faced college kid dead on the street. We both saw it, didn't we? It isn't some phantom story my brain cooked up is it?"

"No Kate, that was real."

They turned under the covers to face each other. Kate was checking her internal systems, thinking, yes I was out for a while. My mind caught a breather. It will do it will have to do. She slowly stroked his shoulder and arm while thinking, I have been with this man three times. So it will be. She could see they were both paying with their innocence. She said, "You can't imagine how this one inside me is reacting to this late breaking news."

"No, I can't, but you can tell me if you want. We both caught a few winks didn't we." He looked into her eyes. "How about this, I'm grateful you are right there." He leaned in, gave her a long hug, then fell back. Her phone alarm began clattering. Abruptly, the day began.

She pulled down the covers on her side of the bed. He remained in bed in order to give her free reign of the room. She took her clothes from the closet, gave him a final deep look, and went into the bathroom, stepping out dressed a short while later. Hanging her robe inside his closet she said, "I can't thank you enough, you know that though don't you."

"I'm glad, no, I'm grateful you are letting me help you."

"You sure are something. Now be honest, do you still really want to go with me to the clinic? You don't have to you know. I expected to do this part on my own in the first place. You've done enough already helping me get a little sleep."

"Without a doubt."

Even though she meant every word, a nagging internal accusation that he was too close to this, too over the top, simmered in the arguments she was having constantly with herself. "Alright then mister, I'll have a car reserved for us and I will see you in the lobby at 8."

They didn't kiss. They weren't those people anymore. She left. He remained in bed. But by 7:30 Bainbridge was at the coffee station. This time he sat with a sight line to her elevator. The elevator delivered her to the lobby. He stood. She made a hesitant wave and quick smile as she walked over. "How about a tea?" he asked.

"Yes, we're early. Let's sit here. I'd love a green tea with lemon."

He brought that and another coffee for himself. She sniffed the warmth of her tea. Bainbridge said, "This is the only moment in time I will ever bring this up, but hear me out, will you?" She chose not to look at him but he could tell she was listening. "Okay, one and done. I'm a salesman, always have been. I can see things other people can't make out sometimes. Okay, stick with me here. I went through with my vasectomy so I would never have another kid. But that's not where I am right now is it? I don't have a right to say this. I know I don't."

"Daniel, finish it, say it."

"Me, finding out only a couple of days ago that you're pregnant and with my baby, has me all spun around. But I do know one thing, I can be ready to be a dad again. That's where it is right now for me. The whole business from diapers and formula right through 'til the cows come home. That's my lane really. I've got time and I've got space. Taylor and Russell, they are my greatest people. But when you get down to it I'm only with them half of the time. Again, I know I have no right to spring this on you, but..."

"I want you to process this now. Go on, say what you need to say."

Bainbridge saw that she genuinely wanted this out of him. "I have more in me. There is room. And the guys? They are young enough where a new sister can fit right in. They could be close. I know what you're about to do and I respect your decision, but this option had to come out in the open between us. I can take full custody or we can share custody. Any way you want to share it."

"Oh god, these days all start out at full blast." She took several sips of tea, which seemed to revive her. She knew that these words at this time were hardening her. On some level she had to agree that hardening her up was the best thing for what she was about to do.

"I went through that option, Daniel." She held on to any energy she had banked. She was surprised and annoyed to be confronted with this issue at this time. She was not going to invest any emotional energy but was willing to process the topic with him. The man could use some slack and she could afford to give it to him. "I went through every possible outcome weeks before I told either of you men. You nursing my child? In what world would that appeal to me? There hasn't been a single option I haven't reworked a hundred times. You're telling me you are somehow grateful the vasectomy was a failure? That after several days knowing you could be a father again, you want to be or could be?

"While we're on options, let me point out an option you may not have come to yet. Tomorrow or the next tomorrow you are likely to find another woman and maybe you will have a baby then." She finally moved her eyes to his. "I heard you out."

"Absolutely. Thank you."

"It is time to get the car."

He felt the sting of dismissal. Admittedly, she had heard him out. He straightened his attitude and aligned his thoughts to offering whatever help she would take from him.

"You're driving. I had the valet put into the navigation the address to the clinic." When they were strapped in she said, "You are driving so you have someplace to sit while I'm in there. I'll be the only one allowed in, I'm sure of that."

While he drove she said, "I heard what you said. I know you'd be a good dad I can see you already are. You understand there are other issues, many other issues really. A big one for me is delivering Heather. Delivering Heather took my body about as far as it can go. To my last good place. There was no more. Her delivery went on and on. You probably think you understand some of this but you don't. She came through as such a big baby I didn't think I'd ever recover from it. Maybe I never have. Do I love her? Of course I do. But I don't know if I could love another one. I never wanted to go through that again.

"You see how it is, Daniel? You came here to be close to this. So, do you see who I am? I am more concerned about me than anybody else. I really, really believe I can't make it through another birth without some serious permanent harm being done to me. That potential outcome makes me more afraid than anything else in my life. I'm terrified, can you understand? To top that off, I am already a terrible mother and I would be worse, not better, a second time around. I refuse to be that woman."

The navigation system told him to take a right in 700 feet. "It is normal what you're feeling Kate," he said. "Your first obligation is to your own health. Everything else follows from there."

"Sounds good saying it, doesn't it? You are quite something I tell you. Leaving everything back home and coming all the way to Denver. Truth is, I'm glad I wasn't alone the whole time. Really, I didn't know I would appreciate it as much. It has been something of a help." The car was pulling into the clinic's parking area. "Should be a couple of hours maybe. I'll text you."

She threw her door open and went towards the nondescript brick building without once looking back. It had a small sign beside the heavy-gauged grey metal door that read in little bold letters, 'Women's Care Center.' He heard a buzz coming from the metal door and the sound of a latch snapping open. She was in.

He parked in a nearly empty lot with the clinic in front of him and a bank at the other end. The sun began to warm the interior of his car. Two hours meant that he should stay close, but maybe walk around a little. He sat in the quiet of the car. In a conscious effort not to drift off to sleep he called Taylor. They talked and then he had Russell get on the phone. Between them all it was confirmed. They were coming over to his place to stay in about ten days.

He didn't tell them he was in Denver. Just said he was checking in and saying hello. He left the car to take a walk but he got no further than leaning on his hood. The outside was crisp. He shouldn't have moved around. Now he had to pee. A block down from the parking lot was a McDonald's on one corner and a Burger King across the street.

With that in the books, he waited in line, eventually buying a dark roast coffee. If anyone thought he'd be feeling guilty he had dragged Kate through his final pitch, they would be forgetting he is a salesman to the bone, built to say what has to be said. And he was perfectly capable of hearing no. He spent most of his time drinking his coffee while leaning against the hood of the car.

Eventually he folded himself back into the driver's seat and began thumbing his phone for messages. He listened to a voicemail from a Jack Stillman who is thinking about selling his house and wanted Bainbridge to help him do that, and one of his agents forgot the passcode to the door lock on a monster house out by the marsh. It was at that moment he heard the latch on the big front door snap and watched the heavy door open. He looked at his phone, surprised to see that an hour-and-a-half had blown by.

Dan left the car and walked rapidly towards her. She looked fine, as she'd looked when she went in. She took the steps on her own before he could reach her and there were no hitches to her movement. "Kate, how you doing, lady?"

"I'm good. Really. Let's just get to the car." Once inside the car she looked at him. A long empty silence ensued. There was no depth to her stare. "I'm alright, everything went as it should. I am so lucky to be in the care of those doctors. They are so special to me. I researched the hell out this place and could not have made a better choice. Please, please get us back to the hotel. Don't look at me like that. I know, I know you must have some questions. We can go through it but not now. I want to close my eyes and be quiet for a few minutes while you drive, okay?"

It took no more than ten minutes to leave the car with the valet and be in the hotel lobby. Not a word had been spoken. Bainbridge's eyebrows were pulled up in severe arcs.

"Just for now," she said, "I'm going up to my room to see if I can take a nap on my own. Either I sleep or I don't, I'll take it one step at a time."

"All I need to know is that you are feeling okay."

"That I am," Kate replied. "I'm going to take some time with myself. Tell you what, we will do dinner, yes? It will be where we talk."

"Perfect, that is all fine and everything, but I've got to tell you though, you look, well, like I should take you right to your room."

"Not at all. I will see you tonight. And I'm paying this time, so bring an appetite" They were at her elevator. It was established. Dinner at six. She went up with a good soldier smile on her face.

He turned toward the registration counter, then walked across the lobby to his elevator. In his room the TV was tuned to CNN. You could barely hear the chatter about a LeRoy Watts who last night was shot down by Phoenix Police apparently for no good reason other than he was on his girlfriend's porch with a cell phone in his hand.

Bainbridge didn't turn it off but he stopped paying attention. He made his room into a little office. He came in thinking that Kate not really saying two peeps was weird. But the main thing is she seems okay enough. Everything started with that. He sat by his window and set up his laptop, then brought his phone to life. The fact that a child of his was ended that day pressed out everything else. He refused to work with it. It was done. The decision wasn't his to make. Man up. This moment in time ends here.

∽

HE USED his phone as an escape hatch back to another place and time. There were four voicemails to get through, and he gave a quick scan of his text messages and email. He contacted Daliwal about the building inspection next Wednesday for the house the Chungs were buying. Being the listing agent, Bainbridge should be there to open the house to the inspector. Good business was any business. Then, a call to Meghan Polatano covered some pretty tender ground. She asked what had transpired with the baby. He told her that Kate went through with the abortion. And that even though she seemed physically fine, she hadn't wanted to talk about it all.

It was Meghan's opinion that she was in a very normal range of behaviors. "Admittedly, we are meeting up for dinner in a couple of hours," Dan told her.

Polatano asked how he was feeling and he told her It is complicated. "Nobody asked me to be here, but I felt I shouldn't be anywhere else. She shouldn't be alone with this. And, I mean, I didn't want either of them to be alone in this."

Polatano understood what he meant by "either of them" but chose to skip that, reminding Dan that he had support, that he wasn't alone either. "You have my office number," she said. "Call me in a week, set up an appointment and I'll let you know where we are."

The Meghan conversation went on way too long. There was barely enough time to shower and begin packing all his stuff for tomorrow.

At the entrance to the dining room Bainbridge was greeted by a waiter who seemed to expect him. He acted as a guide weaving him through tables to Kate, seated at her favorite place. Bainbridge took his chair.

"Kate, you look great. I mean you look well, are you well?"

"Relax Dan, I'm fine. I do very well with alone time. It is a complicated process doing me. And now, here we are. Let's order up and I will tell you about what is happening."

"Great idea. Let's put the waiter to work."

She ordered a minestrone soup and a chef's salad involving walnuts, goat cheese, and sun dried pears over mixed greens with a balsamic drizzle. He thought he was detecting too much of an upbeat tone from someone who hours ago experienced an abortion. Maybe it was an indication of how right she was with her decision. He went to order the shrimp scampi. Kate pleaded with him not to.

"Nothing seafood, nothing that likes to get wet please, for the good of us both."

"Fine," he said, "I can go in the other direction. The pork chop, applesauce, double mashed potatoes, green beans, and a bottle of house red should get me through some of this don't you think?" He could see her relax and busy herself with a reply.

"If that doesn't do it for you, we'll keep throwing money at it," she said.

"You'll be having some of this bottle of red? If you like?"

"I think that would be perfect for you," she said. "But I'm thirstier for something else. I'd like an iced tea with a lot of mint pounded into it." When the waiter was clear of the table and on his way she continued. "We can relax now, yes? I'm thinking there's a chance you have some questions about what went on this morning?"

"Oh, you are the funny one. No, I thought we did a good job of covering all the bases. After that, anything you are willing to share with me, well that is what I'm here for. You've changed from this morning, Kate. You look, I don't know, lighter. There is more of you present then I've seen since I got here."

When the warm bread bowl arrived they each found the cornbread. The buttery corn grain gave them pause for a few moments.

"Lydia is known to say that there are fewer calories in flattery, so why not enjoy every one of them. About my morning, you should hear this once. Let me start by asking you a question. Do you know the name of the boy we saw die last night?"

"No, actually I don't.

"Jamie Burke."

"I didn't even try to find it. How did you come up with it? Local news must have covered the accident in today's news block. Is that it? Did you catch his name on TV?"

A different member of the waitstaff brought the soup, salad, and drinks to the table. Kate's glass of iced tea was frosted and deep green with the mashed spearmint leaves. She looked over the brim of her drink and studied him. He looked like he could use a haircut. It was clear to her he was putting out effort to maintain his little smile.

"I'll tell you how I know his name. It starts with me going into the clinic this morning and meeting my doctor. I have a gold standard doctor, pure gold. I went through my entire checklist with her. She never rushed me. First off, I wanted her to examine me. Am I physically okay? Is there anything I should worry about? She already had the charts from my first delivery. We did the examination right then, from hands on to looking at my charts. She could find nothing wrong with me, but she was super quick to point out there was no absolute predictor to what another delivery would do to me."

Their soup and salad bowls were taken and replaced by their entrees. Bainbridge elected to pour more of his own wine, bringing it up to the rim of the glass. He swallowed a good quarter of the glass and then addressed the opportunity to work through some of the pork chop, which he began sawing through with gusto. His first juicy bite made him very glad he was hungry.

"Kate, Christ, please. I had no right to push that on you. Especially this morning."

"No, no, no, remember? I had a checklist of my own and I finally had a doctor I could believe in to go through your points this morning, along with a million other situations I'm faced with. You should hear this too, I suppose. The doctors agree, it is possible you could, with training, nurture a child through infancy. You would have to be an Olympian to make it through."

"I have to admit I'm no Olympian"

"Obviously," she said with a small, nasty laugh.

"Wow, now you're just trying to make me feel terrible."

"Oh, you don't have to worry. I wasn't thinking about your feelings at all. No, those are yours to have all by yourself. I, on the other hand, was there to puzzle through my whole list. What it would look like if I stayed on with the pregnancy... Oh, there were many more."

"Yes I get it, you finally had your professional to consult with. It must have been a massive relief."

Bainbridge was already aware of changes in Kate. He was not going to jump the gun after what he'd pulled that morning. Kate hadn't arrived at what she wanted to tell him. His job was to get her there. "Can you tell me any more about what the doctor told you?"

She left a third of her salad on her plate, slowly placing her folk at an angle along the rim. "On the option of continuing being pregnant, Doctor Warren was emphatic that if I went on with this, I should expect a cesarean delivery. She also said she would want me on a four day a week yoga and physical training regime from now to delivery. That's about 28 weeks of serious conditioning." She scanned Bainbridge for any expression indicating he was catching any part of what she was saying. To her eyes he seemed to be maintaining a fish face.

"The nugget for me is – if I'm not mistaken, there *is* a nugget here? Are you telling me you're going to have this baby after all?" He was hearing himself saying these words and thought he sounded curt. He was stunned. But in a good way.

"Oh yes, that is exactly what I'm telling you mister. Let me get to the rest. I hadn't changed my mind at that point. Nope. Doctor Warren wrongly believed I was leaning in that direction so she thought we should take one more step. She called in her physical therapist so I could imagine better what that regime would look like, flesh it out a bit. Give it a hard look, I think she said. The woman who came through the door was barely holding back her sobs."

"Wait, wait, you are having this baby say, it."

"Yes, Daniel, I'm having your baby."

"I'm blown away, I don't know what to say and I don't know what to feel," he said.

"Don't feel anything right now, take it in."

"Is this because I asked you to consider it?"

"Look at me. I was going to go through this possibility with my doctor whether you were in Denver or on Mars."

To be at some level of control during this conversation Bainbridge retrieved the wine bottle and poured the remainder into his glass. His mind was settled on nothing. It was best described as skipping along. She wanted to get him clear on why she changed her mind. She would explain it once, this was his time to hear it.

"The physical therapist was a total mess. She was choking up after every word. She told the doctor she couldn't make it through the rest of the day. It was impossible for her, poor thing. As she went on, it turned out that last night her nephew was run over. Killed while riding his bike home from work. Our Jamie Burke, gone, she said. He was only thirty-two and now he's gone.

"I knew who she was talking about. You know what I mean here. He died of a broken neck; you know. And he was an accountant in hospital administration. She also managed to tell us that her sister was in total ruin. It was pretty clear she needed to be with her. Naturally, the doctor told her to go immediately. She left but the sadness stayed in the room."

"What are the chances, Kate? What are the chances?"

"I have no idea. I don't think anyone does. But I do know that was the moment I felt a shift inside me. I could feel a balance that hadn't been there in weeks and weeks. And then, of course, I heard our girl, yes our *girl*," She nodded her head at him and saw that the statement had not flustered him. "From inside me I actually heard her call out, 'I will give life a try!' She really did. On a dime, she changed her mind.

"You have to understand, Dan. All day yesterday the only thing she would say was she wanted no part of this violent, mad world. She called it a viral planet with an environment going downhill in the next 80 years. Yesterday, she gave an unrelenting speech in which she refused to live in a place that did not want her, nor to be in a place where it would take an epic level of struggle simply to survive. She'd be living through it her whole life. She insisted that it would be no big deal if she missed out on it.

"Then this morning she heard about Jamie Burke and changed direction completely. She must have told me seven times in two minutes that, and I quote her, 'death can't have every minute of every day.' She wants me to let her go for it and I will, I will."

"This is good, good news! We are really going through with this."

"There it is, Daniel Bainbridge. You are going to be that father you talked about. Still sound good to you?"

While the waiter tempted them with choices from an extensive dessert menu, Kate could see that Bainbridge needed more time with this news. He was pushing the little menu a few inches along the tablecloth and finishing the last of his wine. A lazy smile was roosting on his face. She ordered mixed fruit with a scoop of lemon sorbet. Without dealing with the menu, he ordered a piece of apple pie with slice of cheddar. The waiter pointed out there was no pie available. Bainbridge wanted to yell out to the entire room, 'I don't care! There is a baby in the house!' But he did no such thing, he excused his error, guessing there must be a chocolate cake. He was assured there was a locally famous chocolate cake, and ordered that.

The moment the waiter stepped away Bainbridge said, "You've gotten past your worry about how it can damage your health? I believed you and I think you believed yourself when you said, 'you were in no shape mentally or physically to have this baby.'"

"Let's face it, in a life full of unknowns it is best we do the choosing in what we believe."

"Agreed, there is the power and beauty we give to our beliefs."

"And this morning I chose to believe my daughter and my doctor."

An ample fruit bowl arrived as did a piece of chocolate cake the size of a travel bag. The two of them swapped desserts. They both saw it as the correct adjustment.

"Believing is one thing. Doctor Warren connected me to an OBGYN back home to work with me and the baby. That's in the mix. And our girl made it very clear to me that she will go much easier on me than Heather did."

Bainbridge laughed while trailing a very difficult grape with his spoon.

"The power of motherhood. With that you can reach places I cannot go. Speaking of beliefs, I do believe you can talk to her, I really do."

"Of course! It is true. She really does talk to me. I am not speaking in metaphor."

"You're lucky. I can't wait to talk to her myself. This Jamie Burke, Kate, we had nothing to do with his death. You do know that don't you? Let's get this out. You were too close to the edge, but you were on the curb. I did yell. Maybe I startled him. But we'll never know. He was nearly flying, and as far as the car zipping down the road, I didn't see much of that either. Jamie Burke is dead. It's sad. It is brutal. But we are not at fault."

"I can agree with that, but if it didn't mean anything then why did we have to see it?" Kate pleaded. "John makes decisions way differently than I do. He comes to a conclusion about something and then tries to bend the world to fit his ideas. John's not alone. There are plenty of people like that. You, I'm not sure how you make your big moves. But me? I always try to see how the world is setting things up. Once I see how it's going, I try to help it along.

"You should know I'm always trying to see what forces are in the mix. I make my decision based on what I see around me. There are no broken pieces they can all fit in an ever changing pattern. Take you, I didn't set out that day to meet you, but here we are now with a baby on the way. I didn't have an idea about you and then set out to make you happen. That's not how it goes with me. Life puts the clues out there and I try to read them as quickly as possible."

"You've made a perfect decision here; I can tell you that."

"We will let it work out, won't we? But Dan, you have to know there are rules. I am the wife of an attorney, which means I did almost as much of John's coursework as he did through law school. The first rule is I am the mother when it comes to this baby: I make most of the rules. From the beginning, day one, she stays with me and Lydia and Heather and John until her fourth birthday.

"The first year she stays exclusively with me. After that, every two weeks you can have her with you for two days at a time. You can take her anywhere, but not more than two days at a time. This next rule is important. Actually they're all important. When she's three, we'll begin alternating months and holidays.

"Then there's the big one. On her fourth birthday, she starts living mostly at your house. She will be brought up by you during her school years. It doesn't mean she won't be staying with me, but her home during these years will be with you. You hearing me? How are you dealing with this?"

"I have no argument with any of it. This is very much how it should go. I'm pumped. This is all good."

"Good then this is the general pattern we will follow."

"Have you told John any of what is going on?"

"Of course I have. I talked to him this afternoon. I will tell you what he said this one time. He made three points. If I was comfortable with the decision, he had no problem with it. He said it was better we have something positive for the two of us to deal with than something negative. It was a good spirit to bring to our launch he said. The poor man is so busy all he can think about is the launch. It went off spectacularly, was how he put it." From her purse she retrieved her phone. She opened it and said, "In fact tomorrow I am flying out from here to Madrid to be with him for a week or so. While I still can visit."

"Oh, oh, I see," Bainbridge muttered. "My god, this is it, we won't see each other for a while will we?"

"Call me in a month and we'll talk. I'll let you know all about what's happening with the pregnancy, we will check up with each other, yes?"

"You promise you will pick up the phone?"

"Oh, I'm not even going to take that on. We live in the same town. In a month, if the phones don't work, come over. We can do lunch or something. To each other and around the town we will be known as friends."

"Yes, yes, yes," he repeated with energy. "Are you sure you want to close up this evening right now. There is this lounge and some really good music."

"Lounge, where?"

"Right here in the Palace."

"Really? Well, alright then. Just for a little longer. It looks like you could use another drink, that's for sure. And I can use a little music to sweep out my head."

"Come on. We will end our evening listening to the piano man."

Bainbridge was amazed that he was showing her a part of the hotel she didn't know. They entered a beautifully large mahogany bar with stained glass. You could hear the piano working through something. The bartender spread his hands apart over two empty chairs at the bar. They settled in. He ordered a double Jameson on the rocks as Kate got comfortable beside him, her eyes to the ceiling, intent on perking her ears to the direction of the piano. She said, "Bring me a glass of what you think is your best sauvignon blanc and another wine glass full of ice."

To Bainbridge she said, "You were there when I had my last glass of wine. Well here is to another last glass of wine."

The piano man broke into a rendition of Ed Sheeran's "Perfect." The song caught them both in a moment of attentiveness to the tender words and beautiful music. When the song ended the singer announced he was taking a break, he'd be back and he was real happy to see so many people here already tonight. Little pockets of applause broke out.

She told Bainbridge, "I haven't heard that song in a while, very nice. Daniel, the dinner gave us most of what we had to say, yeah? Well, I'm done. I'm on a flight to Madrid tomorrow at five p.m. For that matter when do you leave the Palace?"

"I leave for Boston at ten in the morning."

As he said those words, she poured more of her wine into her glass of ice. She thought to herself, we are done as lovers but this man will always be the other man in my life. She had to admit that if there was going to be one, Dan would do in a pinch. "One of the good ones."

She held her glass with casual carelessness and said, "There is John and there is you. As different as different can be. Our second time I was already pregnant. I wanted to have one time with you where there would be no chance of further complications. I wanted to know what just sex felt like for us. You understand? Probably not, I don't fully get it myself.

"After that second time all the pieces in my life started fitting into different shapes for me. This is going to sound rough, but it's getting late and I'm tired. When you left and went downstairs to the party I knew right then that I'd be better with John. And for that matter, and as you said to me, it is best for you too."

She drank some of the cold, watered-down wine. "Do you think I knew how John would come down on all this? I had no certainty at all, but I am his wife, which means I know him better than I know myself.

"To his credit he calmed down considerably as the party clicked along. My arrangements to leave for Denver were made before I told either of you that night. The morning after the party we had a come-to-Jesus moment in which he said he wanted me to do whatever I wanted to do. Have the baby or not have the baby but, he and I are forever and ever."

"It should be noted," Bainbridge said. "You are actually the first woman I have been to bed with since my divorce. It got complicated for both of us right out of the gate didn't it?" They found a little laugh at that comment.

"That day," he said, "we met each other and it went so fast. I couldn't, I wasn't going to stop us."

"I know, I was there." She held his hand. "This one will be part of a wonderful tribe, no doubt, good people all around. She'll be a hometown girl." She brought his hand to her stomach." Tell her something before we are off to Madrid."

Bainbridge lightly cupped her stomach, looking into Kate's eyes he was washed in an intimacy he had never felt until then.

"Take your time," he said. "I'm as happy as I have ever been to know that you decided to join us. We are here for you."

"Very nice," she said taking his hand away. "Talk to me in a month, in a month call me or come over, we live just down the street from each other. On your phone you'll see I sent you the address where you can enroll in an infant care class. You can tell me what you're picking up in the course. For a year or so we have to think Olympic and do Olympic. I can tell you how my first month of major yoga is going. We will do lunch. You can plan on me complaining a lot. "

Bainbridge batted in, "That's great. We'll catch up in a month. Lunch. We always do good lunches don't' we?"

"You stay here," she said. "Listen to some more piano. It beats the TV you have on in your room 24/7. This is a good place for you to be. And me, there is Madrid. Good night, Daniel."

Bainbridge's breath bottomed out. His lungs pressed hard against the ribs in a desperate search for thin air. Parts of his life were shifting at that very moment. A new beginning was shaping him. It had impact. And it was welcomed.

He leaned forward to kiss her cheek but she drew away. They both stood knowing kissing was a thing of the past. He felt stupid and awkward. He reached for anything to say and came up with, "Be careful over there in Spain. The TV says there's some flu or virus running around, especially in England."

"I'm not going to England, Dan. I'm going to Madrid."

Again she took his hand, this time she gave it a small tug and let go. They looked within each other for a long moment. Without words each of them understood or confessed, they did not have a name, but equally they understood a name would come. She turned away and left him to the piano man and the care of a bartender wiping down her space at the bar.

12

THE PRINCESS

"I'm sure, Mrs. Tabor, you'd agree every day is packed tighter than a laundry bag. Nobody is going to tell me any different." Cheryl had walked a direct line along the beach to reach Kate.

"Cheryl, you're going to have to call me Kate or there is no chance we can be friends. It is nice, really, to be talking to someone, don't you think? So beautiful out here. But maybe too quiet today. Unfold that beach chair and sit with me for a bit."

Cheryl slipped the chair out of its sleeve, positioned it near Kate's and sat down.

"Times are shifting," She observed. "We really don't need a mask out here, do we?"

Each of them had one but neither made a move to hasten one out.

"Truth is I've been wearing the mask so long I'm finding it hard to lay it down."

Kate said, "It's probably the fact we finally can take the masks off that made it so I could recognize you. Tell me what's been happening between you and Buckland. Three years ago was the last time I saw the two of you. You made such a lovely couple leaning into each other in the light at the firepit."

"That is nice of you to say. And no parties since then for you? For what three years? I'm sure we would have talked during those. But it wasn't to be, was it?"

"Covid put a stop to our little party, and everybody else's I suppose. Closed up the downtown for a while too, and so much else. Especially the first year."

"I will confess, it has only been the last three months that I've left my mask in my pocket more than on may face."

"John and I were actually talking about hosting another party this year, but we pushed it back to next. Who knows, it is always wait and see now. Do you go to this beach often?"

"Well yes, some. It's really close to where we are living."

"Maybe you can understand. Ariel and I grow tired of the same beach. You know our beach. It is very nice. We do a lot of alone time together. When the weather is good we get out move around from one beach to another. Migrate like plovers. This Old Silver is a good one."

While saying this she indicated her little girl wrapped in a beach blanket napping in the shade the umbrella cast over her. Of course Cheryl had spotted the little one. She was letting Kate direct the drift of their conversation. Cheryl made gentle cooing sounds while taking her in. She said, "Mrs., no, Kate, is that your daughter? Well! A perfect example of busy. There was no daughter the last time I saw you except Heather, and now this sweet Ariel. See? You wouldn't know it until you really take a look, then it's plain as day, everybody is booked solid. Life keeps piling it on and we are playing catch-up most of the time." Pointing to the little one she said, "There is nothing better than a beach nap."

The two women quieted and took in the stillness of the

ocean before Kate asked again, "So tell me all about you two since the days of the fire pit."

"You want to know what I've been up to? There are days and then there are days." Cheryl made a point of featuring her engagement ring.

"Bravo, congratulations! Let's hear a little about that!"

"Yes, alright, I'll give you the slow version. It was about a year ago, this ring came up, and as usual, between Bucky and me the trimmings aren't pretty. Like always, a year ago I was at the plant."

"That would be the building behind Mechanic Street?"

"Exactly. We work hard there, you should know. Putting something together isn't easy. I'm talking about military grade goggles, bulletproof vests, fireproof gloves; a year ago we added a production line of surgical gowns."

"That is incredible."

"Yes, in a way it really is. My mother worked there before me. She was in sales, did really well. Any chance she gets she'll tell you this plant has made one thing or another since the 1950s."

"It is a testament to the town that we have such people who literally make a difference."

"Agreed. Plus, we're well paid for it. And the plant actually tends to keep growing in size."

"That doesn't happen if you all come in just to fool around and chat it up."

"Yes, very true Kate, sometimes though we get knocked off the line. Something comes along and it grabs the whole place. We chew on it all day. It's a beehive that turns into a circus every so often. The news about Senator Roberts got around. It rocked every live soul in the place by ten in the morning. You must know the poor man died, he was older than a hayfield, but age isn't what killed him, remember? No, it was Covid. In this day and age, years after the vaccine showed up. It's a shocker, is all.

He went into the hospital and was dead in five days. Well, that knocked everybody into telling everybody else something that goes like, 'It's too bad. It's sad that he's gone.' People are more shocked because he died of covid than anything else about the man."

"Cheryl, only three years ago I was talking to that man on my deck."

"That's true, how about that? Anne in Human Resources pushed a theory he wasn't vaccinated at all. I heard it twice before I actually got up to Anne's office. I said to her, 'Where did you hear that Senator Roberts may not have been vaccinated?' Anne said, 'I can tell you this Cheryl. I go to the same First Christ Church he and his wife attend. Most of us see the vaccine as a miracle, but there are these base evangelicals. Base evangelicals, she said. What the hell is a 'base evangelical?' And a lot of them. They just want to try to pray it all away pure and simple."

Kate said, "There is usually a simple solution to every problem and most of the time it is the wrong one."

"Exactly. Senator Roberts had support from the fundamentalist sector of that church for years." Anne made the point of saying that a few of those boys could write some very big checks. I'm going to tell you Kate, there is never much left unsaid up there in Human Resources."

"You know yourself there are plenty of churches to be found around here," Kate replied. "Personally, I'm amazed he could get even one of them to put their money into his mouth."

"Kate, over time that man changed. There was something funny about him. You waited for it. He could be talking about the federal school lunch program and when he was winding it up he wove that in with Christ and a never ending jug of wine. You remember?"

"He was a senator for a long time. That's saying something. We both agree he didn't need to die in office," Kate added.

"I doubt we'd be talking about him at all but bear with me."

"Forward girl, march on."

"I'll take you to the cafeteria then." Cheryl looked deep into Kate's eyes and saw that Kate was attached to what she was saying. "My mother even likes Bucky. To be honest, that is neither here nor there. I'm quick to tell her Ma she's not supposed to like him. That makes me look like I'm too easy. She comes back asking, 'Are you two even dating?' She knew we weren't dating or anything like that. I told her, no."

"What do we call it then," she says.

"Courting I told her. Can you believe it? I answered her with 'courting.'"

Kate joined in the joke of it. "He's a different man now isn't he? A few short years ago he was rescuing a leatherback turtle from my beach and now he's running for congress. And why not, I might add."

"Thank you for saying that. He's Buckland now, but he was full Bucky when we were at your place. Can I tell you how this man went about proposing to me?"

"Yes, do, it is obvious you have taken this man on as your little project." Kate saw the child roll out of her towel onto the warm sand. Using one hand in the sand to steady herself she stood and waddled over to her mom. With her arms wide Kate said, "Come here, Sweet Pea." And she hoisted her onto her lap, rummaging in a nearby cooler, from which she brought out a juice cup. The little one settled in, took the cup in both hands, then directly to her mouth. Behind the mug she patiently stared at Cheryl through wide green eyes.

"Oh you have a beauty there. Hello there little miss pretty."

"Don't stop now," Kate said. "We need more about that ring of yours. See it, Ariel? Right there on her finger."

"So the cafeteria again, same day the entire plant is a chattering machine about Senator Roberts. I'm looking through the big windows in the cafeteria. The taco truck is set up and a little line of three people was there before he opened. Bucky came in and took the plastic chair beside me. He said, 'Hey' in this elongated, exhausted voice like he'd just carried a sea chest up two flights of stairs.

"'That's not one of your best hellos,' I said.

"He tried for a smile but failed. He said, 'I'm heavy with responsibilities. This is a day that weighs, well, heavy on me. Some days weigh more than others and this is one of them. Didn't start out that way but by nine it all came down on my shoulders.'

"I looked at his shoulders and there was nothing there and I told him so. He said, 'This morning I put all of what I do in my life directly on me.'"

"Go, Buckland!" Kate gave a modest cheer. "You keep telling me the story, but let's walk a little."

All three stood and took the ten yards or so to the water's edge. They walked slowly along the shoreline. Ariel held her mother's hand for a time and then scampered along, finding feathers, and the empty shell of a crab, and more than a few smooth pebbles. Kate watched Ariel taking a long moment to study something in the palm of her hand that was too small to see from where Kate stood. For that matter, there might have been nothing in her palm at all.

"So he quit his job and then what?" Kate was prodding Cheryl for more.

"Basically, you're right. His spin on it was, he made himself his own boss. He said it was an awesome responsibility. This ring was about two years ago now."

Cheryl spotted a man pacing towards their group. He came closer. The sun was behind him. Eventually she could make out that it was her landlord, Dan Bainbridge. To her he appeared as an out of context visitor. She started thinking something must be up with the condo when he said to Kate, "Hey, I'm right on time I hope. Hello ladies. Not a bad thing, beaches."

While he talked, Kate held up the little girl and placed her in the cradle of Bainbridge's arm. Cheryl relaxed and became aware that Dan wasn't there with any landlord issues at all. Her own thoughts came to a standstill. She observed Dan as he was saying, "Oh Ariel, smart girl, that's right always stay hydrated," he purred. They all walked to the umbrella and chairs. Bainbridge put Ariel down in a small pile of beach towels. "And hello, Cheryl, good to see you. How is everything at the apartment?"

"Great, absolutely," she said. "The best thing we love about it is it's just off the bike path. We really do, we ride to Woods Hole, the canal. Can't beat it, the closer we get to the election the more mornings start off with Bucky doing an hour on the bike. My man is busy-busy."

"Cheryl, it's all over town. You've been newly minted operating manager. The surgical gown division at the plant, it's good to be you, am I right?" Bainbridge boasted.

Kate interjected with a question of her own., "You two seem to know a lot about each other."

"Bucky and I rent a condo from Mr. Bainbridge."

For Kate's benefit, Bainbridge said, "When I moved back to my Shore Road house I must have told you I chose to keep the condo as a rental. These two birds show up the first day the rental went to market. And Kate, they are great tenants. I must say. What are we. it is getting close, maybe a week before the election. How is Bucky holding up?" Bainbridge was at that moment kneeling down and letting Ariel stand. She wandered over to Kate's oversized beach bag.

"Yeah, well he's nervous. And the election isn't a week away. It's only a few days. Buck always acts like a golden retriever that's been in the house all day, so it's hard to tell. Still, he's ahead in the polls so it can't be all bad.

"Hey now, great seeing both of you. I appreciate so much the chance to talk to you Kate. So, so much. I'll let you do most of the talking next time, I promise. But I can't let you go yet. I just remembered one of the reasons I came over in the first place and that was to tell you how grateful we are for the settlement your husband got for us. Of course we've thanked John but when I saw you I said, I should thank her too.

"A chunk of that settlement is in Bucky's campaign. To think, an inch change in that old woman's aim. And, well, you know, some days the bad stuff is looking the other way. Remember guys, vote Bucky!" Cheryl's was a well-practiced, intentionally underplayed cheer.

"Oh, you're not leaving, please Cheryl, not just yet. You sit a minute. I'm giving Ariel over to Dan. I need to tell him a few things and then I'll be right back over here."

To a talkative person like Cheryl, Kate's request made her feel indebted to the woman in a good way.

Ariel had been rooting around in Kate's beach bag, pulling out a rolled towel, an apple, and a clear plastic water bottle. She placed each one carefully onto the sand and then returned each one back into the sack. She was talking away to each object telling them one of her stories. It seemed the towel would not fit anymore and because of this Ariel abandoned the task and her conversation with an apple, water bottle and towel.

They walked a few paces away from Cheryl and Ariel. He said, "Today will be fini. The remodel to my Shore Road house is finally and actually finished."

"Nice," she meant it. "You've been living with construction since the day you moved in there."

"You are so right. It went from a new roof to the interior, and on and on. All the bathrooms, the new kitchen. And today the last project is fini. You'll have to see it. And will, of course. What used to be my old office is now Ariel's bedroom and full bath. Bingo and done."

"You have all the furniture, everything?"

"Yup, all of it. New couches, chairs, beds, bureaus, desks, TVs, right down to sheets, blankets, towels, curtains, and rugs. It is done, believe me. Finally. You have an open invitation. You saw it when I moved back in. Now it's at a whole new level. I've got my kitchen back. In a few weeks, why don't you and Ariel come over for lunch?"

"Why don't I bring John along as well?" They both laughed. "He won't, we know that. But he's always invited, right? And I know you well enough to say there is no way you could choose the wall shades, the upholstery and furniture without help."

"Yes, right, that's true. Aubrey helped, and I hired a consultant from Rothman and Hayes furniture."

"Oh, Aubrey. That is so nice of her, don't you think? That reminds me, I must visit Aubrey's shop and have my colors read. By the way you I suppose you should know, John has booked rooms in Paris for a week. He is calling it 'Ariel's First Business Trip.' Of course, Heather is going with us. I'm taking her out of school for this. She's a senior and doing great. She can afford the time. There will be plenty to learn, with us in Paris for a week."

Using her short legs, Ariel managed her way over to her daddy in precise capable steps. Bainbridge picked her up and returned her to the sling of his arm. They were leaving.

"It's time for the big reveal. Say goodbye to Mommy and Cheryl," Bainbridge requested. But Ariel would not be convinced to do it. "No, no, no."

"She's an obstinate little thing," Kate said. "She is almost three and still won't get out of her diapers. I'll have to work harder on that I suppose." She leaned in and gave Ariel a kiss on the forehead. "You two play nice." She watched them leaving for a moment and then returned to her chair and Cheryl. "Thank you a bunch for hanging in there"

"Oh, it's not a bother at all. I mean it." Cheryl was not about to needle into why Kate had given her daughter to Cheryl's landlord, Dan Bainbridge. If Kate wanted to share anything, she would.

And Kate, knowing Cheryl's capacity for chitchat, felt a protective need to not get into an explanation with her. "I do want to know more about that proposal and ring business."

"Alright, we are back at the cafeteria, again," Cheryl emphasized. "Bucky is telling me, 'We've had a good thing right here, haven't we? I've been here six years, maybe more, and it has been nothing but good to me.' On the cement walkway between the door and the truck he gets down on one knee and holds up an engagement ring. 'Cheryl, it is us. It has always been us. I want you with me on the big stuff in my life. Marry me please? Do that for us and everything else will work itself out.' To be honest with you Kate, I had issues. I have tell you.

"'That is a big ask,' I told him,"

Kate could picture them on a sidewalk. She could see Cheryl being surprised and awkward with him kneeling there.

"My eyes were watering, but I could see there was a ring sitting in an open box being held up to me. I could see that.

"'Put that ring away and get off your knee,' I tell him. 'I might have been more sold on the engagement idea if you hadn't followed that up with, 'I'm quitting my job to run for congress.' Like was I wrong, Kate, I don't know."

"You have your own reactions; you feel what you feel."

"We'll go in sit, eat, and talk. He is a plateful, this guy. We've hung out a little since I started working at the plant. He's a good guy and all but, I hadn't gone to work thinking about getting married at all, let alone to him. I said, 'You live with your mom, you do know that don't you.'

"'Yes, presently I do,' he told me. 'And it is also true I've saved a decent pile of money doing so.' There was this plan he nursed for three years or more. He expected Roberts to age out at some point. He didn't think he'd die of Covid. He also did not expect him to die when he did. 'This is that moment,' he told me. 'And it won't be coming back. I have to act now or no.'"

"'Why, why do you do this?' I asked him. 'Of all the things you could do?'

"That's a very good question to ask," Kate reassured.

"He said, 'I want to help on a bigger scale.' While everybody in the plant was talking about the poor man's death, Bucky was pitching himself to me for congress. 'I was going to propose to you today regardless. The Roberts thing just came in and changed a few things is all. It is a sign. I'm changing who I am.' Can you beat that?"

"He seems to be a man comfortable with big decisions," Kate added.

"I thought to myself, somewhere in that turtle whisperer brain you planned for our proposal here at work? While we were in line at the taco truck? I'll try to be as close as possible to what he said. 'Well, not exactly, but yes. Right here in front of our friends and where we see each other almost every day. I want you to marry me. We can do a lot together.' When he said that I started to believe him. You know it. I see a path for us I really do."

"Those are some fantastic things to hear. Do you remember how you were feeling when you heard those words?" Kate inquired.

"I remember. I felt like I wasn't alone for the first time since I became an adult."

Kate asked, "He quit his job? That makes sense if you are moving toward what he is planning. Did he tell you how he planned to finance the campaign?"

"I am the same way. 'I'm thinking, he's asking to marry me right after quitting his job?' Basically, he said the obvious, he'd been working for six years while living at his mother's place. He's going to borrow off those savings. The man is as cheap as a goat. He does have his campaign office downtown, and not in our spare bedroom, thank you Jesus. He puts in about six days a week. He goes all around the state. There are thirty-five and counting farmer's markets I've been to with him. It is our Saturday morning ritual. Must say, there are a lot of nice towns and people in this state."

Kate chuckled. "Men can get tiring don't you think? They make too many things a competition. Everything doesn't have to end with a winner and loser. I haven't heard how that engagement ring ended up on your finger."

"Well, that's when I said to him, 'It's not like you're falling off the moon. Hear me out. You're going after this for two years. At the end, if they have knocked you on your ass, which is very likely, you'll do something else that has a job attached to it. Like running the heat and air in a plant something like this.' I pushed it. I said, 'Be honest with me Bucky. Can you come back to what you were and be happy about it?' He came up with 'We are the connective tissue.' I still think it's a gross picture, but he went on with it. He opened a hinged box and there was a very big diamond for a guy who quit his job. I let him slip it on my finger as he said it was his grandmother's engagement ring. His own mother insisted I have it. What do you think, Kate? Sometimes I feel it's too big. Does it suit me?"

"Oh come on girl," Kate pretended to be looking with studious attention. "The ring is perfect for you. Really. Very lovely and in a beautiful old-school setting. This takes me back to John's proposal. He presented me with a thin band of gold. Here, see? No stone at all. I'm not even sure he knew there was a difference between an engagement ring and a wedding ring. It was before he started law school. We were in Boston Common. Unlike you, I can't remember anything exactly about what he said. I do remember saying yes about five times in a row... This was lovely," Kate added as she found her phone. She stood and Cheryl knew their conversation was over. Cheryl collapsed her beach chair while listening to Kate directing her driver to come and gather her beach things.

"I loved your story Cheryl. This was a perfect beach day, thank you very much for sharing."

"It was wonderful to get to talk with you, bye." Cheryl slung the strap of her chair casing over her shoulder, faced into the sun, and marched her way off the beach.

∼

WITH ARIEL lightly pulling his ear and patting his cheek with her closed little fist, they walked across the beach to the lot and his Volvo. He opened the rear door and strapped her into a child's car seat.

"Daddy, this is for you," Ariel said, "It is from the beach." She opened her hand and there for him was the second angel tear that had been gifted to him in this life.

"Oh, Ariel, this is spectacular! And so generous of you to give it to me." He used his thumb and index finger to twizzle the ocean-formed green glass from her open palm. "What you found is called an angel's tear. See it looks like one, doesn't it?"

"It is for you Daddy."

"I will show you another one I have some time. I'll keep the two together and safe. I love it, thank you Ariel." He offered her fruit strips, which she gladly started chewing on. When he shut his driver's side door he thought to himself, how did she do that? How did she know to give it to him and not brush it away or simply lose it? She is a keeper. She knows her mommy's name is Kate; she calls me daddy, and she's given John the name papa.

"Daddy, I am smart, you know."

"Of course you are, Ariel. That is one of the first things I know about you."

"Yes I am because when I'm in the water I know how to ride the fish."

"That is incredible, tell me, how do you do something like that?"

"Yes. It's like riding a pony but only it's a fish. Cause I'm in the water. It's fun. They carry me on the waves and they laugh a lot."

"You know something Ariel, I'd like to ride fish. And Russell and Taylor would want to know how to do that for sure."

"Russell can probably find a lot of fish just like me. Daddy, I'll give you one of my fish as soon as we are in the water."

Bainbridge took a turn that brought him onto Shore Road. He asked, "Do you want to know where we are going?"

"Yes I do," she answered with absolute conviction.

"I am going to show you your own bedroom."

"Daddy," she said with dramatic disappointment. "I already have a bedroom."

"That's right, you do. I mean your other very own bedroom. This is your bedroom at Daddy's house, Ariel. We're here! Let's check out your bedroom and hang out at your other home for a few hours."

"Daddy, I peed."

"Nice timing on this one, come on we will go inside and get a dry diaper on you." He unstrapped her, pulled her from the chair to his shoulder and up they went to the side door of their house on Shore Road.

The house held a slight smell of fresh paint and the heavier smell of drying plaster and major tile work. They stood beside the refrigerator door as it made ice and then poured water in her daddy's glass. Ariel began opening the doors to the kitchen cabinets on her level, bending in, taking a peek inside, then leaving it open before moving on to the next. She was pulling open a drawer purposed for pots when Bainbridge knelt to her height.

"Let's go see your bedroom and get you into a dry diaper," he said.

She looked up at him with recognition.

"Oh, yes. Can I have a drink of your water, Daddy?" He held his glass to her lips, she drew deeply, smacked her lips and exclaimed, "Good."

He walked with her alongside him, his hand reaching down, her hand reaching up. They took a stroll through the kitchen, living room, and main foyer to her bedroom door. It opened into a bright room with big windows looking out on the front yard, the room warmed by the afternoon sun.

Ariel raced to the bed, a low toddler model, and did a reasonable somersault on it. She was trying to stand, probably expecting to jump up and down, until Bainbridge lifted her from the bed and required her to stand on the floor. She demonstrated her second somersault and then looked up.

"You wait right there," he said. "I'm going into the bathroom to get a towel and diaper." He hoped she was still in the same sized diaper. It seemed that she had grown a lot in the last month. Against his instructions, Ariel followed him into the bathroom and watched as he filled the sink up with warm water and placed a washcloth to soak in it. Ariel was opening the cabinet doors to the bathroom sink. He took a Pamper from a stack, a hand towel and a bowl.

"What is that Daddy? "

"This is a bowl. A white ceramic bowl. Here you want to hold it for a minute?"

"Sure."

"Hold out both hands then." She took the bowl for a brief moment, then decided she wanted to give it back.

"What is it Daddy?"

"A bowl."

"No, I mean what are you and the bowl doing?"

"Look, I'll show you. I'm taking this washcloth that has been soaking in warm water and I'm going to give the towel a little squeeze so most of the water drips back into the sink, see? Then, I put the warm towel in the…" He pointed and waited until she exploded with "BOWL!" and lots of silly laughter.

He carried everything as she followed him back to her bed. He floated a large towel onto the bed, picked her from the floor, and placed her on the towel. He had her cleaned up and in a dry diaper in what his childcare class would have considered record time. Admittedly, there was important information he learned in that five-week course, but he had mastered the diapering skill a few years back on Taylor and Russell.

She held the indifferent expression of someone in a takeout line. While he hung there, absorbed in his revery, she squiggled off the bed and was across the room. She held her arms out in a graceful, relaxed way, and flew around the room like a butterfly, then came back to him and pulled him by his index finger across to an area below one of her windows. There was a throw rug and a small pile of blocks in all sizes, along with the various parts to a circle. A plastic cone stood to receive the circles when they were assembled correctly.

He learned that she, more than either Taylor or Russell, liked to have many things in her hands. She loved to build block towers, then order Bainbridge to knock them down. They played at that game for a long time in a leisurely manner. Some blocks were chosen with careful deliberative discussion, and other blocks, not so much. Eventually, a small tower would appear. And then it was time for him to break it all down – the fun was obvious in her face. They were stretched out on the rug. Bainbridge asked, "Ariel, would you like an orange?"

"Sure, I do."

He went to the kitchen. He wanted her to have some time to herself in her own room. He peeled the thick giving skin from the meat of a navel orange, pulling it apart into wedges. When he came back she had drifted over to the collection of circle pieces. He sat on the rug beside her.

"These are nice juicy slices of orange. Want one?"

"I do."

"Okay, dig in. But remember to chew really well."

She took one and as she chewed a smile hung on her face. "Daddy," she said, and she took the wad of orange pulp from her mouth. She gave it to Bainbridge as if he knew what to do with it. Which he did. He put the glob on the little blue dish while asking her if she wanted another wedge. She took a second one and, as if in some sort of profound thought, she looked into the distance as she chewed and chewed.

She was tiring. She tried to put a circle together, but in the end she said, "No, you do it."

He clipped two halves into a circle. She took it from him, walked to the cone and slipped the circle over it. She came back, insisting, "Daddy make one more." Which he did by clipping four quarter pieces into a circle.

With perfect solemnity, she said, "Thank you." Taking the circle she went over to the blocks and plopped on her bum. She carefully placed the circle beside her on the rug. Bainbridge watched as she eventually selected four blocks, stacking them into a little tower arising from the center of the plastic ring. Bainbridge could tell by her droopy eyes she was Grade A tired. It was not by accident she was sleepy. His job was to maintain a routine Kate established, which included a short nap time around two. A morning and an afternoon nap time had been in play for a long time now. It was 2:30 and Ariel needed a time out. He picked her up and put her down in her bed. There was no struggle. She understood. After Ariel was tucked in, with a kiss on her forehead, Bainbridge quietly exited to the kitchen.

He made coffee and took the cup to the living room where he thumbed his phone, scrolling for messages. He felt the comfort of normalcy knowing there was someone with him in the house. He felt good and bright and new. Lynne from Meghan Polatano's office wanted him to call.

"Lynne, always a pleasure talking to you, I must say. Yes, it all went through. $2.5 million was successfully transferred to my accounts. Yes indeed, a banner day that was. I talked to my financial guy yesterday and it all worked out fine. Everything is where it is supposed to be. No, I'm not going crazy with the money. What, did you think I'd be calling you from Saint Martin? No not me, I'm here on Shore Road. Though I did pull out some of it and pay off this house I'm in. Yes, the construction is all done. Can you believe it? And it's all paid for. Yes, you're right Lynne. To me everything is about real estate. All right then, make sure you thank Meghan for the hundredth time."

Six of the men who underwent one of Crown's fake vasectomies produced a child. As Bainbridge understood it, they each received a $2.5-million settlement. It was not clear what the others got.

Some things were meant to be. Ariel was one of them. Through the window he could see that Aubrey's car was pulling in. When she reached the porch, he opened the door.

"Aubrey, come on in, hello. Want something. Coffee? Tea?"

"No, no. I just dropped by for a second. Is she here?"

"Oh yes, the princess is in the house. She's taking a short nap."

"That's wonderful, Dan. Obviously, she must like her new room. You see, no worries, right?"

"Without a doubt, no worries. I am very, very lucky, I'm where I'm supposed to be doing what I'm supposed to do."

"This living room is really pretty, Dan. It all came together perfectly. Last time I was here the old furniture just didn't look like it belonged anymore.."

"The whole place is great. You were a huge help, Aubrey. I can't thank you enough."

"Well, you can thank me a little. I came by for a couple of reasons. My brother and sister-in-law are in town, staying with me. I told you about him when we were at Putters last week. That was a funny night don't you think? What got into Francis when he wouldn't take our money for the drinks?"

"If we had known he was in such a generous mood, we would have ordered dinner."

"Well Larry is here now in all his glory. It is nice to have Jolien for a few days to balance off the Larry experience."

Bainbridge chortled. "I've never taken in a single of my class reunions, you have to give Larry props for showing up."

"I know him, I know how he thinks. He's done well for himself over the last ten years. His classmates hadn't met Jolien until this reunion. They're actually going to it tonight. Tomorrow evening they want to take me to Florentine's, but he insists that he won't spend big money on a fancy restaurant if I don't bring a date along. To quote him, 'Someone to join me in the extravagance.'"

Bainbridge added, "They must have set up that reservation way before they came into town. Sure, count me in."

"Good news then," she said. "It'll be fun. Pick me up at 6:30. Now, this isn't for you."

She held up an oversized bag she was carrying. From it she pulled out a woven stuffed doll of some creation. She playfully waggled it in front of his face. It had long legs and long arms. Stitched into its face were eyes at odd alignment with bold eyelashes and big bulbous lips. A rendition of a lanky girl with dreadlocks. Its species was vague but it was unquestionably a happy face guaranteed to generate a smile similar to the one stretched under Bainbridge's nose.

Over the last three years, Bainbridge and Aubrey had developed a relationship as an unattached couple. They were seen at spots all over town. For the last year or so, they had been together at dinner parties that popped up when most of the town began sensing Covid may have subsided.

"Hey, come on, we'll get her up."

Together, they went into Ariel's room. Bainbridge sat on the edge of the bed and used his finger to tickle her ear. Ariel swatted at his finger and came awake. With quiet calculation she looked at both of them sitting at her bedside. It was clear she was adjusting to where she was.

Aubrey leaned in saying in a sincere quiet voice, "Hello Ariel."

"Do you live here too?" Ariel asked.

"No silly, I just came by to say hello. You look very comfortable. Do you like it here?"

"Yes, I do"

"I've brought you a gift. Here is a friend I thought you might like to keep in your new bedroom." Ariel grabbed for the doll and took it to her chest. "Yes, your very own friend. You can keep her in the bedroom and every time you come back you will have a friend here to welcome you."

Bainbridge reminded his daughter, "What do you say when someone gives you a gift?"

"Thank you, Auby." She had yet to get that name right.

Ariel had that woolen doll with her for the rest of the time she spent at the house that day. The four of them, which included Ariel's new friend, unraveled themselves from the bed. Ariel's sneakers were put back on and they drifted through the house and out onto the porch. Bainbridge attempted to help Ariel, but she managed the stairs easily on her own, and soon was in the front yard.

Aubrey knelt beside Ariel. "I'm going now. It was very nice seeing you in your new bedroom. Do you have a name for your friend?"

"I don't know. I will ask her." She brought the doll to her ear, then began nodding her head dramatically as if in agreement with what the doll was telling her.

"Will you share the name with me?"

"Her name is Rhonda. Auby, she says she can be your friend too."

"I would like that very much, thank you. You are a very generous young lady. I'll see you again. Bye. And bye to Rhonda."

While Bainbridge walked Aubrey to her car, reviewing the plans for the following day, Ariel took Rhonda on a tour of the yard. By the time Bainbridge came back he found her in the corner with the oversized rhododendron. The very spot where Larky had been saved by a cat. She sat on the grass, positioning the doll's long legs to sit beside her. "Ariel it is time for us to go."

"No, Daddy no. I have to go back to my room first. Then we can go. okay?"

"Of course," he said.

"You count to ten, no you count to fifty and I'll take Rhonda back to my room and then you come and get me."

"Okay, but fifty is a really big number."

"Good, it should be."

"Alright then here we go. One..."

Ariel walked her own way to her room. At her bed she placed her stuffed woolen friend in a way where it was resting comfortably against her pillow. By the time Bainbridge arrived

Ariel was standing beside the bed, one foot over the other, her arms crossed, looking as if she'd been waiting for hours.

"Alright now, come over here Ariel. Let's put this very pretty sweater on you. We are going out for a little bit and we want to be sure we are warm. and then I'll be bringing you back to Mommy's. Hey, you hungry? Would you like some chowder?"

"I do."

"Well me too. We are going down to Putters and get us some chowder."

Francis wouldn't put Ariel down. He brought her to his big window and showed her the island across the waters of the sound. She crawled up on a stool beside Francis, both looking through his big window. Bainbridge listened to Francis giving an elaborate definition of an island, Ariel punctuating his tale by repeatedly asking 'why.' Everyone, including Ariel, knew this served to spur Francis on.

Bainbridge settled into a booth near enough to catch some of what they were saying. He heard more like singsong and low bass notes than actual words. The food arrived. Ariel was explaining to Francis how you ride invisible fish. Finally Francis relinquished his share of the conversation and carried her and the stool over to their table. There was a bowl of fish chowder, a little basket of bread, and a custom order for Ariel: a cup of fish chowder and a perfect quarter-sized grilled peanut butter and tomato sandwich.

Ariel was light years from the notion of being spoon fed, but when it came to her and fish chowder, it was always a mess. Putter's chowder was kept just warm enough to melt a thin pad of butter, so Bainbridge felt no risk watching her grab her cup in both hands and bring it to her mouth.

"That's fine Ariel but take little sips, just little sips."

She took giant sips that exceeded the ridge of her lips. He couldn't get a napkin there soon enough to stop a blob of drippage slipping from her chin to her sweater. Francis dabbed at her sweater.

"Now here we have two ways of proving who your father is." He was pretending to be talking to Ariel who in fact did have her ears lined up to his voice, but it was Bainbridge he was really talking to. "One is that you are a wee bit messy, just like your dad. The second one is that his eyes look way better on you."

Francis's quarter-sized peanut butter creation was featured. Ariel dove at that like a seagull. Francis placed a small glass of icewater for her to drink. Bainbridge spooned through his and the remainder of Ariel's chowder. Francis talked on. "This must mean your house finally has a legal occupancy permit."

"Oh yes, and a kickass kitchen you're going to have to help me break in."

"Soon enough Danny. But something is coming up sooner, I think. The election is five short days from now. I donated the use of Putter's to Bucky's campaign and they accepted. That day it becomes the campaign's central gathering spot," Francis explained. "Listen, I could use a few friends in the crowd that night. I'm talking nine or ten at night to around midnight. If you could drop in it would be good. To have a familiar face in the crowd, you know. Most elections you know pretty much where it's going by ten. Win or lose, there will be good music, good food and drink right up to closing. But I'm not going to hide it. These things can get a little interesting sometimes. If you were in the crowd and something were to flare up? You, me, and two off duty cops I hired will be my A-Team. Am I right Danny?"

Bainbridge was carrying Ariel to the door as Francis walked beside him, asking Bainbridge to be part of the team. He said to Francis, "Yes, I'll be there no question. It's another reason I have to vote for the guy. If he wins. It'll be a better party to hang out at."

"You've got a bright side. I'm glad to see it Danny."

It was 4:30 now. Time to bring Ariel back to Kate and with no minutes to spare.

Thin, leafy roads guided the Volvo along the shoreline. The car hugged the winding road while Ariel talked to herself some. Finally she broke out of her own conversation to ask, "Is 'price' a real word Daddy?"

"Price is a real word."

"What does it mean?"

His nose began detecting a smell, thick like a haze. Ah, nuts. This is going to be great. I'm bringing her back with a load in her pants. John will be talking about this for weeks.

"Daddy, what's it mean?"

"Price mostly means the amount of money you have to pay to take something home from the store. The store has a box of Cheerios that they put a price on, say four dollars. If you want to take the box home you give them money equal to four dollars and then the Cheerios are yours to keep."

"And I can take them home."

"That's right. They are yours and you can take them home."

"Oh," she said in a thoughtful tone to convey an understanding she really didn't have. Bainbridge knew she would come back to this another time. Their car rolled up to a stop on Tabor's driveway.

The smell was unavoidable, though Ariel seemed to give it no mind at all. Feelings of being trapped and guilty washed through Bainbridge. He had no way to correct this situation unless he went back out and down the street to the CVS. He was weighing that option when he realized Heather stood right outside his car window.

"Hello Daniel, hi Ariel." Heather had soccer gear on, indicating she'd just come from a practice or game.

For reasons that weren't even clear to himself, Bainbridge tried to buy some time. He rolled down the window and said,

"Heather good to see you. I'm wondering if you know how Buddy Rice is doing at NYU?"

Heather stood at the open window, a little put back by the extraneous question. To her credit she rallied and answered, "Oh, you want the deets on Buddy, do you? He's doing great, actually. He's in his third year and already has some production work. His work shows up in several episodes of Chicago PI."

Nodding his head Bainbridge said, "That is impressive."

"For sure. He has a neat studio apartment. NYU is all around him. I've visited him twice. I loved autumn in New York it was a great scene. He is in a nice space. He says he's learning at lightning speed."

By then Heather could smell what it was he wasn't saying.

Bainbridge caved and offered, "Now this isn't pretty. I know. It happened suddenly. We were on the way here. And I went right by a CVS before I noticed we were in this shape. What do you think? Should I go back change Ariel up and then we come back more presentable?"

"No need for that. Let's get her out of the car. It's all good."

Heather went around and opened the back door. She freed Ariel from the car seat and had her standing beside the car while Bainbridge came up to them. Ariel had a reproachful look on her little face.

"This was a very long car ride Daddy," she huffed.

Heather said, "This isn't our first prom together now is it Ariel? For a high school senior I'm putting in impressive numbers in the changing diaper category. It's no bother really. Did you have a good time with Daniel?"

"Yes I did, and I have two bedrooms now."

"You do? Isn't that a nice thing to have. Anything else go on today?"

"Yes, I met a friend."

"A friend. Does your friend have a name?"

"Rhonda."

"You did have a good time, Ariel. Let's go get you changed." She offered her hand and Ariel took it. Together they took several steps towards the house.

"So, I hear from your mother you guys are off to Paris. Nice, huh?"

"Yes, it will be great. I'm told it's a world class city. The whole family will be on vacation. That will be new, that will have some juice to it. Mom says you've finished your house. Now what?"

"Settle in. And that could take a while. It was some project. Seemed like everything I wanted or needed was in short supply. Trying to get the right workmen to the job required biblical patience. There were endless delays with the tile, the windows, the plywood. Even doorknobs if you can believe it."

"Rolling shortages is what my economics teacher calls the current economy."

"Sounds like your high school has the right focus. What about you, what are you up to?"

"Writing out college applications, touring some of the schools. I'm big on actually seeing the ones I'm interested in."

"You'll know the school when you see it. I understand."

"True. Daddy says I shouldn't limit myself to schools that are offering scholarships. I can go anywhere I want. Who knows, I might not want to play soccer anymore."

By that time, Ariel and Heather were at the front step. Ariel turned and broke into the discussion Heather was closing off with Bainbridge.

"Daddy, what is better, a really, really, really tall tree or a really, really, big elephant?"

13

A SPACE AT THE TABLE

More and more "Buckland Sanders for Congress" signs were sprouting on lawns than you could count in a single day. Kate wondered what they did with all those signs when the election was over. She was seated on her patio. The last time she was with John was this morning when they walked to the elementary school to cast their votes. A brittle day. The salt in the air coming up off the ocean. invigorated her.

During the rest of the daylight, John went to the office, while she and Ariel spent some time at Menauhant Beach, then went into town. When home, while Ariel napped, Kate did her yoga stretches. The day slipped along. Around dark, John was back in the picture.

He sat beside Kate. A little glass-top table held his mug of coffee. She was sipping warm spicy green tea with a large lemon slice floating in her cup. They were taking in the ocean sounds, each wave huffing its last onto the beach. It was 9:30 at night and dark and the air had turned chilly. For no particular reason, they had talked at length about her yoga passion.

"I really, really miss my trainer," Kate said.

John offered, "We must be able to find you another trainer."

"No, she took me through my pregnancy and two years after that, so, no."

"I get it. Most good people are hard to replace," he said. "But it can be done. I have to ask. All that time and you were her only client?"

"For God's sake, no John. I paid her enough, bet on that, but no. During that time she established a full client list. It's easy pickings around here. Problem is, during that time she also picked up a guy and he became a husband and they decided to move out to Montana."

"It is what it is," he said.

"Those words don't make it any better. She and I knew she was training me to be fine on my own, and that time has come now, hasn't it? But my energy, I tell you I'm done in at the end of the day."

"I think that is how it is supposed to go." John blew the steam off the brim of his mug, took a careful draw on his coffee and continued. "Yes, it is a wonderfully busy house since Ariel has come along."

"Wonderfully? That comes across as a little old-timey. I'd say busy, about four times the busy, but it is not just her. Look at us. Our evening, this one at any rate, is starting at 9:30."

"Tell me this isn't good stuff, right?"

"John, of course. And for the record, that little gal is my best buddy. She is a funny one. She studies every move that Heather makes. Heather has been so good with her."

John's phone buzzed and he learned that the driver was out front. They walked along the deck and into the living room, where she gathered up a knee-length sweater and he put a light topcoat over his dark blue suit. Kate continued their conversation.

"Is she too young? Should we put off this vacation idea? What age is it safe now for children to be vaccinated? My god I'm a terrible mother, is it 5 to 11 or 2 to 11? Am I supposed to have gotten her vaccinated by now? I was supposed to get her some form of baby vaccination. Right? Did you even know she wasn't vaccinated all this time?"

They strapped themselves into the wide backseat of their black Suburban.

"No, actually, I'm not up to speed on children's vaccinations."

"Neither am I. Oh, I am such a terrible mother. I'll call Doctor Fryeman and get this all cleared up. Ariel will be on the right side of this issue by tomorrow. She'll be good to go. But John, is it too soon? Should we do this? I've been checking the Covid numbers in Paris. The numbers are decent, by the way."

"And I'm sure you'll check the numbers right up until we leave. This vacation was your idea in the first place," he said. "Are you changing your mind?"

"No, but there are things to consider. Don't look at me like that. What's China up to? What happens if, when the whole family is over there, Pakistan decides to invade India or something?"

"You haven't let yourself get this frantic since your pregnancy days. You can be pretty funny when you're frantic. Calm yourself down. Come on now. You do know that you are being overly whatever." He stroked her thigh and patted her knee. "Let's not overlook the obvious. Remember, I currently work in Paris. I just came from there. It's beautiful and as safe as New York, Phoenix, San Francisco, or here."

"Sure. You are right. That's true. The way I'm acting, a vacation may be the only cure. Why do vacations always happen somewhere else? Do they wear masks on the streets of Paris?"

The Suburban clipped along the night roads. John's mind took some moments to anticipate what men he might see at

Putters tonight but he couldn't get very far with the thought because Kate was leaning into his side vision asking, "Well do they, you were just there?"

"No. I mean some do, but no not really. It's just like here. The country is vaccinated just like here. And just like here, that doesn't mean everybody has taken the mask off. I'll admit, they do smoke like crazy over there, so right out of the gate a lot of that bunch were pretty quick to drop the mask. But there are people as scared as you all over the world. So you'll see a few masks on the street. A lot of the waiters and waitresses still wear them. Not all of them, but some. What you will notice is that the more expensive the restaurant, the fewer masks on the staff. I always wear one when I'm traveling by air. We will mask up while taking the plane. That's a given. Whatever works, we do, am I right?"

"To my credit, Ariel has her passport, I made sure of that. You, me, Heather, I know we've all had our round of booster shots. Lydia made us some of her stylish cloth masks. I remember when she was making her cloth masks for everybody who walked in, including some of the National Guard. There's a lot that goes into this you know. I have copies of the vaccination and booster documentation. All I'm asking is a little appreciation, that's all. Just a little appreciation for what it takes to do all this."

"Kate I do appreciate you. You know I do. There wouldn't be any of this without you. I love you. We love you." He looked deep into her eyes to see if this was doing any good. "Now come on, this isn't what we're doing right now, is it?"

The Suburban rolled along the streets very close to Putters. Seven or eight huge buses were parked nose to tail along the border of the parking lot, with cars extending much further down the street than that. The Suburban slowly paced along the parked buses using the thin lane that remained of the street. He came to a stop where the white clapboard corner of Putters began.

They exited the SUV and went between the first bus and the building into the crowd filling the parking lot. John held her hand and wove them through the standing room crowd to several long tables with buckets of canned beer in piles of ice, and jugs of water with tubes of large paper cups beside them. Slices of pizza were available from stacks of pizza boxes.

John pulled two beers from the ice. He popped one and gave it to Kate and popped another. They moved slightly left of the action at the tables, stood in the shadows near the building and took in the crowd. Both were surprisingly thirsty and grateful for the sweater and topcoat. Three distinct smells wavered in the air: weed, whiskey and beer.

Kate noticed there were more than a few bald-headed men wearing masks with "Buckland Sanders" stenciled across them. There were also a lot of women that gave off a twenties and thirties vibe. There were hundreds of people in the parking lot and a couple hundred more on the beach, most dressed in their rendition of office casual. There was one dude with a decent-sized American flag on a short pole, moving from the beach and laughing with three other people, toasting the flag with their half empty beer cans.

Tabor knew this evening wasn't on Kate's top ten things to do tonight. He also knew she would be good about it – she could do two hours, sometimes four, at any function thrown at her. And in high heels, as she was always quick to point out. When business needed her she could get behind it. Otherwise she left business to him, which worked out well for both of them. To ease her into the night's strategy, he thought he'd carry the conversation they were having on the ride over.

"The Paris rental we have is beautiful. A huge apartment

right where it should be. You'll love it. But I think of all of us, Heather is the one that will probably not want to come home."

"I know," she said. "I know. While she's over there I don't want her getting any ideas of going to a university anywhere in Europe. She can pick any school she wants in America and that way we will all be happy. You have to be with me on this point. And you are?"

"Yes, certainly, I am with you one hundred percent. Before we get too far ahead of ourselves here, do you have any idea what schools she has been thinking about seriously?"

John had been noticed by then. A man in a leather jacket cut to the waist, an open collar white shirt, grey dress pants, and black loafers, was standing in front of him shaking his hand. Kate also noticed his four-day growth of black beard and a heavy gold watch on his hairy wrist.

"All right, all right, all right, I'd hoped I'd see you here tonight," boasted John. "Kate, this is one of the good ones. This is Alan Burr of Electric Tech. Alan; I'm surprised I haven't introduced you to my wife Kate until now. Queen of all her realm."

"Kate, it's a pleasure and one we will have to repeat at more length. But could I just pull your husband away for a few minutes?"

"That doesn't surprise me Alan, I can manage. In fact I encourage it."

They both saw the wisdom in that. John went only a few steps away and the two of them drilled into some conversation, but not before they grabbed a couple of fresh beers. Kate shifted her focus. On her sharp left against the restaurant wall a large screen displayed a whiteboard tallying statewide results. Numbers had been changing all night. Buckland Sanders held a solid nine percent lead. This was around ten o'clock. Kate was aware, as was everyone else, that Anthony Milch had stumbled badly three weeks ago when it came to light that he was almost completely financed by Brock Cushing. Cushing's factory in upstate was dumping yellow goop into the Chicopee River, which ran into the Connecticut River. He had been trying to kill two rivers over the last three years. Some phase of the case was constantly on the news. Cushing's business had been booming.

Over the last month, the CEO of a large mutual fund, heavy with state pension money, had wallpapered the television screen in support of Milch, like he was some savior of the state's economy. Meanwhile, Bucky's single ad continued to roll through, county by county, along with a small dose of platform ads paid for by the party.

Kate became aware that the man who stood beside her was Daniel. She found her cheerful voice and said, "I'm not surprised to see you here but I am surprised to see you *here*." She pointed at the ground right beside her.

"Well, this is some jamboree isn't it? Nice to see a familiar face in this crowd. What do you think? Looks like Bucky is on his way."

"It does look good for him, who would have thought?"

"Yep, by now 85 percent of the vote has been counted. It will be hard to knock him off the lead at this point."

"Are you wearing a Putters Staff shirt? Are you working at Putters now?"

"Yes, for tonight anyway. Francis asked me to help out with this, be around, you know? He thought he could do with a couple of security guys, but by seven o'clock, he tripled that number.

"Hey, I saw Heather a few days ago when I dropped off Ariel and she was talking about her college search."

"Oh she is focused, that one. I like the way she attacks a problem from multiple angles."

"That's a good way to be."

"It is not the only way to be, but it is a good one. She likes to take her time, sit on things. We've all learned to wait her out. Let's see now, we've been to Yale, Duke, Colombia, Brown, and after Paris, I've already booked a visit to Tallahassee."

"Tallahassee, how did that come into it?"

"For almost one reason and one reason alone. FSU has the number one women's soccer team in the nation. You didn't know that. I didn't know that. But she did. She arranged a date where she will meet the coach and have some time to talk about the sport with someone at that level. Oh yes, visiting schools has become a real thing for us."

"This is one of the good puzzles to be figuring out. You two really have a travel bug going."

"It is more like I'll simply be there when she makes the right decision."

When John returned, moving towards Kate, he saw she was talking to one of Putters staff people, only to realize it was Bainbridge.

"With all the people around here, I'm surprised you found us so fast. What, have you got a job working for Putters now? I can suggest that with the extra cash maybe you can restock your diaper supply."

"Good to see you too, John. No, I'm sort of security. So, if anything happens to break out, I'm the guy that steps in and stops them from leaning on your neck."

"You actually believe you would have any effect on a crowd of this size?"

"John, this has been fun, I have to keep moving, enjoy."

Bainbridge was swallowed up within six paces. John said, "At least out here, Buck seems to have the young crowd with him."

"Oh yes, like us," Kate shot back.

"The young don't vote in the numbers they should. It was a sad fact in past elections."

"Well, it seems to me," she said, "A lot of them are burned

out on most days. I mean look at it, the younger you are, the more work you have to take on. Whether you're a waiter or on Wall Street. The young are also having the babies. My point is a lot of them don't show up because they are worn out. And I include showing up to vote. But this looks different. There sure are piles of them here tonight. Where do we fit in, does having Ariel make us young?" They gave each other a quick, deep look and laughed.

He said, "I'm going with, we are on the young side of mature, Let's go inside. What do you say we hang in a little longer and hear Sanders make his first acceptance speech?"

"You're right. It's bound to be only a few minutes from now. Why not? Look, even in the little time we have been here look his margin is up 38 percent!"

"Miltch tanked. It's over, he has no road to victory. Let's get inside and do a little time."

Kate pulled a mask from her sweater pocket, put it on, and followed her husband into Putter's brightly lighted main room. There was a warmth and buzz inside, and oddly, a less dense crowd. There were more men in suits, more women in jewelry and dresses. Kate was offered a "Bucky for Congress" face mask by one of the organizers. She took it and placed it in her sweater pocket.

Tables similar to the tables outside offered buckets of canned beer in piles of ice and large urns of clear water, more pizza. Kate pulled out two beers, handed one to John and they migrated towards the little stage set up in a corner of the hall. There was a single small podium supporting two microphones and a blue banner with "Buckland Sanders for Congress" arched overhead.

The music in the hall was just below conversation level. It was a feed of contemporary folk music broadcast out of Boston University. Mateo Abruzzi talked to John. Abruzzi was the state's attorney at the head of the team seeking damages from the Cushing Corporation. Kate ignored them and studied the stage. She could see a side view of Cheryl standing just beyond the limits of a solid black curtain that lined the back of the stage. She was talking to someone, tapping on her phone. Then she took a single step and was out of view.

Mateo said his goodbyes, Kate marveled at the familiar expression his face held at all times. She said to John, "A few days ago, at the beach, Cheryl Sanders stopped for a while. She thanks you for what the firm did when representing her husband."

Tabor thought for moment and then, "Meghan, that's who handled him. He is lucky to be alive."

"Yes, and what else can you remember about him?"

"He will forever be known as the one I couldn't keep away from that blue turtle. Or from hoisting it off our beach right in the middle of our party. I asked four times for him to leave the thing alone. He wouldn't listen, and that's when I started to like this guy."

"Exactly, and that was our last great party."

"Covid swamped us. No one wants to think about it anymore, but it hit right after that party and it hit hard."

"I was pregnant and delivered Ariel just as Covid first came on. The hospitals were filling up. I was never more afraid in my life. You could see the worry in the faces of the nurses and even the doctors. That fear is like a stain in my head, I can't seem to rub it out. Well anyway, Cheryl and Bucky are sweet. She said they are using some of the settlement to finance this campaign."

"It is sad, but I can't imagine us ever hosting that sort of party ever again."

"Agreed," she said. She pulled down her mask and took several careful sips from her beer. "Here is the deal," she said.

"Tonight will be whatever it wants. But in Paris? No work. In Paris we are just tourists."

The well-lighted hall fell instantly into pitch darkness. The undercurrent of music was also silenced. It was an abrupt transition. The crowd went from a buzz to silent anticipation. Kate noticed the light from a cellphone appear onstage seemingly suspended in thin air. Someone walking to the podium. She became aware of her own phone glowing at her side. So was John's in his hand, and the phones of most everyone in the hall. Everyone was lighting the darkness with the candle power of their phones. On a large screen beside the podium, a camera broadcast the view from the stage taking in the dots of light from the crowd inside, out through the open double doors to the outside darkness also sparkling from the hundreds of phones waving back.

Bucky's voice penetrated the darkness.

"I owe this win to hardworking people everywhere! I am so proud to be working for the people in my district and to a larger extent all the people in this wonderful state. Those of you who showed up at the voting booth, including these brilliant points of light we see right here at our headquarters. I am grateful, I am honored, and I am here telling you it is official, our voice is going to Washington!"

As light returned, a rousing cheer was heard. Bucky adjusted the mic. "That was a little bit of fun right?" Another burst of cheering. He had the sleeves of his white shirt rolled up to the elbows and was also wearing dark grey pleated dress pants and soft black Skecher shoes, not to mention a wide smile for having been in that winning moment before the crowd. "Some people move mountains and some people climb them. We have both of those types with us tonight. It's official, I am going to Washington to represent people that want to be partners with the planet."

With his election now a point of fact, everyone cheered, shook each other's hands, clapped, did little jigs, and cheered some more.

"We are way beyond the time where we can just be takers. The Earth needs us to wake up. And in this state, we have. We've all worked hard to get to this night. We are not alone. There are others in Washington with similar priorities. You didn't elect me to take apart our government. I will be going to Washington to help government become stronger. Because a government that works for the people needs to be as strong as the challenges we face, and bright enough to have some real answers."

The crowd roared and clapped.

"We will partner with the planet. Clean energy isn't just a cliché. It is the only choice we have. What we are faced with is real, on some level our very survival needs to be looked after."

Another wave of cheering.

"We amp it up, right? That's what we do," he said. "Right now, we need to make our relationship with our earth as important as our military defense spending."

The applause was thunderous.

"We will do better at protecting our air, our water, land, and forests. We will manage them, not exploit them. I won't get too nerdy on you, but listen…"

There was a collaborative groan in the crowd as they playfully acknowledged they wanted as much as he would give of his thoughts tonight. Kate pulled at John's sleeve. John could lap up this political preamble all night long but he understood she had reached her limits. He used his phone to notify the driver.

From the stage Bucky noticed several couples pulling out of the crowd, but by now had developed the instinct to direct his attention to the ones that stayed.

"All creatures rely on the Earth's systems, not just us. It is not as simple as cut a tree, plant a tree. We will know more and do more in the way we use the sun and the wind over the next four years than has been known or done over the last twenty and this state right here wants to be a part of that."

Roars and whistles of approval.

"The industries are already there and the pioneer companies have a proven track record. You know it. I know it. For that matter even the automobile industry knows it. We want to scale it up. Jack it up. We have big expectations for our state and our nation. We must redirect a large sector of our technology and manpower to being the world's leader in creating renewable sources of energy. The time is now." Bucky tapped his chest with an open palm and turned to acknowledge another person coming on stage. "I've had as much time with this mic as I should. Let me introduce my newly minted, very lovely wife, Cheryl!"

Cheryl stood before the crowd in a navy blue vintage pencil dress with capped sleeves. She took time to scan the crowd and allow the noise to momentarily recede.

"Hello everyone, I'm Cheryl Sanders, and I'm as proud of Bucky— Congressman Sanders as I can be. It is true. Give him half a chance and he'll surprise you, too. The energy and the environment, sure, but you hired him to do more. There is a health care system to protect, and the people that work in it, from the EMTs to the aides, nurses, and doctors. We love you for choosing that field and we will find ways to recruit our finest to follow in your footsteps.

"Probably everyone here knows Bucky was all over the state. We couldn't keep him just in his district. What you don't know until now is he made a point of meeting as many electricians, plumbers, carpenters, mechanics, and road crews as he could fit into each visit. Well, a whole little army of them joined our initiative to mentor sharp-minded people for solid careers in those fields. If you want to work in these fields, we stand ready to help. Remember that ad of his where he said we've got to start seeing every job as a valued career track? Well our boy means it. And he means it when he says we will find a way to provide substantial financial support to any citizen of our state going to any of our wonderful community and state colleges or universities."

Huge cheers reinforced her comments. Someone started chanting, "Let's do it! Let's do it!"

"I knew that would get a reaction. The only ones up this late are the young or the young at heart. Am I right?"

"Get it done! Get it done!" Became the cheer.

Bucky eventually damped it down by talking above the chant.

"I don't know if 'Get it done' is exactly right but 'We can do better' sure is. My district has a subway system older than anyone alive at the present time. You think that might need some help? We have rolling shortages in everything from dairy to housing. We need to pivot, scale up. I thank every one of you for this opportunity. I thank Cheryl above all."

He then turned to the black curtain behind him. The two halves of the curtain were drawn apart, revealing twenty or so people, including Cheryl's mom. But it was mostly his staff people. Francis was back there, too, along with four or five politicians from the city.

"I hope everyone on this stage feels like I couldn't have done it without you, because that is exactly how I feel."

"You have the right man here," Cheryl said. "That's a sure thing. And now it's time to call it a night. We did our work and we did it right. We wish you all a very, very good night. Be safe in your travels. I want every single one of us to get home and get a good night's sleep. Tomorrow we will all pick up where we left off. There is no time to waste."

ACKNOWLEDGMENTS

I would like to acknowledge Kit Dunlap and every person and every hour spent with what was the Buzzards Bay Writing Group. Additionally I wish to acknowledge Cameron, Kristen, Ron, Sally and Ed, Paulette and Dennis as early readers who saw something worthwhile and contributed in kind. To Ariel who is so very generous with her craft and was an extremely important editing guide. It was solely because of my wife, Carol, I gained association with Ariel. Carol too has acted as a valued editor and helped chart some of the major sea changes in the story. I am sure she agrees it is time to find some other readers out here in the world. It does get down to one thing though – you – holding this book in your hands right now. Without the time you put in the story can't be told. Everyone in it, everyone who helped write it, welcomes you to Angel Tears.

ABOUT THE AUTHOR

D.G. Radford is mostly known publicly for his teaching career. One that has led him from teaching second graders to teaching junior and senior high school to undergraduates and graduate school students. He has played guitar most of his life but admits to being unusually average. Radford credits his poetry with helping him keep his pen on the paper. He believes that eating an oyster is where both parties to the act are on equal footing. He has four fine young men who allow him to call them sons. He is something of a Civil War buff mainly because the news today can be so disturbing he at least knows how that era turned out. He wishes he had put in more time and effort into coaching little league baseball and town league soccer. The American author he admires most is Hemingway. Radford will cook you a savory meal and proceed to talk your head off. If you are not careful he will borrow every good idea you have ever had and make it his own. He splits his time between Falmouth Massachusetts and Venice Florida. On some level it has to do with being a libra.

Made in United States
North Haven, CT
20 March 2023